CRY OF THE CHILDREN

Recent Titles by J.M. Gregson from Severn House

Lambert and Hook Mysteries

AN ACADEMIC DEATH
CLOSE CALL
CRY OF THE CHILDREN
DARKNESS VISIBLE
DEATH ON THE ELEVENTH HOLE
DIE HAPPY
GIRL GONE MISSING
A GOOD WALK SPOILED
IN VINO VERITAS
JUST DESSERTS
MORE THAN MEETS THE EYE
MORTAL TASTE
SOMETHING IS ROTTEN
TOO MUCH OF WATER
AN UNSUITABLE DEATH
MORE THAN MEETS THE EYE

Detective Inspector Peach Mysteries

BROTHERS' TEARS
DUSTY DEATH
TO KILL A WIFE
THE LANCASHIRE LEOPARD
A LITTLE LEARNING
LEAST OF EVILS
MERELY PLAYERS
MISSING, PRESUMED DEAD
MURDER AT THE LODGE
ONLY A GAME
PASTURES NEW
REMAINS TO BE SEEN
A TURBULENT PRIEST
THE WAGES OF SIN
WHO SAW HIM DIE?
WITCH'S SABBATH
WILD JUSTICE
LEAST OF EVILS

CRY OF
THE CHILDREN

A Lambert and Hook Mystery

J.M. Gregson

This first world edition published 2013
in Great Britain and 2014 in the USA by
SEVERN HOUSE PUBLISHERS LTD of
19 Cedar Road, Sutton, Surrey, England, SM2 5DA.

British Library Cataloguing in Publication Data

Gregson, J.M.
  Cry of the Children.
  1. Lambert, John (Fictitious character)–Fiction. 2. Hook,
  Bert (Fictitious character)–Fiction. 3. Police–
  England–Gloucestershire–Fiction. 4. Detective and
  mystery stories. 5. Missing children-fiction.
  I. Title
  823.9'14-dc23

ISBN-13: 978-0-7278-8286-8 (cased)

All Severn House titles are printed on acid-free paper.

Severn House Publishers support the Forest Stewardship Council™ [FSC™],
the leading international forest certification organisation. All our titles that
are printed on FSC certified paper carry the FSC logo.

MIX
Paper from
responsible sources
FSC
www.fsc.org   FSC® C013056

Typeset by Palimpsest Book Production Ltd.,
Falkirk, Stirlingshire, Scotland.
Printed and bound in Great Britain by
TJ International, Padstow, Cornwall

Do you hear the children weeping, O my brothers,
Ere the sorrow comes with years?

Elizabeth Barret Browning

To Lesley and Malcolm Pease,
long-time friends and splendid people

ONE

'**A**LL THE FUN OF THE FAIR!'
It took Lucy Gibson a little while to get all of the words on the poster. They were scrawled in big blue letters and Lucy wasn't used to reading everything in capitals.

She was a good reader now. She'd heard her teacher tell her mum that she was coming along fine, after a difficult start. These weren't big words, any of them, but it took her a while to make out what the notice said because of the capitals. And she didn't quite understand what the strange punctuation mark at the end meant. Mrs Copthall had told them about exclamation marks, but said they weren't to worry too much about them yet. Lucy had promptly dismissed them from her thoughts – there were quite enough difficulties with this strange business of reading, without struggling with things Mrs Copthall said she shouldn't worry about.

The man used his staple gun to pin down the edge of his poster, then stood back like an artist to admire his handiwork. He looked big and powerful to Lucy. Squat and powerful, an adult might have said. But to Lucy Gibson the man was tall as well as wide; when you are seven, all adults seem tall. Even the girl standing beside her, Daisy Cornwell, seemed tall to Lucy, though she was only nine and looked thin and bony to the adults who controlled the world.

It was Daisy who now took Lucy's hand firmly in hers, conscious of her responsibility and very proud of it. It wasn't far from the school to the road where they lived, scarcely more than two hundred yards. There were no major roads to cross. That's what Lucy's mum had said when she asked Daisy to bring her daughter safely home from school. Nevertheless, it was a responsibility. Daisy's mum had stressed that to her and told her to come straight home and keep a tight hold on Lucy's hand. From the lofty experience of her nine years, Daisy recognized the tone in her mum's voice. Adults, and mums in particular, always fussed about things that were really quite straightforward.

But it was the first time she had done this, so she was being very grown-up and responsible. 'We'd better get you home,' she said officiously to Lucy. 'We don't want your mum getting worried, do we?' That was the kind of silly question adults asked; Daisy felt herself very much an adult today.

'What's a fair?' said Lucy.

'It's good, the fair,' said Daisy. 'You'll enjoy it. That's if you're allowed to go. It costs money.' That was all you needed to say. If things cost money, grown-ups always became keen on them.

Lucy looked doubtfully after the big man who had put the poster up on the noticeboard on the edge of the common. He was now stumping away towards the battered white van in which he had come here. 'Why d'you have to pay?'

Daisy gave the superior smile that comes from experience. 'You pay to go on the rides. They'll be putting them up tomorrow, ready for the weekend.'

'What sort of rides? Donkeys?' Lucy frowned. She remembered racing along the sands and screaming, whilst a rough man trotted beside her and told her to hold on tight. She'd pretended to enjoy it, because she'd been told it was a treat, but in truth she'd been glad when it was over, glad when she'd no longer had to feel the rough coat of the donkey scratching the tender skin on the insides of her bare legs. She didn't want donkeys coming to the common. That was a place where you threw tennis balls and tried to catch them, and patted friendly dogs.

'No, not donkeys!' Daisy Cornwell shook her head with a condescending smile at such ignorance. 'There'll be proper rides, with things going round and round and up and down. You pay to go on those. You can ride on a motorbike or on a little bus or on the footplate of an engine.' She couldn't remember what else there had been. It was a whole year ago now and she'd only been eight then, hadn't she?

'I can't drive a bus. I'd fall off a motorbike.'

'You don't have to drive, silly.' Daisy's immensely superior experience edged her voice with contempt. But she found it difficult to explain exactly why small people didn't need to drive. 'They're toy ones, fastened to the floor of the ride. But big enough to sit in. You pay when the man comes for the money. Then you go round and round and up and down on the ride. It's good. Your parents pay for you and wait for you at the side.' She looked down at the small, round face that was gazing at her so trustingly. 'Yours might go on with you, because you're still small.'

'I'm not *that* small!' The protest sprang readily to Lucy's lips because she'd made it so often.

'They won't want you going on the big rides on your own. Not at your age.' Daisy knew that she wouldn't be allowed to go to the fair on her own either, but she wasn't going to admit that to Lucy.

'Shan't go, then. Not bothered.' That was Lucy's unthinking, petulant reaction, her seven-year-old determination to assert herself in the face of this condescension from the bigger girl who was holding her hand so firmly. She knew that she wanted to go to the fair really, that her heart was eager for this new, exciting, perhaps frightening experience. It was all right being frightened when you had your hand held by a grown-up person and could bury your face in your mum's coat if it got too bad.

She told her mum that the fair was coming when Daisy delivered her to her home. She acted as if she knew all about fairs and had been eagerly awaiting the arrival of this one for weeks. Her mum seemed to accept that.

'They grow up so fast, don't they?' Lucy heard her saying to their neighbour over the garden fence a few minutes later. It was a thing Lucy often heard her mother saying; she didn't know why she said it, but it seemed on the whole a good thing to say, because other people always agreed with her about it.

Mrs Gibson had greater things than fairs to worry about at present.

They had fish fingers and chips and peas for tea. Lucy liked that and left a very clean plate, which always pleased her mother. She felt better when she'd eaten. She'd only just started at the junior school and it was hard work after being one of the big girls last year in the infants. Mrs Copthall told them that they were in the big school now and had to work hard, and they didn't get the rest period they'd had in the afternoons in the first school, when they'd laid their heads on the desks on top of their arms and closed their eyes for a little while.

And you had to be careful at playtimes. You had to keep to your own bit of the yard and out of the way of the big boys and girls. They played their own games and didn't want little kids getting in the way. There were all kinds of things she was having to learn, as well as the things in the classroom which the grown-ups seemed to think were the only things that mattered. She came home very tired, but she always felt better after her tea.

They had homework now. Lucy had welcomed the idea at first, as another acknowledgement of her new school status, but after six weeks she had decided it was a nuisance, when she wanted to be playing with her toys or stroking next door's new kitten in the garden. It wasn't too bad tonight, because her mum seemed preoccupied with other things and was just as anxious to have it out of the way. She reeled off the ten words she had to learn to spell and was pretty sure she'd made a couple of mistakes, but her mother didn't seem to notice. She slammed the book shut as if she was as glad to be done with it as her daughter was.

Lucy talked about the fair again as she was putting on her jim-jams and getting ready for bed. 'There's different rides. They go round and round, faster and faster.' She added the last bit herself to make it sound more exciting. Mrs Copthall said you had to use your imagination to make things more exciting when you were writing. She wasn't writing now, but you had to practise, didn't you?

'We'll talk about it later in the week. You need to go to sleep now. And I need to get on with my jobs downstairs. There isn't time for a story tonight. I expect you'll be reading your own stories soon. You're getting to be a big girl now.'

Everyone told Lucy she was becoming a big girl. She'd liked it at first, but she was bored with it now. People seemed to say it when they couldn't think of anything else to say. Or when they didn't want to talk about what you wanted to talk about. She said stubbornly, 'I really want to go to the fair. All the others in my class will be going.' She'd no idea whether that was true, but it was usually a good argument, one that the grown-ups found hard to reject.

Her mum kissed her forehead. 'I expect you'll be able to go. Perhaps Matt will take you.'

Lucy wanted to say that she didn't want to go with Matt, that she wanted her dad back, that she wanted her dad to take her to the fair. But that would only upset her mum, and she didn't want to do that now, when she was lying flat in her bed in her clean jim-jams and could still feel the cool touch of her mother's lips upon her forehead.

She still felt vaguely unhappy when her mother had shut the door and gone downstairs. It was going dark early now that October was here. She'd liked it better in the summer when the sun was still an orange glow behind the curtains. Her dad had been here then, coming up to tuck her in on some nights. Now it was Matt who was the man in the house and he wasn't here all the time. Matt was all right, she supposed. He was kind to her, in a curious, careful sort of way. But he wasn't her dad. Mum said she'd soon get used to Matt, and perhaps she would. But she wasn't sure she wanted to get used to him.

Lucy Gibson stared up at the ceiling for a while, then fell fast asleep.

The men were erecting the fairground rides when Daisy took Lucy home from school on Friday. They were powerful men, who wore only dirty white vests and torn jeans above their trainers. Most of them had lots of tattoos. Some of these had words that Lucy couldn't read; some had snakes and lions and tigers; all of the designs rippled and flowed with the movements of the men's bodies. There was just one woman working with them; she was young, but she had tattoos as well.

The two girls stood well back from the wooden structures which were growing before their eyes. All this movement and effort had to be accorded a certain caution. Everything was urgent, as if these people were working frantically towards a deadline. If you got too near to the action, things might fall on you or hit you as the builders turned quickly, and it would be your own fault if that happened.

Lucy held the hand she clutched a little more tightly as she watched the sea of dark-blue limbs moving above her. 'I don't like tattoos,' she announced to Daisy. She'd only just decided that, after watching the men and the woman whirling their limbs in swift activity for several minutes.

'My sister's got one,' said Daisy. She paused for a moment, waiting for a reaction from her young charge. They watched a brawny man whirl a strut of wood which seemed impossibly long. 'My mum doesn't like it, but Pat says it's better than the ring in her belly-button that she might have had.'

'Belly-button,' said Lucy appreciatively. She liked that word – it had a good sound and it was just rude enough for her to enjoy repeating it. She could see the man's belly-button when he lifted the wood above his head and his shirt shot up and showed his stomach. She wondered if he had tattoos lower down on his belly, on the bits you were never allowed to see. Perhaps he even had them on his bum – he seemed to have them everywhere else. She giggled a little to herself at that daring thought, but didn't say anything. She wasn't allowed to say bum. She wondered if Daisy, who was two years older than her, was allowed to say bum.

There were dragons and unicorns on one of the round-abouts. That was the one that looked almost complete now. The dragons looked very battered, with shiny noses where people had clung on to them and paint missing at the sides where thousands of legs had clambered across them. They were the least frightening dragons that Lucy had ever seen, nothing like the ones in books which had fierce red faces and belched out fire from their nostrils. These dragons looked as though they might make quite good pets, like Mr Chadwick's old Labrador which lived at the end of her road. Did dragons have warm pink tongues, like old Barney? She rather thought the dragons on the roundabout would have warm pink tongues.

She told her mother about the dragons and the unicorns when they got home. Her mum didn't listen to her properly; she was busy giving Daisy a bar of chocolate for bringing her daughter safely home all week. Lucy thought she'd like to ride on the unicorn and clasp her hands around its horn, where so many thousands of hands had been before hers. She knew

all about unicorns from a story they'd had when she was still
in the infant school. She hadn't actually seen one. She checked
the forehead of every horse she met, but she hadn't yet found
one with a horn or even a bump that might grow into a horn.
Unicorns must be quite rare.

She chattered on about the fair, but she didn't mention the
men and their tattoos. Her mum didn't like tattoos and she might
stop her going to the fair if she thought it was run by people
with blue pictures and blue writing all over them. Lucy decided
she didn't like tattoos much herself. They were frightening
things, especially when you didn't understand what they were
about and they bulged and rippled as people's bodies moved
beneath their skins.

Her mum let her set the table, because Matt was coming
tonight. Lucy laid out the cutlery with great care, remembering
the order her mum had taught her and placing each knife and
fork and spoon precisely as her tongue flicked each side of
her mouth in turn. Mum was very pleased that Matt was
coming. 'You'll have to be a good girl and keep quiet. Matt's
been at work all week and he'll be tired.'

Lucy wished she could be as excited as Mum about Matt.
But all it meant to her was that tea was going to be late, when
she was hungry. Mum said she could watch television whilst
she waited, and she put CBeebies on and sat in the big armchair
with her legs stretched out as far as they would go in front of
her. After a little while, she wandered into the kitchen and
stood on one leg with both hands on the back of a chair,
watching her mum at the stove. 'Will it be long?' she asked
plaintively.

'Not long now, love. Matt will be here soon. He rang to tell
me that five minutes ago. He's very thoughtful about these
things, isn't he?' Lucy's mother seemed to be reassuring herself,
but Lucy wasn't interested in that. Instead, she looked at the
table and thought of when her dad had sat beside her and helped
her with her food. She must have been very small then. She
was a big girl now, as everyone kept telling her, and she must
get used to a new situation. That was what her mum said. Mum
seemed to say it almost every day now. Lucy wasn't quite sure
about Matt. She thought she liked him, as people said she should.

But he wasn't her dad, was he? Everyone said she must move on when she pointed that out. She wasn't quite sure what 'move on' meant. She wasn't going to forget her dad, whatever they said. But already she was finding it difficult to get a proper picture of him and how it had been between them. She wished she could see her dad more often.

And then Matt was in the house, ruffling her hair and smiling at her and calling her 'young 'un'. He went into the kitchen with Mum and shut the door firmly behind him, and they were quiet for what seemed to Lucy a long time. She heard her mum giggling a couple of times and whispering, so it must be all right.

Then the door burst open and there was food and noise, and both Mum and Matt were fussing over her. 'And what have you been up to this week, young lady?' said Matt when they were all sitting at the table with Mum's cottage pie and fresh green beans in front of them.

Lucy wished they'd just let her eat. She was hungry and she hadn't mastered this thing grown-ups seemed to do without any effort: talking whilst they were eating. When she tried to do it, she was told not to talk with her mouth full. The world seemed to get more confusing as you got bigger. It didn't seem any easier when her mum said brightly, 'Tell Matt about the fair,' and then turned to him herself and said, 'She's been getting more and more excited about it. She hasn't been old enough to appreciate a fair before.'

Adults were like that. They suddenly spoke as if you weren't there. They asked you to talk and then made some remark that somehow left you very little to say. Lucy said, 'I can't talk about the fair now. I mustn't talk with my mouth full.' Then she smiled down into the last of her cottage pie, feeling that she'd really said something quite clever.

They had strawberries and ice cream for afters, because Matt liked that. 'Make the most of this,' her mum told them, 'because these are probably the last British strawberries you'll have this year.'

'We'll do that, won't we, Lucy?' said Matt. Then he smacked his lips extravagantly over his first mouthful, like some of the boys did over their puddings at school. Lucy thought he looked a little ridiculous, but she realized that he was trying to please her, so she gave him a weak smile as she conveyed her own strawberries carefully towards her mouth. They didn't taste as good as the strawberries she remembered from the summer. But the ice cream was nice, so she ate it slowly, making her enjoyment last as long as possible.

Matt insisted that she sat on his knee after they'd left the table. He hugged her tight and then ran his hand softly down her shin. Lucy supposed he meant well, but she couldn't help thinking of her dad holding her like this and making her laugh whilst he bounced her up and down. Mum made her recite for Matt the four times table she'd learned this week. She managed to do all of it, with only one prompt from Matt, which she wouldn't have needed if he'd given her just a second more time to think.

He applauded very loudly, clapping his hands together very near her ears. He said he'd always known she was going to be clever and what a big girl she was becoming now. Then he bounced her very high on his knee, so that her bottom banged against him and her skirt climbed up above her pants, even though she tried to hold it down and almost lost her balance. 'Too much!' she shouted, and she dropped between his knees to the floor as soon as she could.

'You mustn't make her sick,' warned Lucy's mum. But she was laughing at how happy they seemed together.

Matt offered to read her a story, but Lucy was relieved when her mum said she'd do it. It didn't last long, and Lucy sensed that her mum was anxious to be away and back with the man downstairs. 'He's good fun, isn't he, Matt?' she asked her daughter, and Lucy, anxious to please, nodded vigorously. She didn't trust herself to speak, because she might have mentioned her dad, and she knew her mum wouldn't like that.

Her mum went out, then came back only a moment later, whilst Lucy was still staring at the ceiling. 'Matt says he'll take you to the fair tomorrow if you're good in the morning. Aren't you my lucky little girl?'

It was the first time Lucy had been allowed to be little for ages.

TWO

Detective Chief Superintendent Lambert was deeply depressed. He found any sort of police corruption disturbing, and to him this was one of the worst instances. The fact that it was petty compared with the major crimes of violence that made the headlines excused nothing. It was the stupid crimes that were somehow the most depressing.

John Lambert didn't think he was much good at bollockings, though there were some junior members of Oldford CID who would have disagreed with that view. But on this occasion he would have no difficulty. These men were not only fools but fools who should have known better. He'd arranged to see them on Saturday morning because the station was quiet then, which meant that their humiliation would be less public. Now he wasn't sure whether he should have afforded them even that consideration.

They were sitting outside his office when he got there. They sprang to attention as he approached, as though they were army infantrymen or trainee policemen. But their trainee days were long behind them. Lambert left them standing stiffly upright for a moment, whilst he looked them up and down without disguising his distaste.

'At least you're here on time!' he said sourly. Then he was annoyed with himself for lapsing into something so banal and for suggesting that he might be lenient.

There was a little pause whilst the men wondered how to respond. Then the taller of the two said, 'Do you want to see us separately or together, sir?'

'You might as well come in together. You've been equally stupid, as far as I can make out. I don't want the same feeble excuses trotted out twice over.'

Lambert took his time over moving the papers to one side of his desk and sitting himself down in the swivel chair behind it, letting them stand awkwardly and feel too tall in the low-ceilinged room whilst he scanned the three envelopes that were his morning post. It was a good thirty seconds before he looked at the men again and snapped, 'You'd better sit yourselves down, I suppose. I can't speak to you whilst you're standing there like prisoners.'

They hurriedly pulled out steel and canvas chairs from the corner of the room, sensing that the two small armchairs were not the right seats for them. Neither of them had been in this room before, though they both knew all about John Lambert, who was the sort of policeman around whom legends were created. He was such a successful taker of villains that the Home Office had accorded him an exceptional three-year extension to his service, at the chief constable's request. To them he looked very severe, very old and very unyielding.

And now they were here as villains themselves, sitting still and awaiting his wrath. They sat as upright as guilty schoolboys before the headmaster, not daring to look at each other, not daring to look anywhere save at the long, lined face on the other side of the big desk. The head of Oldford CID looked at them without speaking for a moment, allowing his distaste to manifest itself in a tightening of the lips beneath the long nose and the merciless grey eyes. It seemed a long time before he spoke. 'You've been stupid buggers. But you know that. Every stupid bugger realizes he's been stupid, when it's too late.'

The smaller of the two glanced sideways at his companion before he said, 'Yes, sir. We acknowledge that, but there are certain extenuating—'

'I'm not interested in your extenuating circumstances. They don't apply for policemen. Still less for experienced CID officers. Still less for an experienced Detective Sergeant. You should have learned that a long time ago. How old are you, DS Padgett?'

'Twenty-seven, sir.'

'And you, DC Kennedy?'

'Twenty-four, sir.'

'Quite old enough to know better. I wouldn't try offering callow youth as your defence when this comes to court.

Because it's going to come to court, you know. The Crown
Prosecution Service told me that yesterday. And so it should.
No one should get away with this, and least of all experienced
CID officers.'

He let the rebuke drop like lead into the silence, which
extended until DS Padgett felt an overwhelming need to break
it. 'We were provoked, sir.'

Lambert looked at him for a moment, which stretched out
long after Padgett had begun to regret the phrase. 'Do you
know how much you sound like those young thugs we arrest
in Gloucester every Saturday night? You'll need to come up
with something much better than that in court. Otherwise,
you'd better keep your mouth shut and leave it to your brief.'

Kennedy felt an unwise impulse to support his colleague in
the face of the chief superintendent's contempt. 'We were off
duty at the time, sir. It all blew up out of nothing. It happened
very quickly.'

'I'm sure it bloody did. Brawls usually blow up out of
nothing. And they invariably happen very quickly. All of which
you know very well by now. That's why they warn you in the
first weeks of police training that you have to keep cool
and keep control of yourselves. Both of which you signally
failed to do.'

Lambert tried not to think of himself in his twenties, tried
to shut out any thought of the impulsive things he might have
done then, when there were fewer checks on coppers and fewer
people anxious to provoke them. He looked at the cut above
Kennedy's eye and the blue-green bruising that coloured
Padgett's left cheek. 'You didn't even have the sense to choose
the right side, by the looks of it.'

It was the first semblance of humour he had accorded them.
Padgett was encouraged to say, 'We didn't have time to choose
sides, sir. It all happened so quickly. That's the way with
football violence.'

'Don't talk to me about football violence, DS Padgett. We
were handling football violence in the bad old days, before
all-seater stadiums and segregated crowds and all-ticket
entrance. Before you two were even in nappies.' He looked
at the two pale faces, which looked so out of place on these

young, powerful men. They were gazing at their feet like chastened schoolboys. He was suddenly even more annoyed that grown men should have reacted like this. 'You got yourself involved in a bar-room brawl; you behaved like particularly ignorant sixteen-year-old schoolboys. Every police instinct should have told you to back off, but you let your fists take over. Wanted to bully someone, did you?'

DC Kennedy felt it was his turn to speak. He had an odd feeling that they should alternate in confronting the Lambert wrath. 'We were trying to keep order, sir, not disrupt it.'

Lambert stared at him for so long that DC Kennedy eventually felt compelled to lift his eyes and look at the man on the other side of the desk. He immediately wished he hadn't done that and dropped his gaze again to the shoes he had polished so assiduously before coming in to confront the chief.

John Lambert wished he hadn't mentioned bullying. It made him feel he was using rank now to do a little bullying himself. But he was genuinely fiercely annoyed with these men and he hadn't yet reached the real reason for that. He said, 'You were a couple of fools to get involved and you know that, whatever you try to trot out in the way of mitigating circumstances. I expect you'll be happy to let your brief use all the arguments you find so contemptible when they're used on behalf of common criminals. But that's not the worst of it. That isn't what will lose the two of you your jobs, is it?'

'No, sir.' DS Padgett knew better now than to try to defend himself or Kennedy. He had caught the genuine anger that was driving Lambert's tirade.

'No. You tried to cover up your role in this brawl. You put pressure on a witness to retract his evidence. The two of you sought out one of the men you had hit and used a combination of bribery and threats to try to get him to change the statement he had made in this station.'

Kennedy said desperately, 'We didn't offer any direct bribe, sir. We simply suggested that—'

'I'm not interested in what you simply suggested, DC Kennedy. You know as well as I do that the CPS wouldn't have charged you unless they thought they had a strong case. Contrary to what you might think, they don't like bringing cases against the police. It's tiresome, time-consuming and a waste of resources that should be applied to other things. I suggest you now get together with your brief and either refute the charge or produce the best "mitigating circumstances" plea the bugger's ever heard.'

'Yes, sir. I think we can show that we—'

'I'm not interested in hearing what you think you can show or what you intend to cobble up. Consult your bloody brief about that, not me. I'll take the verdict of the court on this, in due course. You've brought disgrace on the police service as well as yourselves with this. It's that service that is my concern, not your miserable skins. Don't expect any sympathy from me if and when the Crown Court finds you guilty! Now get out of here!'

They shuffled to their feet and departed as rapidly as his fierceness indicated they should. John Lambert stared at the blank wall opposite his desk for a long five minutes. Police corruption always appalled and depressed him. Yet, despite what he'd said, he knew he'd end up doing his best for Padgett and Kennedy in due course. He'd be telling whoever would listen in the hierarchy that they were foolish rather than vicious young men, who would surely learn from this experience and give good service in the future.

And yet . . . and yet. If they were found guilty of trying to pervert the court of justice, they would deserve no sympathy, so that he hoped his routine pleas would be ignored. It was a ridiculous contradiction. He slammed the door behind him and went home very depressed. He thought as he drove, 'God give me some real crime and let me dispense with this sort of rubbish!'

By the end of the weekend, he would be heartily wishing he had entertained no such thought.

Lucy Gibson went to the fair that Saturday. She waited all day to go whilst she did other things that were boring.

She was forced to go into Hereford with Matt and her mum. There she had to walk round shops, when she wanted to go to the cathedral or the castle. She wouldn't even have minded a walk by the river, where there were lots of things to see and people to watch, but she had to trail round shops with her mother, holding on to her hand, whilst the adults tried to buy things that were of no interest to her.

She had to sit and watch her mother try on winter coats and parade up and down for Matt to decide which one was best. Her mum was like a silly girl with Matt, prancing up and down and giggling at his comments. Lucy would never have thought of that, but she heard one of the mums at the school gates saying it about another woman who'd got herself a new man. So that's what her mum was being, in this shop and in front of other people – a silly girl. Lucy tutted silently to herself with all the righteous puritanism of a seven-year-old.

Then she had to watch the terminally boring business of Matt buying himself a new electric shaver, whilst her mum giggled and asked questions that Lucy did not understand but which the salesman's reactions told her were silly. Matt made a great show of trying out different models and discussing with the man behind the counter what you got for the extra money with the dearer ones. Then he bought the cheapest of them, which Lucy felt she had known from the start he would do.

They had their lunch in a café in the middle of the town. Lucy was told it was a treat for her and she would normally have enjoyed it. But the place was crowded and it took them a long time to get served. Lucy couldn't help thinking of the summer and her visit here with just her mum, when they walked round the grounds of the old castle and then had tea in a much nicer café beside the river. Matt bought her a milkshake at the end of the meal as a special treat, then asked her when she'd finished whether she'd enjoyed it. 'Too sweet!' Lucy said decisively. Her mum told her that was rude and ungrateful. Probably it was, Lucy thought to herself. She couldn't remember ever saying anything was too sweet for her before.

It seemed ages before they finally reached home. Then her mum insisted on parading up and down in her new coat, to make sure she'd made the right choice. Lucy asked again about the fair, even though she'd been forbidden to mention it again. She was told she must be tired and needed a rest before she went out and got excited. She was sent to her room to read her book and calm down. She talked to Donna, her favourite doll, and told her how stupid and annoying grown-ups could be.

When she went down again, Matt was sitting with his arm round her mum on the sofa. Mum had her head on his shoulder; her eyes were closed and she was nearly asleep. She had what Lucy thought was a stupid smile on her face. She scrambled up when she heard her daughter and said she would make them tea and cake. Lucy followed her into the kitchen, not daring to ask the question that shone out from every feature in her small, anxious face.

'Matt's going to take you to the fair,' said her mum. 'That's good of him, isn't it? And you must promise to be a very good girl for him.'

Lucy clenched her lips and nodded firmly three times. She didn't want to go with Matt, not on his own. But she wouldn't risk being told she was a naughty, ungrateful girl and wouldn't be allowed to go, as had happened two weeks ago when she'd been hoping to go to the cinema. 'Won't you be coming?' she said.

'No. I'll stay here and wash up and tidy the house. You'll be going after tea, like a big girl. You are a big girl now, aren't you?'

Not again, thought Lucy. When do you get old enough for people to stop telling you that? She nodded mutely, not trusting herself to speak, not wanting to say anything that might see her forbidden to go to the fairground. The fair had been withheld from her for so long now that it seemed the only thing that mattered in her life. Eventually, her mum said, 'It will be a good chance for Matt and you to get to know each other better, won't it? Well, I should say even better, because you already know each other quite well now, don't you? It's very important to me that you two get on with each other, you know.' And then she suddenly bent forwards and hugged Lucy so hard that her daughter felt she couldn't breathe. Grown-ups did things like that. As she smoothed her dress, Lucy felt that they should give you some sort of warning before a hug like that one.

She put on her prettiest blue dress for the fair, with the pale blue beanie her mum had bought her in the summer. She wondered as she set off with Matt whether she should have put on her trousers, but it was too late to worry about that now. He'd said she looked very nice when she had stood waiting to go, and Lucy had managed to produce a small, tight smile for him by way of thanks. Mum said she should put on the coat she wore for school, but she said she'd be all right with the dark blue fleece, which went better with her dress.

Matt held her hand tightly in his when they got to the common. When Lucy saw the number of people at the fair, she was suddenly glad of Matt. She didn't like crowds, especially crowds of grown-ups. The rides, which had looked so attractive when they were being built, seemed very noisy now, with people clinging on for dear life and other people shouting and laughing at them from the wooden paths at the sides. Everyone except Lucy seemed very much at home here. She held on to Matt's hand and leaned against his leg, feeling a reassuring warmth through his trousers.

'We'll be all right, won't we, Lucy?' said Matt. Before she could answer, he bent down suddenly and hoisted her high in his arms, holding her against his shoulder so that she could see over the heads around her. She pulled her dress down as low as it would go over her legs, but there still seemed to be a lot of them bare. It was cold now. It wasn't quite dark yet, but the raw bright lights above the raucous noise of the fairground made it seem so here.

Matt took her on a ride called the Caterpillar. The carriages went up and down and round and round, and it wasn't really frightening, once you had got used to the noise. Then the canvas cover came up over the top of them and everyone screamed, and Matt put both arms round her and held her tight against him. She was glad he was there in the sudden darkness, which might have been very frightening with the cars still rattling forward on the bumpy track. But she wished he wouldn't hold her quite so hard, or pull her legs against him with his big rough hand. She wished it was her dad who was there in the noisy darkness, but she knew it would have been rude and ungrateful to say that to Matt. Her mum had warned her about being rude and ungrateful.

Matt wanted her to go on another of the rides, where

motorbikes went up and down and round and round, but she was frightened of that. 'I can't ride a bike yet,' said Lucy. 'Not even an ordinary pedal bike.'

'They're not real bikes, Lucy,' said Matt with one of his big, loud laughs. 'They're fastened to the floor and they just go round and round and up and down like the other things. You'll be perfectly safe. I'll come on with you and ride right behind you. I'll make sure you don't fall off.'

The ride had stopped whilst he spoke and the people who had ridden were coming excitedly down the steps and shouting to each other. A big boy said there was 'nothing to it', and Lucy moved hastily out of his way as he jumped the last two steps and flung his arms up into the air. She saw one of the girls in her class away to her right with her mother, but before she could make any contact they had disappeared into the noisy darkness.

And then, before she could speak or scream, Matt was swinging her high in the air and setting her down astride the motorbike. And then the ride was moving again, slowly at first, then much faster than Lucy wanted it to go. She clung hard to the handlebars in front of her, which were much too big for her small hands, and felt Matt's body hard against her and his warm breath on the back of her neck. 'You'll be all right with me, little 'un!' he shouted in her ear.

Lucy bent low over the smooth wooden frame of the bike and clung to it with her arms and her knees and her feet as the speed increased and she heard excited screams around them. The man taking the money swung athletically about and took money from people for the ride. Lucy couldn't understand how he did that without losing his balance and falling off and being crushed. She was afraid for him, until he disappeared from her sight and her mind, and she clung again to the bike and her own safety, whilst Matt pressed himself hard against the seat and her, like a protective shell on a tortoise.

By the time the music slowed and the ride came to a halt, she had become accustomed enough to the movement to be excited as well as frightened. She didn't nod her head at Matt, but she managed a sickly smile when he said, 'That was good, wasn't it? You're a big girl, now that you've been on the motorbikes!'

Lucy was a little breathless, but she was pleased that she had been on the motorbike and the big ride, now that it was over. Matt took her over to the shooting stall and said that he'd try to win a prize for her. She had to hold on to his trousers whilst he put both hands on the rifle and peered though the sight, then shot at the little moving targets ahead of him. He won her a little rag doll with a Chinese-looking round face and delivered it proudly into her two uplifted hands. Lucy would have liked the great big teddy bear in the middle of the prizes, but Matt said no one won that and it was only there to make people pay to try for it. He said the guns weren't really very good and the sights on them weren't true.

They went over to one of the smaller rides, which was quiet now that most of the younger children had left the fair and gone home to bed. It had an old-fashioned bus on it with a horn you could honk. She preferred it to Thomas the Tank Engine, because the bus was very like the one Lucy remembered from one of her favourite books when she had been small. She hadn't gone on this ride earlier, because the bus had always stopped opposite other children rather than her and they'd been on to it and honking its horn before Lucy could get there.

Now there weren't as many children here. And this time when the ride was over and the roundabout slowed, the bus came to a halt right opposite Matt and Lucy. She looked up at him automatically and he smiled down at her. 'All right,' he said. 'If you still want to go in that old bus, even after you've been on the big rides, you can do. But this will be your last ride. It's getting late and we don't want your mum to be worried, do we? We must go home after this.'

Lucy was in the bright blue bus before he had finished speaking. Matt smiled and waved at her as she waited for the ride to fill up and the man to take the fares. He watched her face concentrate as the ride began to move slowly and she grabbed the wheel and gave her first vigorous honk on the horn.

Matt took the time to think over his relationship with Lucy's mother. He wasn't sure how deep he wanted to get in with Anthea Gibson – everyone said don't touch anyone with kids. But she liked him and she was good in bed; that was surely a good start and it made his life more pleasant having a few creature comforts to look forward to these days.

And Lucy was a nice kid, when you got to know her. She had lovely bright eyes and a nice smile. And she had that smooth, perfect skin that you only really got with girls of her age. And that lovely soft . . . but he mustn't think about things like that. That way disaster lay. He directed his thoughts to the rounded flesh of the child's buxom mother: that should surely be enough for any man.

Lucy relaxed a little as the ride made its third circuit, enough to remember that she was with Matt. She waved to him as her bus swung swiftly past him. He watched her go past, twisting the wheel hard to her left, then pressing the horn hard and continuously. She got a long ride because there weren't as many small customers around as there had been earlier in the day. Lucy waved the arm of the little rag doll she'd decided to call Molly at Matt as she grew more confident. He'd take her straight home after this, so she'd better make the most of it.

Matt waved to the joyous girl and smiled at her. He was thinking enthusiastically of the night ahead and his lovemaking with the eager Mrs Gibson.

Then, after what seemed a long time, the ride was slowing and Lucy was giving him a hasty wave before her last sounding of the bus's horn and her final twist of its wheel. The bus stopped on the other side of the circuit from Matt. Lucy must be exactly opposite him, he reckoned. He'd wait here for her. If he went round to the other side of the ride to meet her, she might go the opposite way and they'd miss each other. He didn't want her to panic.

But Lucy didn't come. Matt peered into the darkness, wishing that there weren't so many lights in his face to dazzle him and make things even ten yards away so indistinct in the gloom. He went round to the other side of the roundabout, then back to where he had stood whilst it was operating. All the other children on it had rejoined their parents and left now. He went back to the other side of the ride and yelled into the darkness. 'Lucy, if you're hiding, come out! This isn't funny! This isn't a joke!'

But Lucy didn't come. Nor was there any answering shout. Matt raced round the ride another three times, then roared off into the blackness beyond it and into the wood beside the common. He yelled Lucy's name hopelessly into the night air.

THREE

L ambert couldn't remember being quite so tired on a Saturday evening. Surely he must have been as exhausted as this many times before, when he'd worked long hours in the garden? But that was a different sort of fatigue; he loved unwinding in the garden after the rigours of his working week.

That was the kind of fatigue he loved to feel in his ageing limbs, the sort he still occasionally eased away with a hot bath and a long soak, lying with closed eyes and shutting out the problems of the world. Soon it would be time for the autumn clear-up in the garden, when you threw out the annuals, divided the odd perennial, took in the dahlias and then lay in the bath planning your garden work for the spring. Perhaps he'd be able to begin that next weekend, after the clocks had been put back.

It was wonderful to have grandchildren, to see the second generation beyond your own growing up and preparing to take over. But youngsters had boundless energy, and their swift growth reminded you constantly of your own accumulating years. On this pleasantly sunny autumn afternoon, he'd taken the boys to the common with his son-in-law and played football with them for a while. He'd become breathless far too quickly; he'd been secretly relieved when Richard had said it was time to pack up if they wanted to visit the fair at the other end of the common.

The boys were seven and five now. John Lambert had been delighted when Harry, the five-year-old, had asked if Grandad would go on to the ride with him and sit in the engine with the cheerful face which looked so like Thomas the Tank Engine. John had folded his legs awkwardly within the cabin, whilst Harry had stood self-consciously on the footplate and pulled the cord which made the whistle sound each time they passed his father and George, standing and waving at the side of the ride.

Each boy had ridden on three of the smaller rides at the side of the fair. Then Grandad and Dad had taken them for their last ride, a special treat on the least frightening of the big roundabouts, the Caterpillar. The boys had clung wide-eyed to the adults as the cars had accelerated and moved more swiftly round the undulating track, then screamed with delight and excitement like everyone else when the canvas hood came suddenly over them and left them in noisy darkness. The sound of the wheels rattling beneath them over the rails was suddenly much louder, and even George, who had spent much of the afternoon asserting his senior status, clung hard to his grandad's arm through this new experience.

Then it was home to the meal Christine had prepared for her family, and amusement at the boys' tales of the football and the fair and Grandad's pretended fear of the Caterpillar. John had stood at the door with Christine to see their daughter Caroline and Richard and their grandchildren drive away, the boys waving furiously at them through the windows as the car disappeared into the gathering darkness.

As the grandparents dropped happily into armchairs and sipped the glasses of port Christine had set beside them, Lambert found himself fighting to stay awake. 'I didn't used to be like this,' he announced resentfully to the ceiling.

'None of us used to be like this,' said Christine firmly. 'Get real, John. You're getting older like everyone else. Chief superintendents don't have a divine dispensation to keep their energy whilst the rest of the world ages around them.'

'I had a depressing morning.' He preferred to blame that rather than his happy efforts with George and Harry for the exhaustion he now felt.

'You weren't at the station long. What was it that left you so depressed?' Christine gazed at him steadily over the top of her glass. Her question came softly, but it was a challenge nevertheless. For years during the early part of his career, when her children had been small and she'd felt isolated with them in her home, John had shut her out of his working life completely. He'd worked long hours as a detective sergeant and then as a detective inspector without even being prepared to reveal the cases he had been assigned to. Often she'd picked up more from

the press than she had from her husband about his successes
and failures. He'd been away so much and cut himself off from
her so completely that their marriage had almost failed. The
union that now looked so solid and unshakeable to his juniors
at Oldford CID had almost foundered on the rocks of his passion
for results.

He had realized later, much later, that he had been driven
above all in those days by a fear of failure. He had confessed
as much to Christine now, but that hadn't prevented them from
sailing very near to the rocks of divorce in those early years.
Christine still wondered what might have happened if she had
not resumed the teaching she loved when the children reached
school age. Now they were so solid and had been through so
much together that it seemed as though she was studying two
other people, ignorant and vulnerable, when she looked back
to those years. Yet her instinctive reaction when he mentioned
his work was still to encourage him to talk to her about it.

John gave her a small, tight smile, as if he wished to convey
to her that he understood all of this and was sorry for the past.
'You'll read about it, in due course. Two CID men in their
twenties have got themselves into trouble. They used their fists
in a brawl outside a pub before a Bristol City football match.
They were off duty at the time and no doubt didn't announce
themselves as coppers.'

'It's daft, but it's the kind of thing young men get themselves
involved in before they realize it's happening.'

John Lambert smiled sadly. 'That's more or less what they
said. If that was all they'd done, I'd have given them an earful
and sent them on their way – possibly even left that to someone
further down the line. But they've now done much worse.
They tried to pressurize a witness into withdrawing his
statement. They'll end up in the Crown Court in a couple of
months' time.'

Christine knew that he was only speaking about what would
become public knowledge in due course. He still never
mentioned anything that should remain confidential; she understood that and respected him for it. But at one time he would
never have mentioned anything that went on in the Oldford
CID section, however trivial. He had shut the doors on her

when it came to that dominant section of his life. She said gently, 'I know how it upsets you, any sort of police corruption.'

'It affects us all, the publicity these idiots will get. The public tar us all with the same brush. We're all corrupt and all on the take.'

'That's the way life is, John. Some people always want to believe the worst. It's not confined to the police.'

He shook his head sadly, then grinned at her, suddenly and unexpectedly. 'You're right about me getting old. Perhaps we should discuss what we're going to do when I retire.'

Christine Lambert was a wise woman. She knew that, with husbands, you sometimes had to give up whilst you were winning. She said, 'Let's leave that until the time comes. You've got a few more years in you yet, super-sleuth.'

She used the term one of the tabloids had created for him a year earlier, which she knew he hated. It was part of a private code between them, and he grinned his recognition of that, then switched to happier themes and talked for a pleasant ten minutes about how quickly and attractively George and Harry were developing. He was fully alert again for the BBC's *Match of the Day* and managed to shout at the screen three times after Christine had retired to bed. Not too bad a day after all, he decided.

It rained overnight, but only a little light drizzle. A weak early-morning sun was beginning to pierce the autumn mist as Lambert drew the curtains back. He'd be able to get out into the garden by late morning. Dig over the vegetable plot and leave it ready for the first frosts.

The phone rang early. That was never a good sign at the weekend. Christine answered it, then passed it across with a sigh of resignation to her husband. She went back into the kitchen and left John speaking in low tones into the mouthpiece. Most of the talk came from the other end of the line; his contribution was a series of terse questions about time and place.

His face was drawn and grey when he came to her and spoke across the table and his untouched toast. 'It's a missing child. A seven-year-old girl vanished last night. Disappeared from the fairground. She still hasn't been found. I'm going in straight away.'

Christine listened to his clipped phrases, nodded grimly and went with him to the door. They looked at each other but didn't wave as he reversed his big old Vauxhall in front of the bungalow, then turned swiftly through the gates and into the wide and dangerous world outside. Both of them were thinking of their two joyous, innocent grandsons, who had so enjoyed the fairground rides the previous day.

'Why didn't I hear about this last night?'

The station sergeant looked at Lambert apprehensively. He could have said that he wasn't on duty then, but that would have been buck-passing. Something in the chief super's manner indicated that he wouldn't appreciate buck-passing. 'It wasn't reported until five to ten, sir. It was midnight by the time a uniformed PC had brought in the first statement from the mother. There's no father around.'

'What was a seven-year-old doing around the fairground at that time?'

'I gather she disappeared much earlier, sir. Around half past seven, I believe. They spent the evening hoping she'd turn up, I think.'

Lambert didn't ask who 'they' were. This was all second- or third-hand information and he wanted something more direct.

The station was unusually busy for a Sunday morning. A missing child brought in male and female officers in numbers no other emergency prompted. Lambert assembled the CID staff and made the initial moves. He directed Detective Sergeant Hook and Detective Sergeant David to go to the girl's home and divine whatever they could there. Bert Hook was experienced and sensitive, and Ruth David was intelligent and alert to all the possibilities in a situation. And it was always advisable to have a woman to speak to a mother in these appalling circumstances.

Detective Inspector Rushton would coordinate and computerize the vast array of information that would accrue unless the girl was found alive in the next few hours. Lambert would go immediately to the point where the seven-year-old had last been seen. He was a dinosaur among modern chief supers in demanding to be out and about in pursuit of a solution, rather than coordinating the investigation from behind a desk. But DI Rushton did that job very effectively and Lambert's methods worked. His chief constable was enough of a pragmatist to tolerate and encourage him.

Bert Hook and Ruth David did not speak to each other much as Bert drove the police Mondeo to Anthea Gibson's house. They were an unlikely pair, physically very different. Bert had the sturdy physique of the Minor Counties fast bowler he had been for fifteen years; he was just under six feet tall and broad of shoulder and beam. He subscribed to Fred Trueman's theory that you needed a powerful backside to bowl fast. He had a countryman's complexion and an air of sturdy reliability. One of his great advantages as John Lambert's bagman was that people assumed he was less intelligent than he was and underestimated him. Beneath his PC Plod exterior there lurked a shrewd brain. Hook had completed an Open University degree the previous year – a source of much police ribaldry but also considerable well-concealed respect.

No one would have assumed that Ruth David was unintelligent. She was seventeen years younger than Bert, possessed a Cambridge degree and had joined the service under the graduate recruitment scheme. She had the tall, willowy figure of an athlete, ash-blonde hair and dark green eyes. She was the source of many male sexual fantasies among the raging hormones at Oldford police station, but with a bearing too formidable for these to give her any problems.

These two very different physical specimens had great respect for each other. Bert had taken the decision several years earlier not to go for the detective inspector role that would undoubtedly have been his by now had he pursued it. But it was Bert Hook who had told Ruth a month ago that she should now be moving on and becoming an inspector. She had said that she didn't need the money and preferred for the moment to remain in John Lambert's team, because she thought she was learning more there than she would elsewhere.

They drew up outside Anthea Gibson's house and studied it for a moment before leaving the car. It was a small end-of-terrace. It looked far too unremarkable and far too much like its neighbours to contain the potential tragedy that was unfolding within it. The police pair stood looking at the unmown lawn and the weed-infested borders of the small front garden for a moment before steeling themselves to approach the green front door.

Anthea Gibson ignored the warrant cards and stared straight into each face in turn. 'Is there any news?'

'Not yet, I'm afraid,' said Ruth David. 'It's early days. We'll have a better chance of finding her in the daylight.' She was ashamed of herself for the clichés, but she had nothing better to offer. 'Mrs Gibson, I know you spoke briefly with a uniformed officer last night, but we're CID. We need a few more details from you to help our search. May we come in?'

'Yes. Yes, I'm sorry, of course you must.' She glanced past them and looked up and down the road, as if she hoped to see Lucy's small face peeping round a hedge and banishing her nightmare.

'And who is this?' said Bert Hook, as affably as he could, drawing into the conversation the heavy, white-faced man who stood in a doorway behind her.

Mrs Gibson looked startled, as if she had thought that she was alone in the house. Then she said, 'Yes. Oh, yes. This is Matt Boyd. He's not my husband. He's – he's a friend. A close friend.'

Bert thought he knew what that meant. 'We'll need to speak to you both, but separately, I think. We find people remember things better when they speak to us alone. Is that all right?'

The pair nodded without looking at each other. Ruth David said, 'I think we should speak to you first, Mrs Gibson – get a few more details about Lucy to help us with the search.'

'I'll wait in the kitchen,' said Matt Boyd. 'I'll come with you to the station afterwards, if that's all right.'

'That will be fine,' said Bert immediately. He wondered why the man didn't want to be interviewed with the girl's mother around. Very few people opted to go to the police station to be interviewed; it was generally something the CID offered as a threat when people were being uncooperative. Probably this man would be trying to hear what they said to Mrs Gibson, but he couldn't blame him for that. Bert shut the door of the living room carefully behind him and went to sit at the other end of the sofa from Ruth David. His colleague was already contemplating the tense face of the woman sitting in the armchair opposite her.

Ruth waited until the room was still and silent, smiling gently at the young woman who was suffering this rare but excruciating torment. 'How old is Lucy?'

She said it easily enough, as though it was nothing other than a gentle opening question, but she was already treading carefully. It was so easy to say 'was' rather than 'is', and there was no retrieving an error like that once you'd made it.

Speech was a small relief for Anthea Gibson. She said promptly, 'Seven and three-quarters last Thursday.' Then she almost burst into tears, as Lucy's voice sounded in her ears. 'I know because she kept telling me that all last week.' The woman's small, involuntary giggle showed how near she was to hysteria.

'Doing well at school, is she?'

It seemed irrelevant, no more than a polite enquiry. But they needed to know that the girl was normal, whatever that blanket term meant. Children with mental limitations were much more likely to be abused or abducted, because vicious people recognized weakness of any kind and exploited it. Less intelligent children were less aware, less ready to defend themselves against initial advances, more liable to disappear in the way that Lucy had. The statistics showed it, and at this stage, when you had so little else to aid you, you fastened upon statistics.

Anthea Gibson knew none of this. She said with a tiny smile and a flash of pride, 'Yes. She's a good reader and Mrs Copthall said her writing is coming on well. She's doing pretty well in maths. Not quite as well as in her language work, but that's girls for you, isn't it?'

Ruth didn't respond to this disavowal of her sex, except with a small smile of encouragement. 'She hasn't had any problems at school that you know of?'

'No. She's always been a good mixer, the teachers say. She likes going to school.'

'And you're not aware of any change in that recently?'

'No. She chats to me about her friends and what's been happening.' Anthea's tense face clouded with a sudden thought. 'I've not been meeting her at the school gates lately. Daisy, a bigger girl who lives next door but one, brought her home from school each day last week. You don't think that has anything to do with this, do you?'

Ruth watched Bert Hook making a note, then said, 'Almost certainly not, Mrs Gibson. But if Lucy doesn't turn up quickly, we'll be talking to people at the school to find out whether they have any thoughts on this.'

'It's not dangerous, you see, the way she comes home. There are no busy roads to cross and we're only two or three hundred yards from the school. And Daisy's a sensible girl, even though she's only nine. I thought it would be another stage in Lucy's growing up.' She suddenly found herself weeping, without any warning. She dabbed at her eyes with a handkerchief that was already sodden.

Ruth nodded, moving without any visible change of gear into the more contentious section of her questioning. 'I know you've answered this question before, but could you tell us exactly when Lucy disappeared last night?'

Anthea glanced automatically at the room's closed door, perhaps wondering, as Ruth did, whether the man they had excluded had his ear against the other side of it. 'We think about half past seven. She was at the fair on the common with Matt.'

'I see. But according to our records at the station, her disappearance wasn't noted until almost ten o'clock.' The two detective sergeants in the room had read the statement made to the uniformed officers on the previous night and knew all of this, but Ruth David was probing, looking for any sign of nervousness. Even mothers had to be investigated in situations like this. She'd already noted that there were no signs of drugs in the house and that Anthea Gibson didn't look like a user.

Now the girl's mother looked hard at her own feet. 'Matt was looking for her. He couldn't believe she'd gone, at first.

He thought she was playing tricks and hiding away from him as a joke.'

'Is that the sort of thing Lucy does? Is she a mischievous little girl?'

'No. She's a good girl. I don't think she'd do that. I said so to Matt.' She dabbed furiously at her eyes again, then looked up to check their reactions to what she'd said. This woman sergeant was pretty. Too pretty, Anthea thought. She asked abruptly, 'Do you have children yourself?'

Ruth summoned her gentlest, most understanding smile. 'No. I've just got engaged. I hope I shall have them, in a year or two.'

Mrs Gibson nodded and sat very upright. Her bearing reflected her view that a childless woman couldn't possibly understand what she was feeling.

Bert Hook had been wondering how to enter the exchanges. He had agreed with Ruth beforehand that she would do the mother-and-child questions and he would come in when they reached the men in Anthea Gibson's life. He now said softly, 'I have children, Anthea. Two boys. They're older than Lucy, but we still worry about them when they're out on their own.'

The woman in the armchair nodded fiercely, as if establishing common ground with this experienced, unthreatening man. Bert said softly, 'I gather your husband isn't around any more.'

Anthea wondered fleetingly where he had gathered it from, but all she did was nod. She was too near to tears to trust herself to do more.

Hook produced an immaculate white handkerchief and stretched his arm stiffly across the gap between them. 'Take it, please, and use it. I shan't want it back.'

'Thank you. I've got some tissues somewhere.' Ruth David passed the box to her from the unit behind her and Anthea blew her nose noisily, as if she needed this vigorous gesture to regain control. 'No. We're not divorced. But I expect we will be. Dean's not around anymore.'

'But he's Lucy's father.'

'Yes.'

'Does he live far away?'

'Not far. Somewhere in Malvern, I think.' She watched Ruth David's perfect fingers as she scribbled furiously, having taken over the note-taking from Hook. You had to be single to have hands and nails like that, Anthea thought inconsequentially. 'I don't have an address. He's moved around a bit since he left here.'

Hook nodded. Malvern wasn't a huge place. They'd need to speak to the father, but they'd find him quickly enough if he was still there. Bert noticed that he was already assuming that the girl wasn't going to turn up today and give them a happy ending. 'Does your husband still see Lucy?'

'At least once a month. More like once a fortnight, most of the time.'

'Could you describe his relationship with Lucy for us, in just a few words?'

She should have expected this, she thought. But she hadn't planned for it. But then she hadn't planned any of this. 'Dean likes Lucy. She likes him. We didn't split up over her.'

'And he enjoys seeing Lucy?'

'Yes. I feel guilty about it. Not about splitting up, but about Lucy and her dad. They got on well together.'

Did this mean that Lucy didn't get on with the man now in the kitchen? The man who had been the last person known to have been with the seven-year-old before she vanished? Hook was at his kindest and most avuncular as he said, 'Please think about this before you answer me, Mrs Gibson. Do you think your husband might be involved in this in any way?'

'No.'

'You answered that very promptly.'

'That's because I've already thought about it. I discussed it with Matt before we rang the police last night. Dean says he still loves me; he wants us to get back together. It's me that doesn't want that. But he'd never snatch Lucy like that. And even if he did, he'd let me know. He wouldn't have me going through this.'

'Fair enough.' But they'd track the man down as quickly as they could, nonetheless. Sometimes you didn't know even the people who'd shared your bed and fathered your child as well as you thought you did. Bitter resentment could drive people

to act out of character. Hook smiled at her again, trying to
take the edge off what he had to say now. 'How long have
you known Matthew Boyd, Mrs Gibson?'

The name sounded strange when they voiced it solemnly
and in full like that. As if it was a different man entirely from
the one who had made her laugh and made her respond so
passionately to him in bed. 'I met Matt just under three months
ago.'

Ruth David recorded that in her neat, quick hand. Such
precision usually meant that a woman was keen. Smitten,
perhaps. So much so that her judgement of character might
be impaired. Bert Hook said, 'And where did you meet?'

'At a singles club. My friend had taken me along.' She
wondered why she needed to explain herself like that, as if
apologizing for her conduct. Everyone went to such places
now, didn't they? Well, everyone in her position. 'Matt asked
me if I'd like to go for a meal. I did and we got on well.
We've been getting on well ever since.'

Anthea wondered if Hook would ask if they had been
intimate with each other. That was an old-fashioned phrase, but
he looked an old-fashioned man. She didn't wait to see how he
would put the question she knew he would have to ask. 'We
became lovers six weeks ago. We get on well and Matt likes
Lucy. He volunteered to take her to the fair.' She'd meant it as
a compliment to him, but now it suddenly sounded sinister in
the light of this awful thing that had happened. Hastily, she
said, 'Matt would never hurt Lucy. He likes her, but not in any
way that's wrong.' That was clumsy, but she wanted to defend
him and she couldn't think of the right phrases.

'Thank you. We'll be speaking to Mr Boyd in due course,
as you know. In the meantime, we need a clear picture from
you of what happened last night. At what time did Mr Boyd
take your daughter out to the fair?'

'About six, we think. Neither of us was thinking that the
time would be important then.' The tears sprang from her eyes
again and she dabbed them away with Hook's gift.

'And you think Lucy disappeared at about half past seven.'

'That's what Matt thinks. She was having a last ride on one
of the smaller roundabouts and then coming home. But when

the ride stopped and he went to collect her, she just
wasn't there.'

'I see. But he didn't report that immediately and he didn't
come back here until approximately ninety minutes later. Or
phone you to let you know she'd gone missing?'

'No. He thought he'd find her. He thought Lucy was playing
a joke on him and would come out from wherever she was
hiding. He didn't want me to worry.'

She was staring at her feet again and Hook knew in that
moment as clearly as if she'd told him that she'd argued with
the man in the kitchen about this. He said gently, 'But when
he couldn't find her, don't you think he should have then tried
to get in touch to let you know?'

'Well, I think he just really wanted to find her himself. He
searched the woods at the top of the common and some of
the streets on the other sides of it. He couldn't believe that
she'd gone.' She looked up at Hook suddenly, wanting to
convince herself as much as her questioners. 'I think he was
terrified of telling me that he'd lost her.'

'I see.' Hook could see that. He wouldn't have relished the
prospect himself if he'd been reporting the disappearance of
the daughter she loved to a woman he'd only known for three
months. 'Was last night the first time Lucy had been out alone
with Mr Boyd?'

Anthea thought for a moment. She hadn't considered this
until now. It sounded sinister when the question was put like
that. 'Yes. But that's just coincidence. Lucy was happy enough
to go with Matt. She'd been looking forward to it all day.'

Ruth David looked up from her notes. 'We're just recording
facts, Mrs Gibson. That's what we do, you see. I hope that by
tonight we'll be recording the fact of your daughter's return
home to you. What happened when Mr Boyd returned here
without your daughter?'

'I screamed at him, I think. I know I turned hysterical. Matt
got me to ring the homes of Lucy's friends before we contacted
the police. He – I mean *we* – thought it might all be a false
alarm. We thought she might have run away for a joke and
then got frightened or lost and gone to a friend's house. That's
why it was so late when you got the call from us.'

That call had come at the worst possible time on a Saturday night, when all the uniformed men and women were dealing with the weekend drunks and trying to shepherd them home without serious trouble. When the only staff available to send here and take statements had been the newest and least experienced young officers on the force. Ruth glanced at Hook and received the slightest of nods, the signal for the pair to stand up in unison. 'Do you have a recent photograph of Lucy we could borrow, to help us in our search?'

The girl looked even younger than her age in the photograph, absurdly innocent and absurdly vulnerable in her blue school sweater.

Matthew Boyd wasn't listening in the hall and never had been. He was in the kitchen with the door shut firmly behind him. He shuffled clumsily to his feet when Hook opened that door. 'You can speak to us here or at the station,' Bert said neutrally to the last man known to have seen the missing girl.

'I'll come to the station with you,' the man said immediately. He did not look at them, nor at the stricken woman who had lost her daughter, as he walked out of her house.

Anthea Gibson watched him leave and fleetingly wondered if he was going to acknowledge her at all as he got into his car. She saw him flick up his hand in the briefest of gestures as he drove past her standing in the doorway of the house.

She went back into her empty home and briefly wondered when she would see him next.

FOUR

The spot where Lucy Gibson had disappeared was being treated as a scene of crime, even though no crime had as yet been discovered. The area was cordoned off with blue-and-white plastic ribbons.

Lambert was intercepted by the manager and chief proprietor of the fair before he could contact the scene of crime team. This was a large, very broad man with a stomach that, in an earlier era, would have been an impressive mount for a waistcoat and watch chain. He seized Lambert's arm and ushered him into a caravan at the side of the fair. He had a smooth brown face, a wide and curling black moustache, and an air of barely controlled indignation. 'This is costing us money. Sunday should be our best day. I own four of the roundabouts working out there. You've shut down three of the smaller rides, which should be pulling in money from children all through the daylight hours.'

Lambert decided he hadn't time for a protracted argument. 'Get real, Mr Davies! There's a seven-year-old girl missing. That takes precedence over everything. I'd shut down the whole of your damned fair if I thought it would help!'

'You couldn't do that.'

'I could and I would if it was necessary. Be thankful that we've let the bulk of the rides and stalls carry on as normal. If your people don't cooperate or we find a need to extend the area of our investigation, we shall certainly do so. You're welcome to complain to my chief constable if you wish to do that. I can tell you now that you won't get a sympathetic reaction. Now, let me move out of here and get on with my work, please!'

It was a relief to sound off at someone amidst his frustration and depression. He had found in this oily and unimaginative man a fitting object for his wrath. He stepped stiffly from the caravan and went over to the civilian in charge of the scene of crime team, a retired detective sergeant whom he had known since his time in the service. The chief superintendent put on the plastic foot covers necessary to avoid any contamination of the designated area and went down the path delineated within it to the man in charge.

'Found anything, Dave?' You dispensed with the formalities when a child was missing. Time was vital. Everyone knew that the chances of finding the girl unharmed decreased dramatically after twenty-four hours.

'Lots of things. At least, we've bagged lots of things. Which ones, if any, will prove significant is anyone's guess at this stage.' The SOCO chief indicated polythene bags with a variety of cigarette ends, a broken comb, a muddy earring, a local paper with a tyre-mark across it. 'No trace of the girl yet?'

'No. We've phoned every relative and friend we can think of and there's an appeal gone out on national radio and television. The usual loonies have already begun to ring in; I expect we'll have a dozen sightings claimed by the end of the day, in all sorts of places. But as yet we've no real news of Lucy.'

John Lambert stated the name firmly. It was important to him now that this was a real girl and that everyone thought of her as Lucy. He had no doubt that Hook and David would come back to the station with a picture of a smiling, carefree seven-year-old. A seven-year-old who by now might be terrified in some isolated building. A seven-year-old who might have endured unspeakable things in the last twelve hours. A seven-year-old who might already be dead. Lucy.

He looked at the still and silent roundabout where Lucy Gibson had taken her last ride. A joyful ride, the man who ran it said. The girl had been smiling happily and waving to the man who had brought her here. A man and a woman from the SOCO team were lifting fingerprints from the bus in which Lucy had ridden and from every other carriage on the ride. There'd be hundreds of them, and all useless. Apart from one, perhaps. But how quickly and certainly could they isolate that one? Even if there was a match with the print of some paedophile who might have taken the girl, how long would it take to establish that match? And what would have happened to Lucy in the meantime?

Lambert fought against an overwhelming feeling of helplessness, the worst possible emotion for a detective. He hadn't had many cases like this in his now lengthy experience, but none of them had ended well. This wasn't the Moors murders, with Brady and Hindley and those awful torture tapes which had sickened hardened policemen. But the outcome might be just as horrific for one small, terrified girl who did not understand how the world had turned ugly upon her.

The photographer was busy, for there was much here that had to be preserved, though most, if not all, of it would prove irrelevant to the case in the end. The ground at the edge of the fair site was damp and soft, for here the stalls and roundabouts had been in shadow for the last three days. Lambert watched the man carefully framing shots of footprints left by trainers, boots and more anonymous shoes, both male and female. Had one of these been left by the man or woman who had spirited Lucy away so soundlessly and swiftly from everything that she knew and trusted?

He walked a little further, to where common merged with woods. This was where the designated crime scene, as delineated by the police ribbons, came to an end. Five yards into the woods, a woman in the scene of crime team was picking up something gingerly with the finger and thumb of a gloved hand, taking care to leave as little of herself as possible on the thing she had lifted.

Lambert went over and held open the plastic bag for her, so as to make it easy for her to deposit her find without handling it further. She did so with extreme care, her tongue flicking at the edge of her mouth like that of a fiercely concentrating child. Once the top of the bag was sealed upon its contents, she looked up at the chief superintendent who was in charge of all this. Then both of them gazed down in silence for a moment, feeling the pathos of her find. There was a muddy footprint across the centre of what lay beneath the plastic. Lambert looked at it for a moment, then made a decision. 'I'll take this back to the station with me. I'm about to speak to the man who was with Lucy last night.'

It was a small rag doll with a fixed and cheerful smile.

*   *   *

Matt Boyd had been in an interview room at a police station once before. It wasn't any more pleasant the second time.

He wondered if the fuzz had left him there to soften him up for what was to come. They hadn't been unpleasant, the two who'd followed him here from Anthea's house, but they hadn't been friendly either. Reserved, he supposed; that was probably the best word to describe it. Careful, perhaps. Well, he'd been careful himself, and he was determined to remain so. It was a nasty business this, whatever way you looked at it. He wished at this moment that he'd never gone near Anthea Gibson at that singles meeting.

He'd liked the woman officer who'd talked to Anthea. She was a real looker, which was a good start, and she'd been polite and pleasant with him, soft and tender with Anthea. Soft and tender; those words set him thinking of Lucy, the girl he'd lost last night, and what might have been. That way madness lay. He dragged his mind back to Detective Sergeant Ruth David. She'd be impressed if he remembered her name and rank. Women liked that sort of thing and it was one of the things he was good at. He'd trained himself, over the years.

But when they finally attended to him, DS Ruth David did not appear. It was the burly Detective Sergeant Hook again, but he had a much taller man with him, who paused for a moment just inside the room to inspect Matthew Boyd. He looked rather like a biologist considering the possibilities of a specimen frog he was about to dissect. Hook said, 'This is Detective Chief Superintendent Lambert, who is now in charge of this case.'

Matt had heard of this man Lambert before, even though he didn't follow crime much in the press. He was locally famous, perhaps even nationally famous by now. He would be able to tell Anthea that he'd been interviewed by the great man. Well, perhaps not Anthea. Perhaps he wouldn't have many more dealings with Anthea, even if this all passed off without any trouble from the police. But he needed to concentrate hard on what was to come in the next few minutes, not think about Anthea Gibson.

He dragged his mind back to the two men who were now pulling up chairs and sitting down opposite him on the other side of the small square table. He must give this all his attention if he was to come through it unscathed. He tried to summon a smile as he looked into the long, lined face and the grey eyes that were staring at him unblinkingly. Lambert said coolly, 'You are not under arrest and you are not on oath. Do you have any objection to our recording this conversation? You are a vital witness in this, the only one we have at present, and we may need to recall what you have to say for the rest of the large team assigned to this.'

'No.' Matt licked his lips. 'I've no objection to that.' In truth, he didn't like it at all. But they had him over a barrel, hadn't they? If he refused, it would look and sound suspicious, and he couldn't afford that. He tried not to notice the recording beginning as Hook set the machine in motion.

Lambert said, 'We need to hear your account of what happened, Mr Boyd.'

'I've already given it. I told the constable everything last night.'

'And both of us have read his account of what you said then. But I want to hear it for myself. Twelve hours have passed since you spoke to our uniformed officer. You may have extra recollections or new thoughts to offer to us. And I'd like an account of everything that happened at the fairground, in case we can pick up anything significant from earlier events. You weren't aware of anyone watching or following you, were you?'

'No. But then you're not even thinking about things like that, are you? If anyone was following us, I never saw him.' He gave a tiny, involuntary shudder at the thought. 'I was giving all my attention to Lucy. It's not easy being a new man coming into the house, when a little girl's lost her dad. I was trying to tread carefully with her.'

'I appreciate that. Describe your relationship with Lucy for us, please.'

Matt had hoped they'd be friendlier than this, that he wouldn't be questioned about how things were between him and Lucy. He told himself firmly that they weren't unduly suspicious of him, that they'd have investigated this with any man in his position. 'I was getting on with her well, when you take all the circumstances into account. The three of us – that's Lucy and Anthea and me – had been to Hereford during the day. We went round the shops and had lunch there. Lucy was perfectly happy with me. I think she was impatient to get home and go to the fair, but I expect any child would have been.'

'Have you children of your own, Mr Boyd?'

'No. My marriage didn't last long. Both of us said, when we split up, that it was a good thing that there were no children to worry about.' He'd had this ready for them. He delivered it in a measured tone and looked just above Lambert's head.

'You took Lucy to the fairground on your own. Was she happy to go there without her mother?'

'Yes, I think so. It was Anthea's suggestion. She thought it would be a step forward. Another stage in Lucy and me getting to know each other.' The last bit sounded hollow in his ears as he recited it, but they were Anthea's own phrases, and thus surely worth using here. He watched Hook writing; the man seemed concerned to write down his exact words, even though they were being recorded.

Then Hook looked up at him and spoke for the first time. 'Was this the first occasion you had been out alone with Lucy, Mr Boyd?'

The words flew at him like an accusation from the calm, weather-beaten face. 'Yes. Yes, I suppose it must have been.'

Lambert said tersely, 'Was it or wasn't it, Mr Boyd? You must surely know that.'

'Yes. Yes, it was. I don't like the tone of your questioning, that's all.'

'I'm concerned with the disappearance of a helpless girl and what's happened to her since. Your feelings are very much secondary to that.'

'All right, I'm sorry. I'm as anxious to see Lucy back as you are. More anxious, because I know her and you don't.'

'So help us get to know her. Help us to understand the state of her mind when she was taken. Because at least two people in this room are pretty sure by now that she *was* taken. Do you think she was?'

Matt tried to control the pulse he felt pounding in his temple.

'Yes. I don't think there can be any other explanation. But when it happens, you just can't believe it's happening to you.'

'I understand that. But we have to record all the facts. When a child disappears, there are very few facts at first. And we need to move fast, very fast, if we are to get Lucy back alive. Tell us what happened at the fairground last night, please. It seems that Lucy was lightly dressed, for a cool autumn evening.'

Matt tried not to consider the implications of this. He had to safeguard his own position. He must give all his attention to that. 'She was in her best light-blue dress. Little girls like to dress up when they're going out for a treat, don't they? Her mum made her put on her beanie, and she was wearing a fleece, but Lucy was almost dancing with excitement. She was impatient to be off to the fair.'

'And she was perfectly happy to go there alone with you?'

'Yes. I've already told you she was.' He tried a flash of candour. 'To be perfectly honest, I think she'd have been happy to go there with anyone, just to get to the rides. She'd been looking forward to it all day.'

'I see. It was still daylight when you reached the common, then?'

'Yes. But with all the lights on the rides and the stalls, it seemed darker and later than it was. Lucy clung tightly to my hand when we got there. It was the first time she'd ever been to a fair. We went to look at the smaller rides first, the ones she really wanted to go on. But they were still very busy, crowded with small children and their parents. Lucy couldn't get into the things she wanted to ride in, like the blue bus on the ride at the edge of the fairground. I said it would be quieter later, when the smaller children went home to bed. I said it would be best if we went away and looked at the rest of the fair and came back later.'

'So where did you go?'

'I took her on a couple of the big rides. She was a bit nervous, as you'd imagine – she isn't eight yet. I took her on the Caterpillar, which is the slowest of the big rides, and then we rode on a motorbike together on one of the others. Lucy liked clinging on to the handlebars and pretending it was a real bike. She's a game kid, and she was safe enough with me behind her.' He was suddenly aghast at his words. 'But she wasn't safe at all, was she? She should have been. I should have looked after her!' His broad features looked in that moment as if they might crash into tears.

Lambert kept his tone even, almost matter-of-fact, despite his theme. 'And what happened next, Mr Boyd?'

'We went back to the small rides, where she'd wanted to go at first. I'd promised her, you see. I remember her tugging at my hand to get me back there.'

'But you weren't aware of anyone following you?'

'No. But there might have been, I suppose.' He shook his head wretchedly. 'My attention was all on Lucy, you see. I wanted her to enjoy it. I wanted her to go home to her mum and say she'd enjoyed herself with me.'

'And she went on one of the smaller rides.'

'Yes. They don't move very quickly, so children don't need adults with them. It's not far from one side to the other on the smaller roundabouts. I still can't see how it happened. I was so unprepared for it, you see.'

'Just tell us exactly what took place, please. Try to leave nothing out.'

'Well, Lucy got in the blue bus she'd wanted to ride in from the start. I think she'd seen the ride being put together on her way home from school and set her heart on a ride in that bus. She was a bit nervous when they started to go round – it's only a small ride, but it was the first one she'd been on by herself.'

'And even at this stage, you weren't aware of anyone else watching her?'

'No. There were parents around me waving to their own children and me waving to Lucy. That was all. If the bastard who took her had been on my side of the roundabout, I'm sure I'd have seen him, even though I was watching for Lucy to come round each time and waving to her.'

'What about the staff? Did you see anyone on the ride paying any attention to Lucy?'

'No. I'd paid the money before it began to move, and I think most of the other adults had done the same. I didn't see anyone collecting fares or swinging around the carriages once it started.'

'Carry on, please.'

'Lucy waved to me, the first three or four times she passed me. Then she got more confident. She tooted the bus's horn and twisted the steering wheel and got really involved. She looked very happy.' He threatened to break down again, but he filled his big chest with a huge breath and regained control. 'They got a good long ride, as I'd said they would. Most of the younger children had been taken home by this time, so there weren't many waiting to get on.'

'But you didn't see Lucy again after she left that little bus on the roundabout.'

'No. I waited for the ride to stop and Lucy to climb out and run to me, all excited. But when it stopped, the bus was exactly opposite me on the other side and I couldn't see across the other cabins to where she would have got off. I waited for a moment for her to come round to me. I was afraid that if I went to collect her, she might choose the other side of the ride from me and panic if I wasn't where she'd left me.'

'So you stood quite still for a moment and watched for Lucy coming back to you. How long would that be?'

'I'm not sure. It seemed a long time, as I gradually realized that she wasn't coming. I was worried, but I didn't really panic at that stage. I thought Lucy would be standing still on the other side of the ride, waiting for me to collect her. She's a sensible girl. I suppose I stood waiting for about thirty seconds before I moved – certainly not longer than a minute.'

'You're probably about right in that guestimate. A minute is a long time when you're standing quite still and waiting for something to happen.' Lambert was thinking of how long a minute seemed when there was no noise and no movement at eleven o'clock on Armistice Day. He dismissed that death-laden image furiously from his mind. 'This is very important, Mr Boyd. When you stood watching and waiting for Lucy, you must have been acutely aware of other adults around you. Did you see any movement towards the spot where Lucy must have been when the ride stopped and she left her bus?'

Matt shook his head unhappily. 'I've been over that moment

a dozen times. I've told myself that I must surely have seen something – someone – who had a hand in her removal. I can see the ride and its lights and the other children getting off it and running back to their parents quite clearly in my mind, as if it were a film loop being run over and over again past my eyes. I can even hear some of the things the other kids said to their adults, but I can't see or hear any sign of Lucy, or any shadow of a movement towards where she must have been.'

He waited for an agonizing moment as Hook completed his note on this. Then the DS looked up at him and said, 'So how do you think you missed her, Matt? Do you think she lost her bearings and wandered off in the wrong direction, or do you think some person or persons unknown abducted her?'

Matt noted the first use of his forename. The man seemed friendly, but was that merely a tactic to soften him up? 'Someone took her, didn't they?'

'It certainly looks like it. But if she wandered off and fell into the wrong hands, it could have been later in the evening rather than by that roundabout.'

Matt thought about it. It was a possibility he hadn't considered. He tried desperately to work out how his answer might affect his own position, but he couldn't think it through. He shook his head vigorously, as though trying to rid his face of a troublesome fly. 'No. I think someone grabbed her as she came off the ride. Probably someone who came out of the wood. It comes right up to the edge of the common at that point. The trees can't be more than a few yards from that ride and the point where Lucy climbed off it.'

Lambert nodded. 'Eleven yards.' He'd paced it out less than an hour ago when he'd talked to the SOCO team. 'Mr Boyd, your evidence is vital. At this moment, you are the last person known to have seen Lucy Gibson.' He bit his lip. Familiarity with dozens of homicides had almost led him to say 'the last person known to have seen Lucy Gibson alive'. He must not allow the increasing foreboding that was weighing upon him to enter his speech. 'You will be asked to sign a statement in due course, Mr Boyd. Is there anything you feel you have missed out in your account of what happened last night?'

Boyd's forehead twisted into a frown above the broad features. 'There's one thing. When we were on our way from the big rides to the edge of the fair where the smaller ones were, we passed a shooting gallery. I stopped and had a go to try to win a prize for Lucy or her mum. She didn't leave me, even when I was shooting. I can remember her clinging on to the leg of my trousers when I had both hands on the rifle. But my attention was obviously on the target I was shooting at, for perhaps two minutes. I suppose someone might have been watching us, sizing up his chances of snatching Lucy.'

'Indeed someone might. I take it this would be only about ten minutes before she vanished?'

'About that, yes. We went straight from the shooting gallery to the small ride.'

'But you weren't aware of anyone skulking around. He or she might have been some distance away, of course – we mustn't rule out women, at this stage.'

'No, I wasn't. It's still my belief that whoever snatched her came out of the woods beside the common. But I don't think I'd have spotted anyone when I'd finished at the shooting gallery. I won a prize, you see. A small one, but I let Lucy choose what she wanted. All my attention must have been on her and the prizes at that moment.'

'I see. What was it you won?'

'A little doll. Just a simple rag one, with a big face and a stupid smile. But Lucy seemed to like it. She kept waving its arm at me as she went round and round in that blue bus on her ride.'

'Just a minute.'

Lambert levered himself up without taking his eyes off Boyd and went out to the bags of exhibits that DI Rushton was beginning to catalogue in the murder room. He returned within his minute, during which Hook and Boyd had exchanged not a word. He held the polythene bag by its corner. 'Would this be the doll you gave to Lucy?'

Matt Boyd's eyes widened in horror as he looked at the contents. 'Yes. That's the doll. It didn't have that mud on it when I gave it to her, obviously. Where did you get it?'

'It was found in the wood you mentioned. The one where you think the abductor took Lucy.'

The three men stared at the small, pathetic item. Matt was conscious that after a moment the two CID men had transferred their gaze to his face, but he could not move his own eyes from that piteous reminder of the girl who had waved at him from the roundabout. Lambert's voice seemed to come from a long way away as it said with quiet insistency, 'We need your account of the rest of the evening, Mr Boyd.'

Matt took another huge breath. He needed to concentrate upon this above all. 'There's nothing else to tell. I didn't see Lucy again.'

'You need to look at this from our point of view, Mr Boyd. You are the last person known to have seen Lucy and there is very much more to tell. You said last night that Lucy vanished at around half past seven. Do you wish to revise that?'

'No, not really. It was probably a little later than that, but not much. When I couldn't find Lucy, the last thing I was thinking about was what the time was.'

'That at any rate is understandable. What is less so is how long you took to report her disappearance to us. Had we been informed immediately, we might have been able to help.'

'Might have cordoned off the area,' agreed Matthew Boyd dully. 'The uniformed man told me that last night.'

Lambert doubted privately whether they would have had the personnel available on a Saturday night to surround such a large area. It was far more likely that they'd have been reassuring the mother that children usually turned up by the end of the evening and trying to explore all the homes to which a small girl might have fled when she panicked. But he felt no inclination to take the pressure off this thickset, apprehensive figure in front of him. 'According to Mrs Gibson, you didn't return to her house until around nine o'clock. Even allowing for the fact that you cannot be precise about the times, that still leaves us with a gap of at least eighty minutes. What were you doing during that time?'

He'd expected the question, but it came across the table from Lambert more like an accusation. 'I thought I'd find her. I couldn't believe she was gone, at first. Then I thought she

must be playing a trick on me – that she'd hidden herself away
and was going to come out and laugh at me.'

'Is Lucy a frisky little girl? Would she enjoy playing hide
and seek with you like that?'

Frisky. Matt wanted to say that she was; it would help to
explain his conduct, surely. But he wasn't sure what Anthea
would have told them and he couldn't afford to contradict the
girl's mother, could he? 'No, not really, I suppose. But I didn't
know her all that well, did I? You pointed out yourself that
it was the first time we'd been out alone together. I suppose
I *wanted* to think she was hiding. I couldn't get my head round
the idea that she'd simply disappeared.'

'But it didn't take you eighty minutes to decide that a
seven-year-old wasn't playing hide and seek with you.'

It was a statement, not a question. That was another signal
that he was on trial here, or at least meant to feel that he was.
What he had meant to deliver as bold and convincing statements
were being made to sound like a weak and desperate defence.
'I looked for her. I went all round the fairground. I asked one
or two of the stallholders whether they'd seen a little girl on
her own, but none of them had. As one of them said, looking
for a kid in a fairground is like searching for a needle in a
haystack. I searched the wood beside the fairground – well,
searched it as well as I could. I needed a torch really, but I
hadn't got one and I hadn't even got my mobile phone: I'd left
it behind at Anthea's house'

Lambert spoke more gently this time. 'Eighty minutes is a
long time, Mr Boyd.'

'I know it is. I suppose part of the reason I took so long is
that I didn't want to face Anthea and tell her that I'd lost her
little girl, when she'd trusted me with her. I even came back
and got my car to search a wider area.'

Lambert nodded whilst Hook made a note of that. 'So you
returned to the house and gave Anthea the bad news at around
nine o'clock. The call reporting that Lucy was missing was
logged at this station at nine fifty-four. Why this additional
delay?'

'I had to calm Anthea down. Or try to – she was
hysterical.'

'Then surely she would have been anxious to let us know what had happened as quickly as possible.'

Again the statement. Again the ringing logic that made his story sound like a pack of lies. Matt said in a low, defeated voice, 'That was me. I thought we should ring all her friends' houses, all the places where she might possibly have gone, before we rang the police. I said that was the first thing they would ask us to do anyway.'

'You may well be right about that. But we could also have been taking other steps, setting a search in motion. Mr Boyd, have you any further thoughts to offer?'

Matt shook his head hopelessly. 'No. I think now that someone snatched her and was away through the woods with her before I or anyone else realized anything was wrong. It seems the only possible solution.'

There were others, but Lambert wasn't about to offer them. He said merely, 'Please don't leave the area without furnishing us with an address, Mr Boyd.'

FIVE

E leanor Hook saw how drawn and tired Bert looked as soon as he entered the house. That wasn't usual for Bert, who generally enjoyed his work, despite his routine protests on occasions at the dullness of it. Tonight he came into their home wishing heartily for a little of that dullness.

'Supper won't be long,' she said.

He looked at her for a moment as if he had not understood, then nodded and slumped into an armchair.

Eleanor got herself a gin and tonic and set a glass and a can of beer on the small table by Hook's elbow. 'Thanks,' he said quietly. He summoned up a small, grateful smile for her, then stared into space. After a moment, he tilted the glass and poured the contents of the can into it with elaborate care, as if he could shut out the rest of his day by this simple act of concentration.

Eleanor sat down opposite him but didn't speak. They had married relatively late by police standards, when both of them were in their late twenties and recovering from broken engagements. It was a relaxed and happy union; they often didn't need words. It wasn't until Bert gave a long sigh and said, 'We haven't found her,' that Eleanor chose to speak.

'You saw the mother?' Eleanor listened to the movements of her boys in the room above her and tried to imagine what it must be like to lose a child as this woman had: snatched off the face of the earth when the little girl had been enjoying a treat. It wasn't even like an illness, where at least you had a little time to prepare yourself for what might happen. The Hooks had almost lost their younger son, Luke, to meningitis a year or so ago. The hours when he had wavered between life and death had been the worst three days of her life.

This must be much, much worse – this sudden removal of your child without any notice of catastrophe. And with it the thought that your little girl must surely be in the hands of someone evil. When you were a police wife, you retained what some people now thought of as the old-fashioned idea of evil.

Hook signalled his return to the world around him with a huge sigh and a belated reply to his wife's question. 'Yes, I saw the mother. I'm sure in my own mind that she had nothing to do with this.'

Eleanor gasped. She'd heard the radio appeals at lunchtime and felt a quite crushing sympathy for anyone close to the girl. She hadn't even entertained the idea that Lucy Gibson's mother might be involved in some sort of unnatural intrigue to dispose of her daughter, but she knew there had been some bizarre happenings in the last few years. The macabre Fred West and his wife had operated less than twenty miles from here. No doubt these things had to be checked out; no wonder Bert was distressed. She said dully, 'Is there a man around?'

She tried to keep her voice as neutral as she could, but you couldn't escape two facts. First, the overwhelming probability was that it was a man who had done this, however the seven-year-old girl had been spirited away. Second, there was a higher incidence of crime in homes where only one parent remained. Eleanor had huge respect for the many single mothers who were struggling to give their children the best chances they could, but the statistics said that single-parent children had more chance of being harmed and more chance of becoming criminals themselves than those in two-parent households.

Hook said evenly, 'There's a dad. He's been gone for a few months. We haven't caught up with him yet, but we will. There's also a new man, a man who's been regularly staying overnight with Anthea Gibson. He hasn't moved in yet, but I think Anthea was hoping that he would. God knows how this will affect the two of them. The girl was on her own with him when she disappeared. Lucy, she's called.' He felt the same need to assert the girl's identity and continued existence as John Lambert had done earlier in the day.

'You'll have seen this man.'

She didn't voice her queries about him, but Bert understood and answered. 'John Lambert gave him quite a grilling this afternoon. You've got to in cases like this. You've no time to spare.' He smiled grimly. When there was a body, however brutal the death, there was not quite the same urgency. When a child went missing, you were trying to anticipate and prevent death. As well as other things, which, for a terrified little girl, might be worse than death. 'The man's called Matthew Boyd. I'm sure the papers will have got hold of the name by tomorrow morning, though not from us. He answered all our questions satisfactorily enough, as far as we could tell. But to my mind there's something not quite right about him. That doesn't necessarily mean he had anything to do with this crime, though.' Hook asserted the caveat of the fair-minded man, even when speaking to his wife.

Bert smiled grimly as he heard the noise of his sons' voices raised in argument upstairs. He was thinking of Jack, his elder son, who always teased him by asking in an American drawl if he was 'playing a hunch'. A hunch is what he'd just voiced, he supposed, when he'd said he sensed something not quite right about Matthew Boyd.

But when the boys came down with appetites honed for the evening meal, there was no teasing from Jack. He said without preamble to his father, 'This kid who's disappeared – was it from the fairground yesterday? That's what they seemed to be saying when we saw the bit on the telly about it.'

Hook nodded. 'At around half past seven or a little later yesterday evening. It was a seven-year-old girl called Lucy Gibson.' At that moment Bert was very glad that Jack and Luke were male and aged fourteen and twelve. 'Why do you ask?'

Jack was at that annoying age when he was still a child but very much wanting to seem an adult. That meant that he said nothing now. Instead, he nodded sagely, produced his mobile phone and tapped the buttons that brought up his best friend from school. He then sank his head towards his chest, covered the mouthpiece and conversed in low tones. His own side of the conversation seemed to be mostly a series of questions.

Then he turned back to his brother and his parents, who were waiting to begin their meal. His face was grave and urgent with his news. 'That was Darren. He told me this at football this morning, but I didn't know then that a kid had disappeared. Darren's kid sister is eleven. One of the guys taking the fares and operating the rides at the fairground tried to molest her yesterday. He stroked her leg and touched her up. She was scared stiff. She ran away as fast as she could, Darren says.'

There is no shortage of civilian volunteers when a child disappears, especially in small rural communities. The problem for the police is usually how to marshal these men and women most effectively. There was little difficulty in doing that after Lucy Gibson had vanished.

The rag doll that she had been clutching when last seen on the roundabout had been discovered in the woods to the west of the common. That suggested that she had been led, carried or dragged away from the fairground on that route. It wasn't a large area, and uniformed police officers and the civilians from the SOCO team searched it diligently in the middle hours of Sunday. Little else of note was found, though much was collected and documented in case it might be of use. A stray glove, a worn and filthy cap, several cigarette ends and various other more disgusting items had been lifted between finger and thumb and bagged, against the unlikely possibility that one or more of them might provide a match with an eventual suspect. The overwhelming probability was that all of this detritus would be irrelevant to the case, but if there was even a faint possibility that one or more of them might become labelled exhibits in a serious crime case in the Crown Court, they had to be kept.

A murder case? The longer the time that elapsed before a discovery, the greater the possibility that this most innocent of victims would become the focus of such a case. No one voiced that thought, but it beat in the brains of every police officer and most of the civilians who were now involved in this empty and heartbreaking exploration.

They spread out in lines across the fields, woods and buildings around Oldford, ten civilians to every police officer, searching thoroughly and generally silently. No one could summon even a false cheerfulness in this situation. For four square miles around the terrace where Lucy had lived, every garden shed, every garage, every outhouse was searched, each one with a drawing in of breath and a feeling of sick anticipation before the seekers opened the doors and scoured the shadowy depths within. Cats watched them intently, dogs barked their outrage, the occasional rat scurried away into the undergrowth.

No small girl was discovered, dead or alive.

By five o'clock, the searchers had moved outside the town and into the fields around it. A few of the elderly and one or two people with other commitments left the volunteers, but most people stayed, well aware of what another cold late-October night without any find might mean. They were lucky with the weather, if nothing else so far. The sun was dropping over the Welsh hills by now, but there were few clouds, which probably gave them half an hour more daylight than they might have had. These conditions also presaged a frosty night, or at least a clear and cold one. No one cared to voice that thought or its implications for Lucy.

The long, disciplined lines of citizens and their police organizers didn't expect to find anything here. Nor did they wish to; the probability was that a child lying in open country who was unable to cry for help or spot the approaching searchers was already dead. They searched barns and other farm buildings, almost invariably in the farmers' presence and with their assistance and suggestions. This was not the tourist Cotswolds, with many unoccupied holiday and weekend homes, but they nevertheless came upon half a dozen holiday cottages where the owners were not in residence. All but one of these were searched with the cooperation of keyholders who lived nearby. The searchers peered through the small windows of the final one, a tiny two-hundred-year-old stone cottage. They could see nothing significant, and police examination of the front and rear doors confirmed that it was most unlikely that anyone had opened either of them in the last month.

Despite the clearness of the sky, the light died alarmingly quickly for the long lines of scrutineers. They searched a final field and the bulrushes round a still and silent pond, then a rambling, tumbledown, almost roofless barn which the farmer had not used for years. It was the home to various rustling and unidentified wildlife, but nothing human.

The uniformed inspector who was in charge of the hunt looked at the long, low outline of the distant ridge of high hills, with the red of the dying sun still visible in the sky above them, then at the lower and much nearer shape of May Hill, a mile or two to his left. There'd been no need to search there; the Sunday walkers who thronged the easy but rewarding slopes of May Hill, from which seven counties might be seen, would have raised the alarm long since had anything untoward been found up there. Unless – unless the lunatic monster involved in this had hidden what was left of Lucy deep in the bracken and far from any path. The sickening impossibility of the inspector's task, even with so many willing helpers, dropped like the darkness upon the shoulders of this decent, helpless man.

The inspector gave a long, silent sigh and drew in breath to make the announcement they all knew was inevitable. 'That's got to be it for today, folks. Thank you all for your help; I only wish we had a better outcome to report. Unless there is some news overnight, we shall resume the search at first light tomorrow. It will be organized and directed from Oldford police station. Please ring or attend there if you are willing and able to assist in the continued police search tomorrow. I should emphasize once more that coordinated covering of the ground is always much more efficient and productive than individual initiatives in situations like this. Thank you once again for all your assistance and please keep your ears open for any scraps of conversation that might give us a clue to Lucy's whereabouts.'

He wondered if the hopelessness he felt came out in the tone of his voice. He hoped not, but he was seized like the rest of his searchers with a sudden leaden exhaustion. When hope died, it affected sinew and muscle as well as brain. He turned towards home and hearth with his heart in his Wellington boots and fatigue in his limbs. There were a few muttered comments among neighbours who knew each other and had come out together to hunt for Lucy Gibson. But otherwise there was silence among the defeated and helpless army of good against evil.

As he dragged his feet wearily over a rise in the ground,

the inspector stopped for a moment and looked to the west. There was a long bend of the River Wye visible from here, running like a dark ribbon of mirror beneath the crescent of moon, which was already sharp and surprisingly high in the sky. In other circumstances, it would have been a view to stop and to savour.

Now, as day crept into night, it filled those who paused to study it with a grim foreboding.

SIX

At the edge of the common on Monday morning, there was the noise of vigorous activity but only the minimum sound of human voices. The men demolishing the fair were not native to these parts and not noted for sensitivity, but they were nevertheless subdued by what had happened there two nights earlier as they took down the rides and the stalls on Monday morning.

Lambert sought out Davies, the proprietor with whom he had exchanged strong words on the previous morning. He was easily spotted, being the broadest man on the site, with a stomach every bit as impressive as anything exhibited on the stalls. He was smoking a cigar and observing the energetic activities of others when Lambert found him. The chief superintendent didn't mince words about the person they wanted to see, and Davies offered his employee no protection in the light of the allegations that had been made against him. 'You're looking for Rory Burns,' he said, 'You'll find him taking down the motorbikes and sidecars from the ride over there. And I wish you the best of bloody luck with him. You'll find he's a rough diamond!'

He tapped his cigar against the beam that supported the surrounds of a ride as he watched them go. Davies had no love of the police, but there was no point in being obstructive when they were on a case like this. He prided himself on his knowledge of public taste and the public pulse, and he wasn't a man to take unnecessary risks.

Rory Burns had a broad face and coarse, mobile features. He was almost six feet tall, with a barrel chest, bulging biceps and impressive forearms. The ease and speed with which he was deconstructing the wooden skeleton of the roundabout showed both how he had acquired his physique and how expertly he deployed it. He was working with a ferocity that would have pleased Popeye or Superman.

Lambert and Hook flashed their warrants before his narrowing brown eyes and suggested he might wish to find somewhere more private for the questions he was about to answer for them. He stared hard at them for several seconds, looking from one impassive face to the other to see what clues he might obtain there. Then he said churlishly, 'Youse can come over here, I suppose.'

He led them away from the roundabout he was working on. He was already suspicious of them and anxious to give nothing away to the filth, but they noted two things immediately. He had a strong Irish accent and he led them not towards the woods into which Lucy Gibson had disappeared, which were scarcely twenty yards away, but over a different route, which involved him moving at least sixty yards away from that spot. Was he simply moving to a place where he felt comfortable, or was it possible that this physically intimidating fellow was unconsciously avoiding the scene of his crime?

Perhaps that was too fanciful; probably he just didn't want to be overheard by his peers. He thumped on the door of a small blue hut at the edge of the fairground activity, then stumped inside when he had confirmed that it was empty. There were worksheets and what might have been duty rotas on a small folding table, but no other paperwork visible. Burns pulled out three stackable canvas seats and motioned them to sit down. The seats were claustrophobically adjacent to each other in the small wooden shed. Hook glanced around with some distaste. 'You don't have your own caravan, then?'

Burns afforded him a superior smile. It was good to be able to patronize the pigs. 'Youse is out of date. Thirty years out of date. We gets ourselves bed and breakfast now. We dosses down for the night over there.' He nodded his head vaguely towards the point where the town joined the common. There were some cheap and dingy lodgings in the older part of the town, surprisingly close to the common. Hook had been into them many times; he suspected they were cleaner and better than many of the places where this man and other fairground staff laid their heads when their work took them into cities.

Lambert said abruptly, 'You know why we're here, Mr Burns.'

The burly man was immediately shifty, immediately transformed from truculence to defensiveness. 'Sure I had nothing to do with this girl who was took. People should take better care of their kids.'

'Perhaps so, with people like you around. We've had a complaint about your conduct, Mr Burns.' That wasn't strictly true, but Lambert knew they could soon translate it into a formal complaint if that became necessary.

'I've done nutting. People think bad of you, just because you come from Ireland and work on a fairground.'

There was no doubt a certain amount of truth in that, but they had more solid evidence to offer. His brown eyes might prove to be a giveaway: they narrowed markedly each time he felt himself under pressure. 'Make a habit of laying those strong hands on young girls, do you, Mr Burns?'

'They make all sorts of things up, these kids. Not fit to be out on their own, some of them.'

'Not *safe* to be out on their own, certainly, with men like you looking for opportunities to assault them. The law takes a very dim view of such things nowadays. But I'm sure you are already well aware of that.'

A hit, a very palpable hit. Rory Burns winced, not with pain but with fear. 'I 'ain't done nutting.'

'Really? We have an eleven-year-old girl who raced home terrified, who thinks otherwise and is willing to talk to us. You could call in your lawyer, if you think that's advisable.'

Lambert divined correctly that this man wouldn't have a lawyer and wouldn't know how to get one. Burns shifted his broad thighs on his seat and said, 'I don't need no lawyer. I ain't done nutting.'

Lambert pursed his lips. 'You'd have to pay for a lawyer, of course, if you wanted one at this stage. You're not under formal arrest. Not as yet. You'll be entitled to a free brief, when you are.'

'I don't need no lawyer, copper.' He licked his thick lips and seemed about to add to that, but then thought better of it.

'Your previous record's not going to help you, of course.'

Another shot in the dark, another hit. He snarled, 'You sods aren't supposed to keep records. Not when there's been no conviction.'

Lambert gave his first smile since he had entered the hut, but it was directed at Hook, not at Burns. 'Very well informed, for a fairground employee, isn't he? A man who reckons to learn from experience, I'd say. Though he doesn't learn enough. If he'd learned the right things, he might have stopped indecently assaulting helpless minors.'

'They ask for it.'

'This one didn't.'

'That's what she tells you. You don't see them climbing all over the rides and flashing their legs at you. Flashing their tits. Flashing their bare arms and bare necks. Flashing their pants, if you know how to—'

He stopped abruptly, looked down at the tattoo of the shamrock on his exposed upper arm, fingered it slowly. It wasn't clear whether he was using it as an aid to thought or whether it had some other association for him. Perhaps it was a token of his Irish origins which he had found useful with the impressionable young, Lambert thought.

It was Hook who responded to the man's sudden silence by completing his sentence for him. '"If you know how to get the angle right and see what you want to see." I suppose that's what you were going to say, Rory.'

The brown eyes glanced up sharply at the first use of his forename. For the first time, there was fear as well as confusion in the dark pupils. He forced an unpleasant smile. 'No penalty for looking.'

'But you were touching, Rory, not just looking. We can produce a young girl to record her evidence on video for a court of law if we need to. And we know whom a jury would choose to believe if we face them with a choice between your word and that of an innocent eleven-year-old, don't we?'

'You're going to frame me, are you? Pity you haven't got one of your clever recording machines going on me now, innit?'

'Know all about those, do you, Rory? Well, I suppose you would, with the things you've done in the past. Been assaulting kids for years, haven't you?'

'I've 'ad pigs like you trying to frame me for years, more like.' But it was token defiance. There was no ring of conviction or outrage in his voice.

John Lambert had been studying his man like a sample under a microscope whilst Hook had pressed him. There had been a thin film of sweat upon his bare arms when they had come here, but now his forehead was wet as well. Burns had now been softened up enough for the main dissection. Lambert said very quietly, 'What did you do with Lucy Gibson after you had abducted her on Saturday night, Mr Burns?'

Again the brown eyes narrowed for a moment in that strange reaction the two men now recognized as characteristic. This wasn't craftiness, as it would have been in other men of his background, but a nervous reflex of tension and alarm. Sure enough, his eyes opened after a couple of seconds into round glass marbles of fear. 'I didn't touch that kid. I know nutting about this.'

'You'll need to do better than that, Mr Burns. A lot better. You saw Lucy on your ride a quarter of an hour before she was snatched. She rode on one of the motorbikes, with her adult guardian behind her. You took the fares from him and you spotted Lucy. When she rode on her own on the small ride next to your big one, you saw your chance. What did you do after you'd rushed her away through the woods?'

The brown eyes shut completely, as if the world's threat could be banished when it could not be seen. But all three of the men in that narrow, sweaty hut knew that they would have to open again very quickly. Burns was now a strange combination of physical strength and mental fragility. 'I didn't touch your damn girl! I finished my stint after she'd ridden on that feckin' motorbike with her man. You can check with Gary Ruddock who relieved me. I had a date on Saturday night and I wanted to get away. I'd been on the rides since ten in the morning.'

His words came in a rush, tumbling one upon another as if speed itself could convince them of his innocence. Lambert said calmly, 'We'd better have the name of the girl. If she can confirm a time for us, she could be your alibi.'

Now there was a pause, so quiet that his noisy, uneven breathing sounded as it bounced off the wooden slats like that of an older man. 'Dora,' he said. 'I don't know her second name. I might have got it from her on Saturday if she'd turned up.'

'You're telling us you had a date with a girl whose full name you don't know, who chose not to turn up and meet you. Not very convincing, is it? Can you suggest how we might contact this girl?'

'No. She's no bloody use to me anyway, now she didn't turn up. Youse lot just don't want to believe me.'

Lambert had a shrewd suspicion that this squalid man had arranged to meet an underage girl who, not surprisingly, had made the arrangement to get away from him and had never intended to keep it. But he couldn't pursue that idea whilst the mystery of Lucy Gibson remained to be solved. He didn't like this man and he didn't like himself for the way he was conducting this interview. It was too rambling and indeterminate. He said harshly, 'You dragged Lucy away through that wood.' He twitched his head towards the invisible trees beyond the thin wooden panels of the shed. 'What did you do to her? Where is she now?'

'I didn't take her. I haven't a fucking clue who did take her.'

'You'll need to prove that, Burns. You haven't a scrap of evidence in your favour.'

It was a mistake. Rory Burns wasn't an intelligent man. But he'd dealt with a lot of police questioning in his twenty-nine years and he knew enough to spot a weakness. 'I don't need any scraps of evidence, copper. Innocent until proved guilty, in this country. The country some of us fought to defend against the IRA scum. You prove I snatched that kid on Saturday, or you fuck off and leave me alone. That's the way it works, and youse lot can't do a feckin' thing to change it!'

He shifted on his seat, made himself a little more comfortable, looked even more squat, powerful and unpleasant. There was no way of challenging his stance until they had some more powerful evidence to fling against him. Bert Hook said quietly, 'We'll get what we need to make an arrest if you did this, Rory. Even people who won't normally help us come forward when it's a child that's disappeared. With your record, people are going to want to believe the worst of you, aren't they? If you didn't do this and you have any idea who might have done it, this is the moment to speak. It's the only way you can help yourself.'

'I didn't do this and I don't have to prove I didn't!' He looked from Lambert's long, grim face to Hook's more fatherly countenance and softened a little. 'You talk as if I approve of seven-year-old kids being killed. I might fancy young 'uns and I might like a quick grope, but I don't like kids being killed – that's something different. I'll keep my ears open around here. If I hear anything that might help you, I'll pass it on. I'm like the other people you spoke of. I don't like kids being raped and killed, either.'

Bert gave him a tiny nod of acceptance. 'You're assuming she's dead.'

'Well, aren't you? Thirty-six hours now, she's been gone. I'd take a bet the poor little sod's dead and gone, wouldn't you?'

Lambert studied him for a moment longer, not troubling to disguise his distaste and distrust. 'You can go now. What are your plans for the next few days?'

'I've four more nights' bed and board booked at my lodgings. Two, Harvey Court. We work through every weekend; this is my time off. Then we move on to Stroud. I won't bloody disappear.'

'Don't even think of it. We shall take it as an admission of guilt if you do. And if you did this, we'll get you, however long it takes. Far better for you to tell us now, if you're guilty, and take whatever help you can get.'

Burns looked as if he might spit in his enemy's face, but he contained himself until he had flung open the door of the shed and lurched outside it. He went back towards his demolition work without a backward glance.

Lambert said to Hook, 'He's got form, that bugger. We bluffed him into thinking we knew all about him when we didn't, but we'd better get Chris Rushton busy on his computer. We need to check up on exactly what Rory Burns has done with youngsters in the past.'

*   *   *

The news the police had dreaded, but increasingly expected, came in at eleven twenty on that cool, clear Monday morning.

Bad news came in a most unlikely shape. Emily Patten was a grandmother, sixty-four years old, recently retired from her work as a part-time librarian and enjoying a brisk walk with her Labrador, Ben, on the picturesque path that runs alongside the River Wye below the old town of Ross-on-Wye. She was exulting in the crispness of the late-October morning, with the sun still quite low in an almost cloudless blue sky. She met few people here at this time, save for the occasional person who was retired like herself.

Most of the people she met were walking in the opposite direction, back towards Ross, and most of them were men. Some of them were considerably older than she was. They found this slim woman with the pretty, small-featured face and the vigorous carriage very attractive, and Emily enjoyed that, even as she told herself how little it meant. Most of them were dog-walkers like herself, and dog-walkers in Emily's experience were invariably not only harmless but interesting. So she accepted friendly greetings, a little banter and a few shameless compliments.

There was no harm in it and not a little pleasure. And if there had been any menace, Ben would surely have come to her rescue. In truth, Emily was not entirely sure of that, since the dog seemed universally friendly to all human approaches. Even in canine interchanges, Ben acted as a fully paid-up coward; his policy was to steer clear of all conflict. He was enthusiastic and indiscriminate in his amorous advances to other dogs, which occasionally embarrassed his owner. But he drew the line at snarls, growls and fights and extricated himself swiftly from all situations that involved them.

Emily carried a tennis ball. She had become more expert in throwing it, now that Ben had left his puppy days behind him. It needed a good long throw to give the Labrador the exercise he needed. She flung it now along the deserted bank of the river, where the grass was short and the ball bounced and ran, so that Ben could race enthusiastically to retrieve it. No wonder he was so energetic, she thought wryly. When they returned home and she resumed the household chores, Ben would stretch himself flat with a contented sigh and doze happily whilst she worked. A dog's life was a pretty good life, in her household.

This was the wrong place to throw his tennis ball, and she knew it. Ben brought the ball back to her with diminishing enthusiasm after her first two throws. After the third, he abandoned it shamelessly. When there was water at hand, it dominated the dog's thoughts and actions.

Whenever opportunity in the form of an easy entry to the water offered, the dog was down the bank and into the Wye. He swam enthusiastically, returning to the shore a little further down the river each time as the current carried him gently southwards and away from Ross. He now emerged to frisk around a septuagenarian whom he recognized immediately as a friend. His mistress yelled a desperate warning, which she saw was too late. She knew what was about to happen, but she was powerless to prevent it.

Ben convulsed himself into forty pounds of boneless muscle and shook himself with a convulsive energy that extended from nose to extremely mobile tail. Hearing the man's good-natured shouts of alarm, he accepted them as a compliment and redoubled his efforts. Thirty seconds of intense activity left the dog transformed from sopping to merely damp and his new friend liberally showered in the waters of the silver Wye.

'I'm terribly sorry!' gasped Emily Patten, arriving precipitately just after the event.

'It's quite all right,' said the white-haired victim, feeling foolish rather than wounded. 'I saw it coming – I'd have got out of the way twenty years ago. But now . . .' He lifted his arms hopelessly and humorously, a willingly abject figure of fun. Ben certainly found it amusing. He gave himself a second, subsidiary shake, watched his two human companions leap ineffectively away from him, and then came forward for the stroking he felt was due to him from his dripping victim.

'I used to have a Labrador myself,' the man said. And Emily understood in that moment that everything was accepted and everything was forgiven. They exchanged indulgent thoughts about the Labrador breed and its production line of likeable rogues like Ben, then moved affably on their different ways.

Emily decided that she would walk as far as the next big curve in the river. That would give her a brisk round trip of four miles, though Ben's energy and curiosity had carried him at least twice as far as that already. After another two hundred yards, she would turn back and follow the path gently up-river with the autumn sun on her back. Meantime, she mused with a pleasant melancholy upon life, and her own life in particular. In another ten or fifteen years, she would be as old as that pleasant and tolerant man who had just accepted his dousing from Ben. Those years would pass very quickly, she knew. She wished that she could pin herself exactly where she was and enjoy the years she had left with all the faculties and all the knowledge she had at present. She thought she was probably happier now than she had been at any stage in her life.

These reflections were interrupted by Ben's abrupt disappearance again towards the river, at a point where there had been a little subsidence and the bank dropped away steeply towards the quietly moving waters beneath it. Emily called him repeatedly, skirting the point where he had disappeared cautiously in the belief that he would emerge at any moment and re-enact his galvanic plunging and localized shower-bath.

The dog did not respond to his name. His mistress peered cautiously down on his activity at the edge of the river. Ben was not swimming and being carried downstream, as she had expected. He was investigating something at the edge of the water. He grasped what looked to her like cotton in his strong jaws as she watched. Then, digging his paws into the wet earth behind him, he dragged his trophy first to the edge of the water and then on to the muddy lower section of the bank. His tail wagged vigorously with his excitement.

Blue clothing. Long, wet strands of childish hair. Emily Patten knew what Ben had found seconds before she gazed in horror at the pale, dead face of Lucy Gibson.

SEVEN

Lambert received the news that the girl was dead as he was driving to see her father. He listened to the first sombre details and was assured that the post-mortem examination would be done immediately. Child murder leapt ahead of the varied multitude of deaths in other minds as well as his.

Neither he nor Hook spoke for several miles as they drove up the A449. They had worked together for many years. Each knew that the other was thinking of his own children, and, in Lambert's case, grandchildren. It wasn't long before they ran into the small town. Both of them could have used a little more time to compose themselves for the things they had to do and the news they had to give.

Dean Gibson had been discovered by the police machine. He was living not in Malvern but in the ancient town of Ledbury, some eight miles nearer to their base at Oldford. He was lodged in a mean little terrace of houses that ran away from the main street and down towards the modern wasteland of a supermarket car park. What had once been a quiet street was now a noisy and unpleasant spot, though handy for the centre of the town and its amenities.

The door needed a coat of paint. The woman who opened it would also have benefited from a little restoration. She was overweight, though not drastically so; her waist had almost disappeared, but she was shapeless rather than obese. Her hair was lank and grey and escaping from the single slide that was her only attempt at control. There was a greyness also about her complexion, which suggested that her sour face saw little of the clean country air around Ledbury.

She looked at them curiously when they announced themselves and presented their warrant cards. She didn't like policemen and wouldn't normally have welcomed them into her house, but murder had a grisly and universal glamour which no other crime possessed. She wanted to be able to relate accurate details about the CID interest in her lodger to her neighbours and her daughter. For a few days it would give her an importance that she had never felt before.

'His room's on the landing. Second door on the right.' She clutched Hook's arm as her visitors moved past her. 'He wasn't here on Saturday night. I don't know where he was, mind, but he wasn't here.' She invested her words with all the heavy import she could give them. Bert sensed that the man behind the second door on the right of the landing couldn't expect much support here. For no reason he could analyze, Bert hoped he wouldn't need it.

Dean Gibson must have heard the voices downstairs. Probably he had heard what his landlady had said to them. The door opened virtually as Lambert knocked, so that detective and quarry almost collided with each other and were left with their faces scarcely a foot apart. It was like a clumsily mistimed move in amateur dramatics, which makes the audience titter when there should be a significant silence.

The room was small and scarcely adequate for three adults, but it did not smell stale. Gibson had opened the single small window, so that the grubby curtain wafted gently and they could hear the noises from the supermarket car park below them. Hook said, 'I'm sure Mrs Jackson would let us use her living room downstairs for this, if we ask her nicely and—'

'I'd rather do it here. More private, like, if you don't mind sitting on the bed.' Gibson wasn't a native of these parts; he had a Birmingham accent, though not a strong one. He took the only chair in the room and gestured towards the single bed. The two big men sat down cautiously on the edge of it. It wasn't comfortable, but they'd questioned people in places much worse than this.

They knew from the file Chris Rushton had already opened on this man that Dean Gibson was thirty-three. He looked much older. His hair was greasy and already thinning drastically; he had a three-day growth of stubble on his chin and cheeks. He was thin and narrow-shouldered, and he had three sticking plasters on his fingers. His sweater had a stain on the front and a hole in one elbow. It was easy to see how his wife might have abandoned him for the far more presentable Matthew Boyd.

Lambert said, 'We had some difficulty finding you, Mr Gibson. Your last address was in Malvern. You seem to have moved around a lot since you left your wife.'

'I take work where I can get it. I don't have a car now. I try to live as near as possible to the place where I work.' He stared at his questioner steadily, but his eyes blinked far more frequently than they should have.

Lambert looked back at him hard, then said tersely, 'You know why we're here.'

'Yes. Have you found her?'

They would have had to tell him, and quickly. Now he had given them the opening. 'I think so. I was notified on my way here that the body of a small girl has been found. I am afraid we are almost certain that it is Lucy.'

Gibson clutched suddenly at his torso with both arms. For a long, agonizing moment he did not speak. When he spoke, it was in a voice quite different from the little they had heard from him previously. 'I knew it. I knew she was gone. If they don't turn up within the first day, they're gone, aren't they?'

'I'm afraid they very often are, yes. I'm very sorry, Mr Gibson. We both are. I know it can't be much consolation to you, but we'll get whoever did this.'

'I expect you will, yes. With all the men and women you can use, you'll get whoever did this. And, as you say, it won't be much consolation to me.'

He spoke dully, but he had acquired a strange dignity with his reception of the news. Beyond that, they couldn't analyze his reaction. Lambert said, 'If you do not wish to speak to us at this time, that would be entirely understandable. We can do this later, either here or at the station. I have to say that the sooner we have your statement, the better it will be, from our point of view. We have as yet no idea who did this and there are other people as well as you to whom we need to speak.'

It was stilted and formal, but formal was probably best in these appalling circumstances. Gibson stared straight ahead of him, his grey eyes blinking steadily but producing no tears. All other movement seemed frozen within him. Eventually, he produced a voice that seemed to come from a distance and belong to someone else. 'Poor little Lucy. Poor, poor little Lucy. She was so small and so innocent.' After a moment, he came back to them, seeming surprised to find them here. 'You'll get whoever did this. I believe that. I want you to do whatever you have to do right now and right here.'

Lambert said quietly, 'Thank you. I think that is the right decision. How long is it since you saw Lucy, Mr Gibson?'

He frowned a little, as if finding it difficult to concentrate on the question. 'Two weeks ago. Two weeks last Saturday. Two weeks before . . . before this happened. Anthea dropped her off in Malvern. I was still in my digs there, then. We had a good walk together, Lucy and me. I carried her on my shoulders when she got tired. Just for a little while. I used to do that when she was small, you see. When all three of us lived together in Oldford.'

They had a brief glimpse with that picture of the bleakness of his life now, of the cruelty of it, for a man with few personal resources who had been cast out into an alien world – a world that demanded more then he had to give it. Everyone spoke of how hard marital break-ups could be for the children, but few saw what they did to inadequates like this. Lambert said, 'How would you describe your present relationship with your wife, Mr Gibson?'

'With Anthea? We get on all right, I suppose. As well as people who've split up normally do, I expect. We said we'd separate for a while to see how it went.'

'A trial separation?'

'That's it. That's what they call it, isn't it? That's the phrase Anthea used. Picked it up from the mums at the school gates, I expect. She did a lot of talking with them, before we split.'

It wasn't bitter; it was dull and resigned. There was a silence, as though all of them were pausing to pin down this situation in their minds. Then Bert Hook said, 'Were you hoping that you'd get back together, Dean?'

Gibson glanced at him sharply, as if he had not expected him to speak. When he replied, it seemed that his words were almost a surprise to him. 'Ye–es. Yes, I suppose I was. Lucy wanted it – she told me that, when we were together. And I must have wanted it, because I haven't settled to anything since I left.' He looked round the tight and shabby little bedroom, as if citing the evidence of that.

'But it hasn't happened. There's been no sign of you going back to the house in Oldford. Not so far.'

'No, and it isn't going to happen. Not with him around, it isn't.'

'You mean Matthew Boyd?'

'Yeah, I mean Matt bloody Boyd. Smooth talker, steady job, worming his way in. Even trying to take over with Lucy. She told me that. Well, he won't be able to do that now, will he?'

He had raised his voice as he spoke, so that his question echoed back off the walls of the cramped room. He must have realized how awful it sounded, for he said in a lower tone, as if by way of explanation, 'He's a salesman, Matt Boyd. He moves around the area. I expect he finds it easy to pick up women. I expect he's had lots of practice.'

'And you don't like to think of him with Anthea, do you, Dean?' Hook probed as gently as a therapist.

Gibson stared at the wall and slowed his blinking. 'I don't like to think of them in bed together. I don't like to think of what they do. That's only natural, isn't it?'

'Indeed it is, Dean. And you didn't like to think of him with Lucy, your little girl. That was natural, too.'

'Only natural, it was, yes.' He didn't seem to notice the repetition of the word. 'I didn't like to think of him with my Lucy.'

'And it hasn't been easy for you to get work, since you moved out of your house and away from Oldford.'

'I 'ad regular work with a builder when I was in Oldford. I can do roofing and lots of other things. Even plastering – there's not many as can do that. But work drops off in the winter. No one wants casuals.'

'And you don't have transport. That must be a handicap for you.'

Gibson hesitated for a moment. 'I got a bike. I get around on that, when I need to. But they don't want casuals in the winter. Not in a recession.' He produced the last phrase with a bitter familiarity; it had obviously been proffered to him many times as he was turned away.

Lambert had been content to observe closely whilst Hook elicited more than the man realized he was revealing. Now he leant forward and said, 'We're almost finished, Mr Gibson. But we need to know where you were on Saturday night.'

'When Lucy was taken, you mean?' He gave a bitter grin at seeing through the question so quickly. 'Well, I wasn't here, as that cow downstairs was so pleased to tell you.' He had been listening to the exchanges in the hall, as they'd suspected. 'I was in the pub up the road, the Rose and Crown.'

'I see. I suppose you were drinking with someone who can confirm this for us?'

'No. I was on my own. I can't buy rounds. I have to make halves of bitter last a long time.'

'But I expect the landlord will remember you. Are you a regular in there?'

'No, he won't remember me. Well, I doubt it. It's busy on a Saturday night.'

'Even early on a Saturday night, Mr Gibson?'

There was so little room in the shabby bedroom that they were almost touching each other. Bert Hook leant forward and rolled up the frayed cuff of Gibson's sweater. There were significant marks on the inside of the man's forearm. Heroin. Bert looked into Gibson's moist grey eyes from no more than a foot away. The man looked down at his exposed flesh. 'They're old marks, those. It's four years since I injected.'

'It's addictive – horse.'

'I was never an addict. I might have become one, at one time. Lucy stopped that. I looked at her and thought her dad couldn't be an addict.'

'But you're still a user.'

He looked for a moment as if he would deny it, then shrugged the scrawny shoulders and pulled down the sleeve of his sweater. 'I take the odd pill or a bit of coke, when I can get it. Since I broke up with Anthea. You get bloody miserable, living in places like this.'

'I know you do, Dean. But don't become a user again. It will destroy you. And if the hash and the shit and the white powder don't, the people who run the industry will.' Any policeman, and particularly any CID man, knows the pattern. People like Gibson don't have the money to indulge the habit. They either steal to continue it or more usually become small-time dealers, taking the risks for the bigger men who supply them. Once you're hooked, you sell to indulge the habit, being paid in drugs, just enough to keep you hooked whilst you sell to new users in pub car parks, in the back streets around cinemas, even outside the gates of secondary schools.

Hook was still staring into the man's face after he had given his advice. He said softly, 'You weren't in the Rose and Crown on Saturday evening, were you, Dean? You were away on your bike to Oldford, weren't you?'

He spoke with such conviction that the jaded Gibson was convinced this was knowledge, not speculation. He was blinking furiously as he said, 'I wanted to see Lucy. It should have been my day to see her, Saturday. But Anthea put me off because of that bugger Boyd. I knew the fair was on. I thought I might see Lucy there. I'd been planning to take her there, before bloody Boyd turned up.'

'And did you see her?'

'No. I must have been too late. I didn't get there until about quarter to eight.'

'How do you know when Lucy disappeared, Dean? We haven't given a time in any of our information bulletins.'

The grey eyes blinked furiously, but they didn't drop away from his, as Bert had expected. 'I don't know, do I? I just know that I didn't manage to see her when I got to the fair.'

Hook looked at him steadily for three long seconds before he said, 'You know Lucy and her background better than anyone except her mother, Dean. Have you any idea who might have done this awful thing?'

'No. I've been asking myself that ever since I heard.'

'You don't know of any odd people who hung around the school gates, for instance?'

'No. You should ask the school about that.'

Hook nodded. 'Members of our team have been doing that this morning. Chief Superintendent Lambert has told you that we only got the news of Lucy's death on the way over here, so we don't have many details as yet. Is there anything you wish to ask us?'

Only now, when prompted, did he ask the question that usually sprang first to the lips of parents involved in this agony. 'Was she . . . did he tamper with her, before he killed her?'

Lambert said as calmly as he could. 'There will have to be a post-mortem. But a preliminary examination by a pathologist has revealed no evidence of sexual molestation.'

They stood up from the hard single bed, straightened the blankets and left him sitting on the single chair, looking up at the small, open window, listening to the innocent sounds of small children with their mothers in the supermarket car park.

By three o'clock in the afternoon, the sun had disappeared, as if it recognized a need to cloak the dismal events in this small corner of the spinning world. The lights were already on in the CID section and in Lambert's office, where four of the senior ranks involved in the Lucy Gibson case were discussing what they should do next on this melancholy day.

'How did the mother take it?'

All of them knew that Lambert's routine opening query involved more than the compassion they all felt for Anthea Gibson. Had there been any tiny signal in her reception of the news of Lucy's death that she might have been involved, or that she knew more about it than she was revealing to them? One of the worst aspects of this sort of crime was that you had to think the unthinkable. Fred West's despicable wife was still in her closely guarded cell to remind them of that.

Ruth David said, 'Anthea Gibson was as stricken as you'd expect her to be. I've no comparisons, because I've never had to do this before. She was devastated by Lucy's death, as you'd imagine, even though she seemed to be half expecting it. Chris went with me; I thought the situation warranted a DI. It was quite bizarre, but I think I was right. I think the lady appreciated that we'd allotted her little girl a senior rank to deliver the final news. Chris was very good with her.'

Chris Rushton hoped he wasn't blushing. Blushing wouldn't improve the image of a DI; as a man who had been promoted young, he was conscious of his image. 'Ruth did most of the talking. I was glad when it was over.'

This was quite a statement for Chris. He wondered if it was unprofessional to confess as much as that. Lambert said, 'As we all would have been. But these things have to be done and have to be done as well as we can do them. It's the least the poor woman deserves. Did she say anything about Matthew Boyd?'

'Nothing significant. I don't think she's seen him since we had him in here and spoke to him. He's working around Oxford this week, she said. She doesn't know when she'll see him again. They haven't made any arrangements, if we can trust what she says.'

'Do you think she realizes he's in the frame for this?'

Ruth David said, 'We couldn't really investigate that. We were there to tell her that Lucy had been found dead. Her main concerns were that her daughter hadn't been raped or assaulted and hadn't suffered very much. My impression is that Anthea is intelligent enough to know that, as the last person known to have been with Lucy, Matt Boyd has to be a suspect until we can prove otherwise. Perhaps she even has her own doubts about him – maybe that's why she apparently has no plans as yet to see him again. But she didn't say anything to that effect, or even imply it.'

'Her husband was at the fair on Saturday night. Dean Gibson cycled over here on his bike.' Bert Hook blurted out the sentences abruptly, like a man downing unpleasant medicine as quickly as he could. He didn't want the pathetic man he had left two hours earlier to be a man who had killed his daughter. He knew his attitude was highly unprofessional; people defeated by life were more rather than less likely to panic and do crazy, irrational things. 'Gibson says that he didn't see Lucy, that it must all have happened before he got there.'

Lambert, who often disconcerted Bert Hook by knowing exactly what he was thinking, now said, 'I didn't like the fairground man, Rory Burns. I wasn't impressed by either his bearing or his attitude. And he's got form. Bert bluffed him into thinking that we knew all about it, when we didn't. Have you turned up the details, Chris?'

'Yes. Only ten minutes ago, though.' Rushton tried not to look too pleased with himself. 'Rory Burns threw up nothing for us. That's not his real name. He's Gerry Clancey. And he's got convictions for child molestation and attempted rape on an under-age girl. Did four months for it. Very lucky to get such a short sentence, I'd say. Used the usual defence – told the court the girl said she was eighteen and led him on. She denied both of those. Clancey was a bouncer in a night club at the time. I expect someone supplied him with a good brief.'

'Good work, Chris. We'll use that when we have another go at him, if we need to do that.'

The DI nodded. He was still absurdly pleased when John Lambert praised him, though he took care not to show it. 'There is someone we should take a look at. There was a complaint against him earlier on in the year from the local school. Probably nothing, but we should look into it. We've got him on our—'

There was a sudden urgent knock at the door. The face of a flustered young female constable appeared as it opened. 'Sorry to interrupt, sir, but there's a woman who's got past the front desk and is demanding to see you. I've tried to—'

She was thrust aside and a small grey-haired woman in glasses stood panting in the doorway. She glared round the four surprised CID faces as if they had offered her some personal affront. 'You need to see Big Julie and you need to see her quick! She shouldn't be out on her own, that woman, and now this is the result! Why the hell don't you do something about her?'

It was the only woman in the room who defused the situation. 'I know Big Julie Foster. And I know you, I think, don't I? It's Mrs Garside, isn't it?' Ruth David glanced at her three male colleagues. 'I think we've more or less finished here for the moment. Why don't you come along with me to one of our interview rooms where we can be private, Mrs Garside, and tell me what it is you have to say about Big Julie?'

She ushered the irate woman away, leaving the three men at once disturbed and relieved. DI Rushton decided that he would need to open yet another new file.

EIGHT

They found him where they had been told they might. He was standing a hundred yards from the gates of the primary school, beside the now deserted playing field where boys and girls played team games.

He looked all of his seventy years, but he was smartly dressed and well groomed. He was around six feet, perhaps three inches shorter than Lambert. He wore no hat, but he had a plentiful head of white hair, which was immaculately parted and brushed. Probably the style of it had not changed in forty years. The chief superintendent said, 'Mr Robson? We need to talk to you.'

He sighed and said resignedly, 'I thought you might. You won't find it very helpful. My house would be the best place, I think.'

Lambert didn't comment. He said simply, 'We have a car over there. We can give you a lift.'

The man seemed to stand more upright as he responded. 'Thanks all the same, but I'd prefer to walk. The mothers will gossip if they see me getting into a police car. And I've had enough gossip to last me for the rest of my life.'

It wasn't far. Dennis Robson arrived as they reversed into his driveway and parked the car outside the small detached bungalow. He didn't seem surprised that they should know the address without guidance. He opened the door and said, 'Make yourselves at home in the living room. I'll get us a pot of tea.' He didn't give them a choice about the refreshment and Lambert decided not to assert himself. You could learn things about a man by studying his surroundings whilst he was absent.

They didn't learn a lot here. It was a tidy but utterly conventional room. There was a good-quality three-piece suite with loose extra cushions which looked as if they were purely decorative. There were venerable black-and-white photographs of a man and woman with two children, one of whom was probably the man they could now hear in the kitchen. There was a newer photograph of a woman of about fifty, looking straight at the camera with a quizzical, humorous expression. There was an oval mirror above the sideboard where these pictures were displayed, a picture of a highland scene on another wall.

Dennis Robson paused in the doorway of the room with a tray in his hands. 'You're looking at my wife, Edith, I see. No child is christened Edith now, is it? I suppose one should be grateful if kids are christened at all. That was taken a good ten years before Edith died, but I like to have it there because it's my favourite picture of her.'

He looked as if he expected them to ask how she died and express their sympathy, as perhaps other visitors who had sat there had done before them. He probably had his reply ready, but he did not get the question from Lambert. These were not social visitors.

Robson set down his tray on the low table in front of the two stern-faced men and poured the tea, watching his hand as he did so. It shook a little with the weight of the teapot, but no more than you would have expected in a man of his years, he thought.

He had given them the Crown Derby crockery, but they did not comment. He was offering them biscuits when Lambert said quietly, 'Where were you on Saturday evening, Mr Robson? Let's say between seven and eight o'clock.'

Dennis set down the plate of biscuits, took one for himself and sat down unhurriedly in the armchair opposite them. 'I expect you know that, Chief Superintendent. I expect that is why you are here. I was walking round the fairground. The one whence Lucy Gibson disappeared.' He was pleased with that rather archaic-sounding 'whence'. The use of the word should emphasize to them how cool he was – in control of both himself and of this situation.

'And why were you there, Mr Robson?'

He took his time again, wondering whether his leisurely rate was annoying them, as it would have annoyed him. 'I like children, Mr Lambert. I like seeing them enjoy themselves.' He decided to be even more daring. 'It gives me great pleasure to observe their innocence, to see the way that small things give them great pleasure. That is a facility we lose quickly as we grow older. I'm sure you've noticed that.' He enjoyed his use of a judicious irony in that last phrase. Let the man know he was getting too long in the tooth to play the great detective!

Lambert was determined not to show annoyance. He was as measured and as calculating as the man who had assumed the trappings of a conventional host in what was certainly not a social situation. 'Were you accompanying any particular children to the fair?'

'No. Edith and I weren't blessed with children, which means that I now have no grandchildren to light up my declining years. It is a source of lasting regret to me, but one I have come to accept.' He looked from one face to the other and rolled out the conventional phrases as if they were his own invention, inviting these guardians of the law to challenge him if they found them false.

'It is not usual to wander around a fairground on your own. It invites suspicion, in today's society.'

'It may be unconventional, but it is not against the law, as you are no doubt well aware. If today's society does not approve, that says sad things about that society. No doubt you two see its flaws more than most of us, having to pick up the pieces as you do. Is that a mixed metaphor?'

His expression said that he scarcely expected policemen to understand what a metaphor was. Lambert said dryly, 'We have more concerns here than a felicitous use of language, Mr Robson. We are questioning you in connection with the abduction and murder of a seven-year-old girl.'

'Crimes with which I have no connection, Mr Lambert. Crimes that I should like to assist you in solving. But I fear I am unable to do that.'

'No one can remember seeing you at the fairground after half past seven.'

'And that is seen to be significant?'

'It is the time when Lucy Gibson disappeared. There were no sightings of her after seven thirty. There are also no sightings of you recorded after seven thirty.'

Dennis felt the pulse racing in his temple. He trusted it wasn't evident to these men who studied him so unemotionally. 'How very convenient that is for anyone wanting to make out a case against me! May I ask who provided you with this information?'

'You may ask, but we won't give you an answer. Information provided for us in this way is treated as confidential. I'm sure you will appreciate that. We have had a large team talking to people who were around the rides and the stalls at the time in question. Your presence was noted. As a lone man without any children, you stood out in the crowd. If you are now able to provide us with any useful pointers towards a murderer, you would no doubt prefer that also to be confidential.'

Dennis volunteered a sour smile. 'I am not able to do that, as you would probably expect. I saw one of the thugs who was collecting fares on the rides looking at the girl lasciviously, but I can't give you more than that.'

'You knew Lucy Gibson, then, Mr Robson?'

Lambert's calm enquiry came as softly as a stiletto slid expertly between the ribs. It left Robson almost as breathless. He wondered if the gasp he felt shaking his torso was audible or visible. Surely it must have been. 'I . . . I've heard the reports since Saturday. I've read what happened in the papers. I thought I must have seen her, that's all. Perhaps I'm quite wrong and the one I remember is a different girl altogether.'

But it sounded feeble, even to him, and he couldn't think of anything to add that would make it even faintly convincing. Lambert turned the stiletto in the wound. 'There have been very few details in the bulletins we have released to the media, as is normal in cases like this one. It would be difficult for anyone who did not already know Lucy to identify her from what has been broadcast or printed.'

'Yes. I heard her age in the radio bulletin. I remembered seeing a girl of about that age riding on her own on one of the smaller roundabouts. I got it into my head that she must have been the poor kid who was snatched. I'm probably quite wrong. I expect the girl I'm thinking of is alive and well and at home with her parents at this moment. I certainly hope so! I've always had too vivid an imagination. The teachers used to think it a good thing when I was at school, all those years ago, but Edith used to say I let it run away with me. That's probably what happened in this case.'

He was talking too much now. They let him run on, watching him entangle himself in the strings of his own verbiage. He looked at Lambert's long, lined, intensely observant face and stopped speaking. But it was Bert Hook who now said, 'Your name was one of the ones we immediately thought of, Mr Robson. That can scarcely be a surprise to you.'

'That's the trouble with you boys, isn't it? Once one has had any trouble with the police, one is damned for ever. When any sort of crime turns up, you don't look any further than people like me.'

Genial Bert Hook could use a stiletto as expertly as his chief when he thought it appropriate. 'Three things, Mr Robson. First, this is not just "any sort of crime". Child murder is the most horrid of all crimes. Second, you are merely one of several people being followed up and questioned. And third, we take note of people who have a history of this sort of thing for one very good reason: they tend to re-offend. It is no more than common sense to speak to them first.'

'Recidivists.'

'That's what they're called, yes. A lot of criminals break the law again. It's something various governments have been trying to correct for the last hundred years, without much success. Consequently, it makes sense for those of us who have to make arrests to look first amongst those who have previously offended.'

'Impeccable logic, DS Hook. I congratulate you upon a well-argued case. But, then, I'd expect no less from a policeman who has recently become a graduate of the Open University. May I offer you my belated congratulations upon that?'

Bert was shaken. He told himself that he should have expected something like this from this oily, intelligent man. But it was the first time any member of the public he had been questioning had come back at him with his degree, and it shook him that the man should have such knowledge. It made him no more than a diligent reader of the local press, where Bert's achievement had been gleefully reported by a police press officer eager for positive publicity. But it took Hook by surprise. He dragged himself back resolutely to the matter in hand and the need to investigate this man who was trying to divert them away from the mistake he had made. 'You're confident that it was Lucy Gibson whose movements you were following at the fairground, aren't you, Mr Robson?'

Dennis forced himself to take his time. He had made a mistake in telling them he knew Lucy Gibson. Apart from that, he was holding his own in this strange game of hint and counter-hint. He had been almost enjoying it until he'd made that mistake about the girl. He recognized now that he mustn't enjoy the game. His position was too perilous for that. He made a play of refilling the cups, of raising his eyebrows in surprise when Lambert put his hand over his. 'I thought it was Lucy until you raised your query. I now realize that I might have been noticing a quite different child.'

Lambert had been watching the two men carefully. He knew Hook's weaknesses as well as his strengths. Bert was much better at handling hostility than flattery. Being buttered up embarrassed and irritated him, even when it was sincere. And Dennis Robson's admiration for Hook might be elegantly couched, but it was anything but sincere. Lambert said brusquely, 'I think you knew Lucy Gibson's appearance quite well, Mr Robson. Were you not the subject of a complaint from the headmistress of her school earlier this year?'

Dennis turned his attention back to the man in charge with an air of relief. 'Why do you bother to ask me questions to which you obviously know the answers, Mr Lambert? Do you need confirmation that you are in the right house, that I am not some recidivist impostor? Very well, I shall confirm for you that the head teacher spoke to me. I shall also point out that the unpleasantness in March was due to the head's overreaction to a hysterical complaint from one of the parents. When your officers came to see me, they found that it was no more than a storm in a teacup. I apologize for the cliché, but it is provoked by an incident which itself represented no more than a clichéd reaction. Modern parents believe that every elderly man they see alone is a menace to their children.'

'The head teacher is an experienced professional. She would have been at fault if she had not reported the complaint to us.'

'And when she did, your equally experienced officers decided that there was no need to pursue the matter further.'

'The family liaison officer and the sergeant who interviewed you decided, Mr Robson, that there was insufficient evidence for a prosecution. They issued you with a warning about your future conduct, did they not?'

'You have done your homework and are well informed, Chief Superintendent. I would expect no less from a man with your reputation. And that homework reveals that no charges were even considered, so that there is no way that this silly business should be thrown at me now.'

'What reason did you have to hang around the school gates and to observe the children on their playing field, Mr Robson?'

Dennis drew in a long, slow breath, then expelled it with equal control. 'I like children, Mr Lambert. I said it earlier, and it's true. I enjoy their innocence. I enjoy watching them at play. There was a time when one would not have needed to account for such feelings. A time when they might even have been considered praiseworthy, in a responsible adult.'

'Even in that time you postulate, the persistent presence of a man with a history of unhealthy interest in children near school gates and school playing fields would have been a source of police concern and action. As you've already acknowledged yourself, you cannot escape your past, Mr Robson. And now one of the children you were observing in March has been snatched and murdered from a fairground, at a time when we know you were present. You must have expected us to come here.'

'I did. I know the way things work. The innocent suffer, especially if they have any previous sort of record.'

'You certainly have previous, Mr Robson. What we have to decide is whether you are innocent in this particular case. The circumstantial evidence is heavy against you. You admit that.'

'I see no point in denying the obvious to people who have a talent for the obvious. I am now telling you formally that I had nothing to do with this crime. Perhaps I should point out something that should also be obvious, but which you seem at present to be choosing to ignore. That is that I have no previous history of violence towards children.'

'I accept that. But it seems probable that whoever snatched Lucy Gibson did not intend to kill her but panicked under pressure. Perhaps he or she was desperate to stop the child from screaming.'

'I like that "he or she". It shows a proper detachment at this stage, even if your criminal turns out to be male. For the record, I'm not given to panic.' Dennis Robson looked at them steadily, challenging them to deny him.

Lambert said softly, 'There are many cases of paedophiles without previous histories of violence who have committed vicious and uncharacteristic acts when they felt under pressure.'

'That's the first time either of you has used that word. I congratulate you on your moderation. Our use of language is curious, is it not? An Anglophile loves England. A biblio-phile loves books. I would claim to be both of those. A paedophile is a lover of children, which I would freely admit to being. But the use of the word has now been perverted to something much more ugly, so that I'm not allowed to be a paedophile.'

Lambert chose not to respond to this. He said formally, 'If we assume for a moment that you have no connection with this crime, I must remind you that it is your duty to pass on to us any thoughts that might have a bearing on this case. Good afternoon to you, Mr Robson.'

As they moved to the door, Bert Hook stopped beside the computer on a small table beneath the window, the newest item in this conventionally furnished room. 'Is there any material on here that you wouldn't wish us to see?'

Dennis Robson smiled, recognizing the question as evidence of frustration. 'Of course not, DS Hook. How could you even entertain such an idea? And you wouldn't be able to investigate without a search warrant, would you?'

He stood in the doorway and saw them away with that contented, superior smile he had striven to maintain through most of their exchanges. He was glad to see they'd come in Lambert's old Vauxhall. One of those garish police vehicles might bring unwelcome attention from a boorish public when you had the background he had.

Robson would have been surprised to hear that John Lambert had voiced just that thought an hour earlier when opting to come here in his own car. As they now drove slowly back towards the station at Oldford, he said heavily, 'We didn't make a lot of progress there, did we, Bert?'

'I shouldn't have made that remark about his computer as we came out. Gives him the chance to get rid of anything incriminating, doesn't it?'

'It might have been better to keep your powder dry. But I suspect it hardly matters in this case. I've no doubt Dennis Robson is an expert in covering his tracks.'

'I didn't like the bugger at all. There's something creepy about him. Something that makes me shudder. I'm usually pretty good at shutting the job out once I get home, but I'll be able to picture that sod clearly when I'm trying to get to sleep tonight.'

NINE

The post mortem-examination of the small, almost unmarked body of Lucy Gibson revealed very little new information.

CID officers investigating murder are interested in how, when and where death occurred. Only on the first of these did Lambert, Hook and Rushton gain positive information. Rushton, who had attended the post-mortem, handed copies of the PM findings to the two older men. 'She didn't die in the river. She was dumped there after death.'

Lambert said dully, 'How was she killed, Chris?'

'Manual strangulation. The marks are on her throat and there are petechial haemorrhages in the whites of her eyes. They're not strong, not even very evident at first sight. It doesn't take much strength to kill a seven-year-old.' Rushton was divorced, but he had one child, Kirsty, of whom he was very fond. She was only marginally younger than the girl whose corpse he had just seen scientifically cut, and all three of them were acutely conscious of that fact at this moment.

The detective inspector coughed and tried to steady his voice as he said, 'The pathologist thinks Lucy was probably strangled from behind, though the marks on her throat had faded a little with the exposure to water. She had been in the Wye for around thirty-six hours by the time her body was found.'

Lambert spoke as much to relieve Rushton as because he thought it was necessary. 'It could be significant that she was strangled from behind. It could indicate that the killer knew Lucy and was known to her. That he didn't want to look into her eyes as he saw her die.'

Even these men with much experience of death were silenced for a moment by that image. It was a few seconds before Hook said, 'But we can't assume that. Who would want to look into a little girl's eyes as he killed her, even if he was seeing her for the first time in his life?'

There was silence again. Normally, they could imagine the emotions of a killer, but child murder once again was different. It was left to Hook to voice the one item that brought them relief as they read quickly through the sparse information of the report. 'It says here that there was no evidence of sexual assault.'

'No. But that means exactly what it says: no evidence. Lucy certainly wasn't raped, and there is no bruising on thighs or groin from any attack or any resistance. And there was nothing under Lucy's nails, but the pathologist made two points about that: first, in a victim of such limited strength, skin or hair under the nails is unlikely, and second, the hours in the Wye might well have washed away any minimal evidence there was from the nails. There is no bruising around genitalia, stomach or buttocks that would suggest any manual attack, but, as the report says, the fact that there is no evidence of indecent assault does not mean in this case that we can discount the possibility.'

Lambert nodded sadly and moved them on. 'Time of death? Can you add anything to the cautious findings here, Chris?'

'He says that he thinks she died within an hour of being snatched at the fairground. He isn't as precise as that in writing, because he's aware that he could be made to look silly in court when questioned about a corpse that has been in water for a day and a half. But he thinks from the stomach contents that she died very shortly after she disappeared. That finding is based on the mother's information about what Lucy ate and at what time, but we've no reason to doubt Anthea Gibson, have we?'

'None at all. Where did Lucy die, Chris?'

'I can't add anything to what's stated here. She didn't drown in the River Wye. She was dead before she was put in the water. So presumably the killer saw the river as a convenient means of disposing of the body and getting away from the scene himself.'

'As you'd expect, there's nothing here about where or how she was put into the river. We haven't yet identified that spot?'

'We haven't. Maybe we never will. The weather has been unusually dry through most of October. If whoever did this chose his spot carefully, he may have left little or no trace of himself behind. I've got six of our team examining likely places, beginning with the points where the river is nearest to Oldford and the fairground.'

All three of them knew the Wye and the paths that ran beside it well. They had trodden them with their own children, enjoying the tranquil beauty of one of the nation's loveliest rivers. Now they were picturing the places where it would have been easy for the killer to dump his small, innocent burden into the dark waters by night. It was important, because a terrified criminal might well have left some trace of himself, one of those 'exchanges' that detectives always hope to find at the scene of a crime. He might have dropped something significant, left fibres of a garment on hawthorn or barbed wire, even left a footprint in the ground at the edge of the water.

Rushton said dolefully, 'It's a needle-in-a-haystack situation. Lucy could have been dumped anywhere between the nearest point to Oldford and the spot where the body was eventually retrieved. That's a distance of approximately eleven miles.'

'Could she have been thrown into the Wye near where she was found?'

'It's possible, but we think unlikely. It's more probable that she was dumped somewhere near Oldford on Saturday night. The body wasn't weighted. It's likely it drifted slowly downstream, being held on the way by various obstructions for periods which we cannot possibly determine.'

Hook was staring unseeingly at his copy of the report, having already scanned it twice. 'The killer must have had transport. Even the nearest point of the Wye must be a good two miles from the fairground. He'd need a van or a car.'

Lambert gave his DS a grim little smile. He knew that Hook was thinking of the girl's father, hoping that the fact that he didn't have a car or a van was now going to let the man off the hook. 'Lucy was a small burden, Bert, and desperation lends strength. If he'd slung the body over his shoulder, he could have carried her there.'

Rushton nodded. He liked the fact that the others did most of the interviewing, whilst he correlated all the information as it came in. In his view, that gave him a certain objectivity about suspects. He said almost eagerly, 'Or Dean Gibson could have strung her across the carrier at the front of his bike. No one would have spotted what it was he was carrying, on unlit lanes at night.'

Hook said stubbornly, 'Matt Boyd had his car. He claims that he came home from the fairground to get it, so that he could search a wider area. And Dennis Robson might well have had his car waiting near the wood, for all we know.'

Lambert was still perusing the report. 'We still have no idea about exactly where Lucy died. She could have been killed within minutes of being snatched, or she could have been killed by the river up to an hour later.'

Rushton nodded. 'We've searched that wood by the fairground and bagged up everything we've found. But it's much too near to the common. All kinds of people use it for all sorts of activities.' He spoke with some distaste, thinking of the unsavoury items he'd seen bagged in the CID section. 'It's my belief we've got nothing crucial from there. But that doesn't mean that Lucy didn't die there. Strangulation of a child needn't leave much evidence.'

Bert said, 'Lucy Gibson disappeared as if she'd suddenly been removed from the face of the earth. There wasn't a sound from her if we're to believe what people tell us. Could that mean that she knew the person who took her and didn't feel threatened – not at first, anyway?'

Rushton looked at Lambert, who said, 'We can't assume that. There's a lot of noise around a fairground. Blaring and distorted music on most of the bigger rides, for a start. It's entirely possible that a child's scream wouldn't be heard, especially if her abductor threw his hand over her mouth to stifle it.'

There was silence in the room. None of them cared for the succession of images they had created. DI Rushton dragged them back to the realities of policing. 'We need a result. The press are hounding us for information. They'll be baying for police blood if we can't give them anything in the next day or two.'

*   *   *

A woman was coming out of the tall Victorian house as they arrived there. They met her at the gate. She looked at them with undisguised curiosity. Hook said politely, 'Could you tell us where we could find Miss Foster, please?'

'You want Big Julie? She in trouble again then, is she?'

'Not at all. We are hoping she may be able to give us a little information, that's all.' He wished he hadn't asked for help. Women like Julie Foster suffered quite enough, without their neighbours telling anyone who would listen that they'd been the centre of police enquiries.

'She has the ground-floor flat at the back of the house. Not fit to be on her own, if you ask me. She needs some kind of warden with her.'

Bert didn't necessarily disagree with that. A lot of people with low IQs had been better five or six to a house with a warden to keep an eye on them and give them advice and assistance. The 'care in the community' system of the last twenty years hadn't worked very well, largely because the community was busy with its own problems and didn't care much at all. He rang the bottom bell of the six available to him to the right of the solid front door.

It was almost a minute before the door was opened to them and a large woman filled most of the considerable space it had occupied. Lambert said politely, 'Miss Foster? I'm Chief Superintendent Lambert and this is Detective Sergeant Hook. We need to have a few words with you, please.'

They showed their warrant cards, but she gave them the merest glance. When reading was a problem, you tended to ignore documents, even when they displayed photographs alongside the print. She looked at the men blankly and waited for them to make the next move. Lambert said, 'May we come inside, please?'

She still didn't speak, but she turned and led them wordlessly down a long, narrow hall to a door on the right towards the end of it. She opened it as quietly as she could, beckoned them in and shut it with elaborate care once they were inside. 'You can't be too careful, you know!' she said to Lambert confidentially. She spoke with the air of one imparting an original piece of wisdom.

She didn't ask them to sit down, so they glanced at each other and sat on the battered sofa, leaving her the wide easy chair with green buttoned velvet covering which was obviously her usual seat. She said, 'I 'aven't took anything, you know. I 'aven't took anything for months, not since that woman copper took the things away and told me to watch my step. I've been doing that.' She looked down earnestly at her feet, as if she was taking the advice quite literally.

'No one is accusing you of anything, Miss Foster.'

'Not yet, you mean.' No one came in here and called her Miss Foster. They all called her Julie – the social workers and the care people and the woman who came to talk to her about her money and how she should manage it. The only time anyone called her Miss Foster was when they were going to accuse her of something. Charge her with something, perhaps. This big tall copper must be very important. Chief super, he'd said. He'd nail her for something if she didn't watch her step.

Lambert was already finding this difficult. He knew what he wanted to ask, but they would need to talk to Big Julie in the right way to get the best information from her. Be sensitive to her disabilities, whilst remembering throughout that she might be a child killer. He glanced hopefully at Hook. He was much relieved when Bert took on the task of talking to this woman, who had the brainpower and many of the reactions of a child, but the physical strength of a powerfully built man.

Hook said, 'It's about the fair, Julie. You were there at the weekend, weren't you?' She looked at him blankly and he said with a smile, 'We know you were, because you've already talked to one of our police ladies, haven't you? You told her that you were there on Saturday night.'

The big woman put her hands together with immense care. Perhaps she thought that the way she set her palms precisely opposite each other before she pressed them together could affect her fate with these strange men. She had a broad face, with a large, flat nose at the centre of it. Her wide, childlike, brown eyes seemed all-seeing, but capable of missing things that were vital to her understanding of the situation. 'Saturday night. I was at the fairground, yes. It's good, the fair, isn't it?'

'Yes, it is. Did you go on any of the rides yourself, Julie?'

'I rode in a dragon on one of the smaller rides. I was going to go on one of the big ones, but I didn't in the end. I don't like going on them on my own.'

'That's what you told our girl in uniform who spoke to you, isn't it? It's good that you remember things so clearly. That's what we want you to do.'

'I've always been able to remember things clearly. They like that at Tesco's. They say it makes me reliable. If Mr Burton says he needs twenty-four tins of baked beans for the shelves, I bring just that many, you see. I'm reliable.' She enunciated the four syllables of the word carefully; it was obviously important to her.

'That's good for us too, Julie. It makes you a reliable witness, you see. Not everyone remembers everything as clearly as you. Did you spend long at the fair on Saturday?'

The broad brow wrinkled for the first time. 'An hour, I think. That's what the policewoman reckoned it must have been. I'm not always good at measuring time and I don't have a watch. I lost it at work. Someone pinched it, I think.'

Hook tried not to be distracted by the harrowing picture he was acquiring of the way in which this limited, brawny woman lived. He wondered whether the estimate of an hour spent at the fair derived from Julie or from the young policewoman who had spoken to her a day earlier. 'You were there for quite a long time, considering you only had the one ride. What else did you do?'

She looked suddenly threatened, as if he had accused her of something dire. As he had, indirectly, he supposed. She said, 'I walked around, watching the big rides going round and round, listening to the music and the people shouting to one another. There was a lot of laughing and shouting, people happy. I like that.'

'Yes. I expect it cheers you up to see people enjoying themselves. I know it does me. Did you speak to anyone?'

Again the frown of concentration, as if it was important to her that she made no mistake here. 'No. Someone shouted at me to get out of the way and pushed me, but I didn't speak to him. I had a go on one of the stalls, where you try to throw rings over prizes. I was trying to get myself a new watch, but a lad at work told me no one ever gets the best prizes. The man on the stall took my money, but he didn't speak to me.'

'Do you have a boyfriend, Julie?'

'No. I did once, but he moved away.'

'Girl friends?'

'Not really. I used to go around with people, but they're mostly married now, see. They don't want to go out with me anymore.'

Hook looked round the high Victorian room. Its filthy ceiling was barely visible; the cheap light fitting threw the light from the single bulb mostly downwards on to the area where they were sitting. This was more a bedsitter than a flat; there would be a single bed in the alcove behind the curtain that covered most of a dark aperture. There were a couple of gloomy Victorian landscapes in battered gold-painted frames on walls that had not been decorated for at least ten years. There was no sign of a book or even a newspaper in the room.

No doubt Julie Foster was confined to this room for most of her leisure hours. It was a depressing place. A small portable television on top of a chest of drawers provided the only relief and the only link with the wider world outside. Julie was thirty-eight now; she did not read and she had only the dumbed-down world of *I'm a Celebrity, Get Me Out of Here* and the like to while away her time. Weekends here must be bleak. Bleak enough to unhinge a woman without the personal resources to cope with loneliness? Bert said almost unwillingly, 'You were all on your own at the fair, then?'

'Yeah. I don't mind, though. I'm used to it. I quite like being in a crowd, especially when people are enjoying themselves. It's . . . well, it's sort of jolly, isn't it? It cheers me up, when people around me are enjoying themselves.'

Bert was filled with a surge of sympathy for this woman who had been given so much to bear and who complained so little. But those feelings were ridiculous. The first thing you had to learn in CID work was to be detached; it interfered with your efficiency if you were not. He had known that for years, yet John Lambert had needed to remind him gently of the principle at intervals during their time together. Bert knew what had to come now, but he suddenly felt unable to move to it.

He looked hopelessly at his senior. Lambert took over with
scarcely a pause. 'You got yourself into a bit of trouble
with the law a few years ago, didn't you, Julie?'

He had spoken quietly, but Julie jumped as if someone had
stuck a pin in her, as that cruel girl had done a couple of
weeks ago when she was stacking the shelves. 'They said that
was all done with. They said that I wouldn't need to worry
about it anymore if I kept my nose clean.'

She lifted her thick fingers to that organ now, as if she
thought that had been a literal instruction. It was a gesture
that seared the emotions of both men. Lambert said doggedly,
'You took a child, didn't you, Julie?'

'Yes, I did. I'd been told you could have a baby without it
coming out of your stomach, that you could . . . I can't
remember the word.'

'Adopt, Julie? You thought you could adopt a baby?' The
word came back to him from the police report and its summary
of the arguments provided in court. It had seemed absurd as
he read it that anyone could have even considered offering
that as a defence. Now, sitting here in the presence of this
helpless woman who so needed someone to advise and guide
her, it seemed quite real.

'That's it, yes. I went to the council offices and tried to talk
to them about it, but no one there wanted to speak to me. I
expect there were forms to fill in. I'm no good with forms.
I need someone to fill them in for me.'

'So you took a baby, Julie. A little girl.'

'Yes. I didn't mean to. It was . . . it was . . .' Her brow
puckered with fierce concentration, but the words she wanted
would not come.

'Spur of the moment, Julie? A spur-of-the-moment
decision?'

'That's it, yes. Spur of the moment. Someone said that for
me in court, but the woman on the bench said it didn't make
any difference. I couldn't see any bench, but they were up
above me, so there might have been.'

'You looked after the baby well, Julie, but it wasn't right
to take her, was it?'

'Ellie, she was called. Smashing little girl. Didn't cry at all.'

'No. That was probably because you looked after her so well.' It was true. The one-year-old had been clean, happy and well fed. Big Julie had bought nappies, jars of baby food and baby milk, and a little teddy bear for her. The child had been expertly bathed and changed. 'You can't just wheel away a baby in her pram and keep her, though. You realize that now, don't you?'

She looked at him blankly for a moment, then nodded her head sadly. 'They'd left her outside the pub, you know. She was there for over half an hour. They said less, but I had a watch then. I didn't move her until she started to cry. Little Ellie.' She looked past him at the damaged mirror on the wall behind him, seeing nothing for a moment except that still vivid moment in her history.

'A little girl was taken from the fair you know. On Saturday night, at the time you were there.'

'Lucy. Lucy Gibson. She was the girl who was taken.'

Lambert felt Hook stiffen on the sofa beside him as she enunciated the name. He didn't even look at his colleague. It was the telepathy they had developed over the years that ensured that his bagman now resumed the questioning.

Bert said gently, 'You know the girl's name, Julie. That makes it easier for us. Is that because you've heard other people talking about this, or did the police lady mention the name to you?'

The forehead puckered in the effort that was now familiar to them. 'I knew Lucy. She came to our store. She talked to me. Her mum said she shouldn't.'

Those few words summarized her present life. Hook strove to keep his tone even as he tried to confirm the picture for himself. 'You knew Lucy before Saturday, then. And she knew you.'

'That's right. I talk to a lot of the children at the supermarket. I like children, you see, and they like seeing what I do at Tesco's. They get bored, the little ones, and they like it when one of the workers talks to them.'

It was the first time he had heard anyone who was a shelf-stacker at the supermarket pronounce that word 'worker' with genuine pride. Someone at the store had done a great job here. 'Did you see Lucy at the fairground on Saturday night?'

'Yes. I said hello to her whilst she was holding on to her dad at the shooting range. He won her a little doll. I went away then, though, because I thought he wouldn't want me speaking to her.'

It wasn't Lucy's dad, of course. It was Matt Boyd who'd won the doll for her. But there was no point in troubling Julie Foster with that now. Bert thought of that doll bagged up in CID, with a muddy footprint across its face, and said fearfully, 'I expect you'd have liked a doll like that for yourself, wouldn't you?'

The big, moon-like, revealing face looked at him in puzzlement. 'No. Why would I want that? It was only a little rag doll. Fine for a kid like Lucy, but why would I want one? I haven't got any kids to give it to. I don't even have nieces and nephews like some, you know.'

'No. Silly of me to ask, wasn't it? But Lucy liked her dolly, didn't she?'

'Oh, yes. She was holding it tight when she was riding in her bus on the little roundabout. She waved at me with the dolly's arm. She looked very happy.'

Now, at last, Hook did glance at Lambert. Julie Foster caught the look and studied first one and then the other of the men's faces. Hook said heavily. 'You were waiting for Lucy and her dolly when that ride stopped, weren't you, Julie? By the wood at the side of the common.'

'No. No, you've got that wrong, mister. I went away after I'd waved to her. Her dad was there and I didn't want him telling me to fuck off. They do that, you know.'

'You wouldn't tell me lies, would you, Julie? It's much better for you to tell us the truth now than to have other people tell it for you later. That's what happened when you took Ellie, wasn't it? We need to know now if you took Lucy away and things went wrong for you.'

'I didn't take her and things didn't go wrong. I waved to her with her dolly. Then I left them to it.' The big face set into a sullen immobility, as blank and inscrutable as a door shut upon their enquiries.

'You don't have your own transport, do you, Julie?'

Hook was expecting a routine negative, which would help

to counteract the suspicion that had leapt into their minds with the discovery that she had known Lucy Gibson before the happenings of Saturday night. But she stood up, moved heavily across the room and opened the top drawer in the scratched chest. She handed them a well-fingered envelope which she had obviously been asked to produce many times before. It contained the log book, insurance and MOT certificate of a Ford Fiesta, first registered eleven years previously. Julie Foster said proudly, 'That's my transport. One or two scratches, but she runs real smooth. She's a little belter. Lad I work with sold it to me. It was his gran's old car. Everything's in order. You check through it all.'

Hook looked dully through the different sheets. 'It's all in order, yes. Did you have this car with you at the fairground on Saturday?'

'Yeah, I did. Parked at the edge of the common. I went for a drive, you see. I like doing that at night, when there's no one to see me. I don't speed, though.' She looked suddenly alarmed, as if it was important that she convinced them of that.

'I'm sure you don't. But are you sure you didn't take Lucy for a ride with you?'

'Course I'm sure. I'm not daft, you know, so don't you go telling anyone I am.' The sudden, alarming flash of temper showed how big Julie Foster might be dangerous if she felt threatened.

'So who do you think it was who took Lucy away?'

But she had closed up on them now. She said only, 'You should ask her dad, shouldn't you? He was with her when she was on the roundabout, not me.'

They had asked Matt Boyd, the man Julie had assumed was Lucy's dad. And they had asked her real dad, too. And the burly thug who had taken her fare on the roundabout whilst trying to look up her skirt. And the man who had watched her on her playing field and at the school gates. And now they were asking this strange, guileless woman whose very artlessness might be her most dangerous quality.

TEN

Anthea Gibson did what the police family liaison officer advised. She avoided the ordeal of identifying the body herself. Her sister Lisa did that for her. Then Anthea left the house in Oldford, which seemed now so empty and silent, and went to stay with Lisa in Gloucester.

Lisa lived quite close to the modern shopping centre of the ancient city. It was a busy place, and Anthea was glad of that. It was helpful to have noise and bustle and lots of people who didn't know her and weren't interested in her. The death that had taken over her life wasn't important to these people, and their lack of interest seemed not cruel but helpful. It bore out the old cliché, which Lisa had used at least twice to her, that life must go on. It was going on all around her in Gloucester, whether she liked it or not.

But Anthea found that she could not exist for long in this strange half-world. It was no more than a substitute for her real life. It was like watching fish swimming past in a monster tank, interesting for a while but not involving you. After a certain time, it wasn't enough. It was good of Lisa to have her and look after her and be anxious for her. This time might bring them closer together, because she wouldn't forget her sister's kindness.

But Lisa was five years older than Anthea and they'd never been especially close. And Lisa had a husband who did not know what to say to Anthea. She also had two boisterous children of her own. Anthea tried to enjoy her nephews, but they reminded her too much of Lucy who was gone. She kept finding herself biting her lip and unable to speak to the boys.

Two nights in Lisa's pleasant modern house were enough for her. She said on Tuesday morning, 'I need to get back home. I've got to face up to things some time, haven't I?'

'But not yet,' said Lisa firmly. 'You need more time before

you go back to an empty house. And you know you're welcome to stay here as long as you like.'

'That's good of you, but you have your own lives to get on with.' She thought of those noisy boys, who laughed with each other and fought with each other by turns, who had already moved on, so that they now had to be reminded by their mother of Anthea's tragic situation. They were at school now and she wanted to be gone before they were back in the house. 'There's a bus to Oldford at eleven fifteen. I'm going to get myself on to that and off home. I'll ring you tonight.'

Lisa protested and said it was too soon, but Anthea caught a measure of relief in her sister's voice. She said determinedly, 'I'll need to make contact with Lloyd's Chemists in Oldford. They won't keep my job open for ever.'

That wasn't true, because the pharmacist had told her to be away for as long as she needed from the shop in Oldford. You needed to have a good measure of recovery before you could cope with the steady stream of sympathy that would come across the counter at you as you served customers in the busy little shop. Anthea only did that for twelve hours a week, but she was conscious in her misery that she was going to need those hours more than ever now if she was to carry on with her life.

The bus took a winding route from Gloucester, so that it could call at numerous villages en route, but today the journey she had always found tedious passed too quickly for her. A pale yellow sunshine was falling low over the hedges. People on the bus spoke of how the hour would go off at the weekend and how it always felt like winter when that happened. Anthea managed to smile a weak agreement when the woman sitting next to her talked about it soon being dark before five o'clock. Anthea was faceless on this bus. No one knew of her tragedy. She wanted to hug that anonymity about her and keep it as a protective blanket for much longer.

She stood for a moment with key in hand at her front door. She had to steel herself to enter the unremarkable house, which was suddenly full of echoes and memories. There were unwashed dishes in the sink, which shocked her. She had never done that before; only sluts did that. The thought allowed her a small smile at her own behaviour, at the thought of her sluttishness. Sluts could never be at the centre of tragedy.

She washed those dishes with brisk efficiency, then dragged the vacuum cleaner from its cupboard and used it vigorously through the whole house. She did not stop even at Lucy's bedroom, keeping her eyes resolutely upon the carpet as she moved the roaring cleaner industriously back and forth. She decided that she wouldn't let this room become a shrine. Then she told herself that it was much too early to be entertaining thoughts like that.

It was almost dark by the time she allowed herself to sit down. She made herself a cup of tea and tried to read the morning paper she'd brought with her from Gloucester. She didn't feel at all hungry. She'd make herself something to eat later. She'd got used to eating early in this kitchen with Lucy, so that her daughter could digest her tea before her bedtime story. There was no need for that now. She slapped her palm hard against the paper for allowing herself to think like that. It made a sound like a pistol shot. She tried to find some interest in the latest *Daily Express* speculations about the royals.

When the bell rang, she didn't want to go to the door. She couldn't face the latest well-meant bout of sympathy, still less the neighbourly rants about what they would do to whoever had done this awful thing. But the light was on and the visitor would know she was in. The bell rang again. Better face the caller and get rid of her as quickly as she could. It was sure to be a woman.

Anthea paused in the hall, took a long deep breath, put on her public face and opened the door. She had a bigger shock than she'd expected.

Matt Boyd cringed in front of her, as if he feared that she would hit him. He gulped and said, 'May I come in?' And then, before she could answer him, he tumbled out more words, 'If you want me to go away, I'll understand. Maybe it's too soon.'

Christine Lambert was feeling the strain of the case. She had been in school today, teaching ten-year-olds in the part-time job she normally found so stimulating. But the tragedy of that other, younger child, who had attended school no more than six miles away, fell over the staffroom exchanges that Christine normally so enjoyed.

Everyone expected that as the wife of the local celebrity, John Lambert, she would know details of this melodrama which they could take and relate to others. It seemed to Christine that everyone thought the grisly glamour of death clung about her and was available to those who chose to carry chunks of it away. Even the classroom seemed to her less lively than usual on this autumn afternoon. The boys and girls sitting attentively in front of her appeared to think that the wife of Chief Superintendent Lambert must surely bring something of the weekend's tragic event into their quiet country school.

She confided some of this to her husband, who for once seemed anxious to talk about the case. Perhaps John thought he could lighten the burden of a child's death by talking to a woman who moved among young people easily and knowledgeably. After a few minutes, Christine realized that this was the reason for John's introduction of the subject. He was troubled and baffled by the death of Lucy Gibson and felt that because his wife had always known more about children and been happier with them than he was, she might have some telling idea to contribute, which he and his team had not yet explored.

Christine didn't mind that, though she feared that when it came to the abnormal adults who must surely be involved in this, she knew much less than John. She said as much when he asked for her thoughts. 'I might know more about children than you do, though you underestimate yourself – you were always very good with our two when there was a crisis. But this isn't about children, is it? It's about some very evil or some very disturbed adult. You've met far more people like that than I have.'

She was right, of course; John knew that. For years he had brought none of his work home with him, so that Christine had known nothing about the central parts of her husband's life. Now he felt guilty about bringing this most disturbing of crimes into the house with him. Christine seemed far more vulnerable to him than she did to herself.

Sturdy common sense wasn't a protection against everything, and least of all against dark happenings like this. He said sadly, 'I think whoever killed Lucy Gibson must be both evil and disturbed. But that can't be my concern. My duty is to bring in whoever did this and let the law and the psychiatrists decide the rest. Whether he or she ends up in a high-security prison or in Broadmoor will be decided by others, not by me, thank the Lord.'

He wondered why he still thanked that Lord he no longer believed in. Force of habit? Or touching wood? Christine felt his anguish; when you had lived with someone for so many years, not everything needed to be voiced. She said softly, 'You said "he or she". Is that just your normal caution? Everyone who's spoken to me has assumed your killer is male.'

'We have one woman among our leading suspects. I don't think she did it. Correction: I hope she didn't do it. I must have picked up that unprofessional approach from Bert Hook. This is a woman of low IQ who hasn't had much out of life. But if I look at things objectively, I know quite well that that's the springboard for a lot of violent crimes.'

'You mean Big Julie?'

He glanced at her sharply. She said, 'This is what happens when you have a child murder on your doorstep, John. One of the teachers is the same age as Julie and has known her for years. She lives within a hundred yards of her. The gossip gets round pretty quickly when the great detective John Lambert comes calling. Julie might even have spread the news herself; she doesn't often have anything to make her the centre of attention.'

Christine was on to things quickly, as she so often was. Now John Lambert wondered among many other wonderings why he so often underestimated his wife. 'Perhaps I should have asked you about Julie earlier.'

Christine shook her head. 'I don't know her, except by repute. There was a time twenty-five years ago, when I was working full-time at the comprehensive, when Julie Foster might have come through into my class. But she was removed before then and placed in a special school. I don't think she had many behavioural problems, but she had a low IQ and was easily led. She grew up in a council home. She didn't have much going for her.'

'And still doesn't, by the looks of where she lives and what she does. I'd say she's had a raw deal from life, but we see a lot of those in CID. Julie's got an old car, which she's obviously very proud of.'

If Christine saw the implications of that, she chose not to comment; instead, she switched the subject. 'The papers say Lucy's father isn't living with her mother any more. I suppose you've had to investigate him.'

'We have. And he's another inadequate, in a different way from Big Julie Foster. He's by no means stupid, but he was missing his daughter and his wife before this happened. I don't think he was coping very well. But that applies to a lot of people, male or female, when a marriage or partnership splits up.'

'According to our local paper, his wife's new man was with Lucy when she was snatched at the fair.'

John frowned his annoyance. Items of information that hadn't been released by the police press officer were now appearing. That was inevitable when a local crime was discussed by all and sundry with wide-eared newshounds around. In this case, it was unlikely that a copper had sold stuff to the media – that was one of Lambert's particular *bêtes noires* about the modern police service. 'There's no evidence for an arrest, though equally we've not been able to clear him yet. There's something a little odd about Matthew Boyd, but that doesn't make him a killer. It might pay him to stay clear of Oldford, though; the local witch-hunters come out in force after a death like this.'

'There've been statistics in the press about the number of active paedophiles in the country. It's quite appalling.'

'It is indeed. The numbers of people collecting child pornography on computers are depressing. We're policing a sick society.' John sighed, knowing he was speaking and sounding like an old man. He had no illusions about 'good old days'; there had been far more beatings of wives and children when he had been a fresh-faced young copper on the beat. Neverthe-less, he found the numbers of people from all divisions of society who were interested in sex involving helpless children deeply depressing. He said, 'As you'd expect, the team has interviewed a number of suspected paedophiles. We've been able to clear all but one. Bert and I saw him yesterday. Very discreetly, I hope. He hasn't any convictions, but rumours travel fast; we don't want the local vigilantes breaking his windows and daubing slogans on his house.'

'Especially if he didn't do it.'

'Especially if he didn't do it, as you say. He probably didn't, though Bert and I both found him a creepy sod. I expect we'd have felt that anyway, knowing what he'd done in the past. When a paedophile has a smooth and educated appearance, it probably just makes you more suspicious. Very unfair, really.'

Christine thought that he didn't seem to care too much about being unfair. It must be difficult to be fair when you were with someone who you knew had done unspeakable things with children. She shuddered a little, surprising herself with the movement; she hadn't been ready for it. She said hastily, 'You took someone in from the fairground, didn't you?'

'How on earth did you know that?'

For an instant, her husband was his bristling alter ego of a quarter of a century ago. She smiled and put her hand upon his taut forearm. 'You were seen, John, yesterday morning at the fairground. Everyone is upset about Lucy, especially now that it's murder, but it's still the most exciting thing that's happened in Oldford for years. When one person sees what's going on, it passes round very quickly, often with colourful additions.'

'Well, the addition someone's made this time is that the man was taken in. He wasn't arrested. He was questioned at the fairground, in a place selected by him, and then sent about his business, which in this case was demolishing the rides and stowing them on the lorries for transportation to their next venue.'

'Cleared, then. I'm glad about that.' Christine was habitually on the side of the much maligned younger generation.

'Not quite cleared. He's a young thug with unhealthy sexual

appetites and a capacity for violence. But there are a lot of those around and most of them tangle with the police sooner or later. We've no evidence to arrest him, but we'll be back to have more words with him, unless we turn up something pretty quickly.'

He was looking very worn, thought Christine. This case was affecting him more than any other she could recall. But that was probably to his credit. John was like a battle-hardened soldier who was still capable of being disturbed by some killing that was especially appalling. She said, attempting to lighten his mood, 'You'll need a psychiatrist yourself, when this is over.'

'I've called one in. Well, a psychologist, actually. I'm meeting the forensic psychologist who is now a resource available to all senior crime investigators tomorrow morning. We need all the help we can get.'

Christine knew all about police scepticism when it came to trick cyclists. She said with only a hint of irony, 'It's marvellous how open-minded and receptive the modern senior policeman can be.'

Anthea Gibson allowed Matt Boyd back into her house. Everything seemed to happen in slow motion as she stood back and allowed him to move past her into the hall.

The man who knew so much about her, who knew her body intimately, who last week she had so wanted to share her life, seemed at this moment a stranger in her house. He behaved like one. He stood awkwardly behind a chair in her kitchen, so that she had to say to him, 'You'd better sit down.' She tried to force a smile and found that she could not do that.

Matt said, 'I've got calls to make in this area over the next day or two. I thought I should come and see how you were coping.'

'I'm coping. Just about. I was at Lisa's until today. That's my sister. You haven't met her.'

'No.' He struggled desperately for something to say. 'I've heard you speak of her.'

She was looking at the table as she said, 'Have the police bothered you again?'

'No. Not since I went to the station with them on Sunday morning. I expect it was just routine. They had to eliminate me from their enquiries. As I was the last person known to have been with—' He stopped abruptly, wondering how he could have allowed himself to arrive here.

'With the deceased. That's what they'd call it now, isn't it? With the deceased.' She gave a huge sigh, as if she could breathe out with it all her tensions. 'Do you want to stay here tonight?'

She'd surprised them both with the question. He said, 'I don't know. I hadn't really thought about it. Do you want me to do that?'

Anthea wondered if it was true that he hadn't really thought about it. He must surely have considered the possibility of spending the night with her when he'd decided to come here and ring her bell. 'You can stay if you like. I might not want to sleep with you.'

'No, of course not. That's understood.' They were like nervous teenagers, he thought, yet they now had more between them than most couples who'd been married for many years. He reached across the table and put his hand on top of hers, trying to ignore how cold, how alien, it felt. 'I want to be with you. I want to help you, if you'll let me.'

Anthea wondered how much he meant that, how much he was merely throwing the appropriate words across the table at her. She seemed to have lost any capacity to weigh these things and make judgements. Perhaps all her emotions had atrophied with the removal of Lucy from her life. Last week she'd been worried that this man wasn't committing enough of himself to her, had been anxious for him to become a greater part of her life. Now he seemed a stranger. Perhaps she wanted to keep him a stranger. But she wasn't sure of that or of anything else. She said dully, 'I'll get us something to eat.'

She opened a can of soup, cut up some of the bread that Lisa had bought for her from the good Gloucester bakery. Matt tried to help, buttering the bread awkwardly and trying to do exactly the things she told him to do. 'I'm not very good in the kitchen,' he said with a nervous giggle. 'But then you already knew that, didn't you?'

She didn't respond, but carried on with what she was doing as if she hadn't heard him. Last week, she'd have said daringly that it wasn't his skill in the kitchen that attracted her, and they'd have laughed together at her bawdiness. Now she was trying to think, but she couldn't make her brain work. Did she want this man in her house? Did she want this man in her bed? Surely her heart as well as her mind should have some emotional reaction to those questions? But she moved around her kitchen like an automaton and felt as much emotion as a robot.

She watched Matt Boyd down his soup, then set scrambled egg on toast in the place she had set for him, with a smaller portion for herself opposite. She didn't feel at all hungry. A few minutes later, she looked down at her plate and was surprised to find that it was empty. She had spoken to him whilst he ate and he had replied to her, but she had no idea what either of them had said.

He said, 'I'll go now, if you like.'

She watched the red second hand going round on the big kitchen clock. Dean had bought that for her, when he had still lived here. It took her a full half-minute to realize that Matt was waiting for a reply. As as if she was offering medical advice to him, she said, 'No, I think it would be best if you stay.'

They went into the lounge and he tried to talk to her. But she sat like a stranger in the armchair with the tall back which she used when she was alone. Only last week, she had curled up with his arm round her on the sofa where he sat now, folding her body comfortably into his as they watched television. He was glad when she said he could switch the box on, because he was finding any sort of talk very difficult. He made comments on the programmes, but she replied mostly in monosyllables.

Matt Boyd wondered how he was going to end this and get out, if he had to do that. There was a place he could stay in the town. He'd had bed and breakfast there two or three times, in the days before he'd known Anthea. But he wanted to stay here – wanted to stay now far more than he would have wanted to last week. He couldn't think why.

It was half past nine when Anthea Gibson said abruptly, 'You can stay the night here, if you want to.'

Matt licked his lips. 'Thank you. I'd like that.'

'But I won't want to make love.' She stopped abruptly and continued staring glassily at the television.

'No. That's understood. You said it earlier, I think.' He made it as emphatic as he could, but she didn't offer any other words for him to bite on. He said desperately, 'I understand that completely.'

A long time later, when he had given up any hope of a response, she said quietly, 'Well, that's OK, then.'

She said she would have a hot drink and he made them tea, finding relief in the simple movements around the kitchen. She stayed in the sitting room and he seized the moment to move quickly out to the car and bring in his overnight case. He handed over her mug of tea, then sat down on the sofa with his own. He said, 'There's no need for the spare room. I'll sleep down here on the sofa. I don't want to be any trouble.' He thought he caught the slightest nod of agreement from her, but he couldn't be sure of that.

She went upstairs and he undressed swiftly, ridiculously embarrassed by the thought of Anthea appearing; she had seen him undress many times before. He was glad there was a downstairs cloakroom in the small house; he would have felt he was intruding if he'd had to go upstairs. He put his pyjamas on and prepared to lie down on the sofa. It was plenty long enough for him, but he wished he had asked her for a duvet or a blanket. He'd have to make do with cushions. He wasn't going to disturb her again.

Then she was suddenly standing in the doorway in a long white nightdress. She looked like mad Lady Macbeth in the school play in which he'd been a soldier long years ago. She said, 'I think you should come into my bed now.'

It was a command, not a query, but one he was happy enough to obey. He followed her up the stairs, feeling guilty that she should now seem more desirable to him than she had done when Lucy was here. He lay beside her in the big bed, carefully avoiding contact, feeling the tenseness seep away inevitably as the heat from their bodies warmed the chill sheets. He fancied that she moved a fraction nearer to him. He rolled on to his side and put an arm tentatively around her. She did not respond, but she did not resist. Presently, against his expectations, they slept.

It was still dark when Anthea awoke. The illuminated figure on the clock radio beside the bed told her that it was five twenty. She slid softly from beneath Matt Boyd's arm; she did not want to feel behind her the erection that she would once have welcomed. He was still sleeping when she stood beside the bed, then padded away from it and crept softly down the stairs.

She pressed the button that would activate the heating, made herself tea and pulled her chair so that she could rest against the warm radiator. There was no sign of dawn yet. It might take more than dawn to raise her spirits today. She shuddered, despite the warmth from the drink within her and the growing heat of the radiator against her thigh.

She hadn't been able to remain in the bed a moment longer. She had been glad to have Matt's arm around her last night. But from the moment when she had woken, she had been appalled. She told herself that her mind was disturbed, that there was no accounting for this clash of emotions, apart from the fact that she was not her normal self and could not expect to be so.

But she could not rid herself of the idea that the hands and arms that had encircled her while she slept had been the ones that had dispatched her daughter from this bewildering world.

ELEVEN

The forensic psychologist was a small, intense woman in her early thirties. She looked to Lambert several years younger than that.

He shook hands and said nervously, 'I thought it better that we had just a private exchange between the two of us at this stage.'

'Very wise. I'm well aware of what your average police officer thinks about psychiatrists and psychologists. We're interfering theorists who don't understand how the real world works. We get in the way of justice rather than help it. We insist on examining the blackest of villains and digging up mitigating circumstances.'

Lambert smiled grimly. 'That's a fair summary of the way I've felt myself at times. In my younger and less enlightened days.'

'I'm happy to talk to you alone. I've no wish to be grilled by a gang of hostile and mainly ignorant coppers.'

Lambert wondered whether to defend the police service against such unscientific generalizations. It would be inadvisable, he thought. Instead, he said, 'If we keep this informal, we're more likely to speculate. And I'd like you to do that. At the moment, frankly, we're wondering where to go next.'

She hadn't smiled so far. He was finding her stiffness disconcerting. He couldn't think of a more serious crime than this one, but the police habit was to keep horror at arm's length with scraps of humour, or at least a wry sense of shared difficulties. Elaine Pilkington said, 'I'm not sure I can be of much use to you here. It's much easier for us when we're called in after a number of serious crimes thought to be by the same person – a serial killer, for instance.'

Lambert wondered if he should apologize for the paucity of what he offered. He said, 'A child killer case is what all policemen fear. Sometimes senior CID officers welcome a more normal killing, as a challenge to their experience and abilities after much duller crimes. No one wants a child murder.'

'Maybe I should be investigating senior policemen who are excited by a good murder.' She looked at him with her head a little on one side. There was no note of humour, but John Lambert hoped she was teasing him. 'I've read what you gave me on the Lucy Gibson case. I can only give you a few thoughts.'

'That's good. Any pointers would be welcome.'

Ms Pilkington pursed lips that did not smile. 'I'm not sure I can offer anything as definite as a pointer. But I'm certainly willing to think aloud with you.'

'Good. We've had a big team investigating this, as you'd expect. They've interviewed everyone known to have been at the fairground at the time Lucy Gibson was abducted. We've isolated five people known to have had opportunity and an interest in the victim. It's difficult to speak with any authority about motive, in a case like this.'

'Your culprit may not have an obvious motive. This isn't a rational crime. Abduction often involves women, though murder less so. Have you any women among your five suspects?'

'One. She took a baby, some years ago. A little girl. She looked after her well in the twenty-four hours for which she held her.'

'Limited intellect? No family of her own?'

Lambert tried not to be impressed. 'Yes. She had a mother who wasn't much more than a kid herself, who's now a heroin addict. Julie grew up in a children's home.'

He passed her a sheet with the details of Julie's past, which Elaine Pilkington studied silently for two minutes.

'From her background, conduct and previous reports, she's almost certainly more unstable than people think she is. But that won't be much help, because I suspect whoever did this is almost bound to be unstable to some degree.'

'I'll make a note of that.'

'It's that "to some degree" that is the snag. Sometimes people who haven't previously manifested personality problems succumb to stress. Do you think whoever did this intended to kill the girl when he took her?'

Lambert tried to banish the thought that he'd hoped it would be he who was putting that question. 'I thought not.'

'I think almost certainly not. It would be far more likely that your culprit took the child with no very clear plans in mind, then panicked when things didn't proceed as intended. Which lets your woman right back in. What age is she?'

'Thirty-eight.'

'Feasible. She sees the opportunity, takes the child without much forethought, simply because the opportunity presents itself. Then finds a seven-year-old has more will and resistance than a baby, and doesn't know what to do except silence her.'

Lambert said with a touch of pique, 'That had already occurred to us as a possibility. We have the psychiatrist's report from the time she took the baby. It mentions personality defects.' He stated it reluctantly, in the interests of fairness. He found it gave him no pleasure to confirm this woman's suspicions. 'It's not my field, but I expect that, as you say, we'll find similar tendencies in some or all of the other four we've got in the frame.'

Ms Pilkington nodded vigorously. 'In greater or lesser degree, as I suggested. The idea may not be much use to us.'

Lambert tried to be pleased by that 'us'. At least this stiff and difficult woman was involving herself in the investigation. He said, 'Do you think the abductor was someone who knew Lucy?'

'Probably, but not certainly. Sorry. I know you'd like something more definite, but we shouldn't rule out a random snatching at this stage. Paedophiles tend to be opportunists.'

'We have one known paedophile among our five. A man of seventy. He has an eminently respectable surface, but previous history. There's something very creepy about him.'

He was immediately sorry that he'd used that very unscientific word, but it brought no visible reaction from his companion. 'There's almost always something creepy about paedophiles, to normal people like us – though, as a psychologist, I shouldn't even admit the concept of "normal". Are you sure you're not influenced by your knowledge of his previous history?'

Lambert said irritably, 'No I'm not! We're used to having to guard against things like that. We do it all the time.'

'Do you think this man was watching and awaiting his chance?'

'It's highly possible. He was at the fairground without a companion, which is very unusual for a man of his age. He probably knew Lucy; he'd been warned off by her school for lingering around the playing field and the school gates. He's ignored those warnings. He has no history of violence. He was suspected of indecent assaults on three children, but no case was ever taken to court.'

'But in this situation, he might have panicked under pressure if Lucy resisted him fiercely. Paedophiles often get off on child pornography and their own fantasies. Sometimes they have little experience of real children.'

'That would apply to this man. He never had children of his own.' He waited, but she made no further observation about Dennis Robson. 'We have one man with a history of violence. He broke someone's jaw and eye-socket four years ago. He was also convicted of indecent assaults on children six years ago. We didn't know about either of these when we interviewed him, because he's been working at the fairground under a false name. We'll be going back to him now that we know about them.'

'What age is he?'

'Twenty-eight. Irish. He worked in Ulster for three years before he changed his name and joined the fairground staff here, but his indecency conviction was in Cork. Violent background there, though he's too young to have been involved in the troubles. He's a thug who follows the fair and is no doubt a valued employee because he's young and strong. He's aroused by young girls. Enjoys looking up their skirts. Enjoys their innocence, I expect, but I'm straying into your territory here.'

She nodded a terse acknowledgement of that but still offered no smile. 'Oddly enough, the fact that he's well used to physical violence makes this man less likely to have panicked. On the other hand, he may find violence a habitual reaction to most challenges.' She frowned a little on that thought, then nodded again, as if admitting its validity to herself.

'Our other two are the people we always interview first in investigations like this. The estranged husband and the new man in the mother's life. Unfortunately, we haven't been able to eliminate either of them from the enquiry as yet.'

'Nor should you, without good reason. This is likely to have been perpetrated by someone who lives locally and who knew the victim previously. How long since the father left?'

'Only five months. And he doesn't deny that he retained a strong attachment to Lucy.'

'How balanced is he?'

'I'm not qualified to pronounce on that. He seems to us a man of limited personal resources who is finding it difficult to claw his way out of a collapsed marriage. We come across a lot of those.'

'Was he hoping to revive his relationship with his wife at the time of this crime?'

It was Lambert's turn to think furiously, so much so that Ms Pilkington said, 'No one's going to quote you. This is a frank and informal exchange of views, as you reminded me at the outset.'

'I think he'd welcome the chance to move back in with Anthea, yes. And a major factor in that would have been his love for his daughter. When we spoke with him, he didn't try to disguise the fact that he'd missed Lucy after moving out.'

'So he might well have snatched her when he saw her happy at the fair with another man. It's a big step from that to murder. But then we're looking for a major departure from normal behaviour in whoever did this. What about the man who's replaced him in the family home?'

'He's thirty-one, which makes him two years younger than the husband. He's a sales rep for a motoring supplies firm. Better looking and a better financial prospect than the husband, who's definitely gone downhill since he was compelled to leave his wife. The new man wasn't living with Anthea Gibson at the time of this death. He was what the pressmen like to call a frequent visitor. He gave me the impression that he was considering moving in permanently and that she was encouraging him.'

'Relationship with the child?'

'Tricky to establish. We think he was treading carefully, trying to establish closeness with a girl who still had strong feelings for her father. Hence his volunteering to take Lucy to the fair, he says. She was really looking forward to it and he wanted to capitalize on that.'

'But you doubt what he says. You think he might have done this.'

'We have to begin somewhere. Unless the culprit is obvious, we always investigate the last person known to have seen the victim alive. In this case, we haven't been able to eliminate him. There was a considerable delay in reporting the crime, which was wholly down to him. About eighty minutes elapsed before he returned to Anthea Gibson with news of Lucy's disappearance. He says he was looking for her in that time, much of it in his car. Even when he returned to the house, he insisted on ringing all of Lucy's friends' parents before he informed the police. She'd been gone for around two and a half hours before he allowed Anthea to call Oldford police station.'

The psychologist stared at him for a moment. 'I think I might have behaved very similarly if I'd lost someone else's child. Wouldn't you?'

'I can't be objective about that. I'm a policeman. I know the way our system works.'

'Has the mother any views on who killed her daughter?'

'She hasn't offered any. She was in no state to be formally interviewed immediately after it happened and she hasn't suggested anything since then.'

'I can't offer you much, Chief Superintendent Lambert, even as speculation. As I said earlier, it's much easier for people like us to be helpful when there's been a series of murders and we can establish a pattern.' She looked at Lambert as if he had let her down in some way by providing only one small corpse. 'For what it's worth, I think that your criminal was local and was probably known to his victim before he seized her. Even if very briefly known, as in the case of your fairground employee. I can't eliminate any of your five, but I think you've very probably got your killer amongst them.'

She stood up, picked up her briefcase and turned towards the door. Then she stopped and turned reluctantly back towards the man she had come to help. 'And there's one other thing. I think you need to catch him or her quickly. Unbalanced people gather excitement from success. Outwitting a big team will give a bizarre feeling of triumph. The person who did this is quite likely to strike again.'

Ms Pilkington gave him her solitary smile at the very end of their exchanges, as she turned away from him. It was entirely mirthless.

Raymond Barrington lived in a council home. He would not have thought that a reason for anyone to be sympathetic towards him.

Children's homes have had much bad publicity in the last thirty years. Some of it is well justified, but the blanket condemnation has been intensely unfair to those care homes and those staff who do an excellent job under testing circumstances. Raymond was happy in the high Victorian house in Oldford, much happier than he had been during the seven years he had watched his mother and a succession of men coming to blows and taking drugs. He was almost nine now; in two weeks' time, he would have the first birthday party he had ever enjoyed.

Mrs Allen, who acted as Mum to him and the five other children in her unofficial 'family', had announced that he would have a little party when he came home from school on the day, and Raymond trusted Mrs Allen absolutely. She was the first adult in his life whom he obeyed and believed unthinkingly. She was a little plump, which was surprising as she was scarcely ever still. She had fair hair and she was always cheerful. She smiled almost all the time, except when someone was really naughty.

It was Mrs Allen who had encouraged Raymond Barrington to join the cub scouts. She wanted him to have friends outside the home and activities away from it, though she didn't tell him that. She'd seen how the cubs, and later the scouts, could add another dimension to the lives of boys who were in care. Raymond was a shy boy. He'd been reluctant to go to the meetings at first, but after a few times he'd begun to enjoy it.

He'd been going for three months now and he raced off eagerly after his tea on this gloomy October evening. Mrs Allen's parting injunction to be sure to come straight back afterwards rang in his ears as he went, waving a hand in the air in acknowledgement but not turning his head to look towards her. She almost always said that, but she'd been especially emphatic tonight. He knew why. It was because of that girl who'd been taken and killed at the weekend. Some perve had taken her, the older boys said, and Raymond thought they were probably right.

You grew up quickly when you were in council care.

There weren't as many as usual at cubs. Parents were worried about letting their children out alone after what had happened to Lucy Gibson, though neither Akela nor anyone else voiced that thought. Raymond Barrington swiftly forgot all about Lucy when the noisy activities got going inside the big hut. They spent some time working on the activities for their badges. Raymond had found knots difficult at first, but he was pretty good at them now. He was looking forward to getting his badges, just as he enjoyed looking up at his bright green cap when he was in his bed at the home.

Because there were only a few of them tonight, at the end of the session they played table tennis, which some of the poorer players still called 'ping pong'. Raymond was the best in the group at table tennis; they had a table in the home and he sometimes played there, when the older ones were doing other things. He was getting quite deadly now with his forehand drive, though Akela told him he must wait for his opportunity and try not to hit it too hard. He won each of the three games he was allowed to play, and he was excited and sorry to finish when the session ended and it was time to go home.

He put his anorak on but didn't bother to zip it up, because he was so warm after the games he'd played and won. He put his green cub cap carefully on his head and set off home with David, the new friend with curly yellow hair whom he'd met at cubs. David went to a private school and lived in a big house near the common, but he and Raymond got on very well at cubs. David said he was going to invite Raymond round to his house for tea and to play one weekend. Raymond rather thought this one might happen; a couple of boys from school had said they were going to invite him, but the parents had put a stop to it when they'd found he lived in the council home.

He said goodbye to the others and went out into the night with David. It was cold after the warmth of the hut. The sky seemed very dark after the brightness of the lights over the table tennis table. He was glad that he had David with him, though he would never have dreamed of saying that. They kept very close to each other as they moved through the night.

'See you next week!' Nervousness made David's voice unnaturally loud. He touched Raymond on the shoulder, then broke into a run and disappeared through the gate to his house and into the darkness.

It was beginning to rain, but it wasn't far back to the big house and Mrs Allen now. Not much more than a hundred yards, Raymond told himself, though he wasn't quite sure how far that was. He broke into a run, but found that rhythm had deserted him just when he most wanted it. His legs wouldn't work together; he almost fell when one of his feet slipped into the gutter. It was silly to get so excited. He was used to the dark, wasn't he? He made himself slow down into a swift walk.

He wasn't sure where the figure came from. It was suddenly towering above him in the darkness. Both his arms were seized, then held together so tightly behind his back that he feared one of them might break. Then his wrists were held in one strong, gloved hand, whilst the other one was placed over his mouth. He couldn't believe this was happening to him. This was the kind of horror he used to scare the others in their beds at night with his stories. It shouldn't happen in real life.

But now something was slipped over his mouth, sealing his lips, closing his panting mouth, so that he feared he might choke. The face seemed far above him, much too high for him to see it properly. Was it a man or a woman, or something much worse, something not even human? He was carried past a streetlamp and the light fell briefly upon them. His assailant was muffled in a coat right up to the cheekbones. Whoever or whatever it was had a mask over its eyes, like the highwayman in the book he'd read last week.

'You're going for a ride, boy!' The voice was scarcely human, growling at him through the material over the mouth. His hand was clutched hard in that huge paw and he was ordered harshly not to speak. There was no chance of that, with the tape that had been spread across his mouth. He looked desperately for anyone coming towards them along the road, but there was no one. He clutched his cub cap with his free hand and flung it away. This awful thing wasn't going to have that.

Raymond thought his assailant was huge. He had dismissed the idea that this was some ogre that wasn't human now, but he couldn't tell from the few words that had been shouted hoarsely into his ear whether it was male or female. It seemed vital not to upset whoever gripped his hand. He must concentrate on breathing though his nose. They were moving quickly now, almost running, but he sensed that it would be foolish to resist.

Raymond Barrington saw the high gables of the home pass swiftly away into the starless night.

TWELVE

There was no delay in reporting the abduction this time. Before half past eight on that damp Wednesday night, the tremulous voice of Amy Allen was reporting to Oldford police station that eight-year-old Raymond Barrington had not returned to the care home. She had rung the cub leader and Akela had confirmed that the boy had left the scout centre at five to eight, accompanied by his friend David Harper. David had reached home five minutes later. Raymond had not been seen since then.

By nine fifteen, in the darkness and drizzle of the late October night, John Lambert, Bert Hook, Chris Rushton and the nucleus of the Lucy Gibson investigation team were assembled in the CID section at Oldford. There were grim faces everywhere. Lambert could still hear in his ears the warning of the forensic psychologist that morning that their killer might strike again. But what could they have done to prevent this? That question merely underlined how helpless they were in the face of irrational and motiveless crimes like this one. Even in a small town, you couldn't cover every street for every hour of night and day.

Raymond Barrington had disappeared on a short stretch of quiet, innocent-looking road near the town centre. Thin, steady rain was now falling from the low clouds as the hastily assembled scene of crime team began their search of the area. They knew pretty well exactly where someone had seized Raymond on that short journey in the dark of early evening. His cherished green cub cap had been found amongst the dying brown leaves of a beech hedge, less than seventy yards from the care home and safety.

They were close enough to the time of the disappearance to corner the offender before he or she had hidden his prey. Or disposed of it. Neither Lambert nor Hook voiced that thought, but each was filled with a desperate haste.

He or she. They went first to Big Julie Foster's flat. Geographically, she was nearest to the scene of this latest outrage. Both men thought that a good enough reason to go there first. Neither of them voiced the thought that perhaps Julie was the likeliest candidate to have perpetrated this second snatching of a child.

Julie wasn't there. The two men glanced at each other in alarm. Neither of them wanted to force an entry, as they would undoubtedly have done if this had been the home of Rory Burns, that fairground thug who had leered up the skirt of Lucy Gibson and not troubled to disguise his interest in small children. Hook moved quickly up the passage at the side of the house; it was but a moment before he was back to report that there were no lights on in the bedsit where Julie spent most of her leisure time. She was presumably out somewhere, rather than merely refusing to answer their ringing of her bell.

Her car was also missing.

Lambert radioed that information back to the murder room at the station. He also directed that members of the team be allocated to visit their three other main suspects immediately, to determine what they knew. The remaining one could be left to them. They were now on their way to the home of seventy-year-old Dennis Robson, known to have studied the playing-field movements of Lucy Gibson and presumably also those of Raymond Barrington, who had attended the same primary school.

It was some time before Robson came to the door. He was wearing grey trousers, an open-necked shirt, soft leather slippers, a comfortable cardigan. The garb of an elderly man who lived alone and had settled down for a quiet evening. Or the carefully assumed disguise of an active paedophile to whom deceit came naturally: a man who had laboured hard to deceive the police over forty years. The CID men didn't feel guilty about such thoughts; policemen were paid to be suspicious.

There were the false flames of a modern electric fire flickering convincingly in the fireplace – just for decorative effect, Robson explained, as the central heating that switched on automatically was quite warm enough at this time of the year. A CD of Kiri te Kanawa was playing softly through the speakers, with the stereo sound directed at the big armchair where Robson sat. The Bang and Olufsen equipment emphasized the purity of the voice and the excellence of the recording.

It all spoke eloquently of a quiet evening at home, with the owner settling happily into quiet and innocent enjoyment which had now been coarsely disrupted. Too eloquently, perhaps? Was this an elegantly staged charade to disguise the darker actions of a man well used to leading a double life? Dennis Robson took them wordlessly into the comfortable room, gestured with a wide arm movement towards the leather sofa opposite his chair, waited wordlessly for them to state their business.

'There's no one better than Kiri at Mozart,' said Lambert. Even with urgency pressing upon his every limb, he instinctively built up Robson's tension by opening with a polite irrelevance.

'A cultured policeman,' said Robson with a relaxed smile. 'I always counsel against the danger of stereotyping.'

Lambert didn't tell him that he had the same recording in his own home. He said, 'Unfortunately, we're not here to discuss the merits of divas.'

'I feared that might be the case. I don't envy you your jobs.' He looked from one to the other of the serious, urgent faces, wondered whether to offer them a drink, decided that might be going a little too far.

'We're investigating a second very serious crime against a child. A second abduction.'

'I feared you might be. I'm afraid it's not altogether a surprise to me.'

'Where were you at eight o'clock this evening, Mr Robson?'

A bland smile, a pause to let them know that he was indulging them by even allowing them to voice their ridiculous suspicions to him. 'I was in this room. It was probably at about that time that I was indulging in a glass of after-dinner port. One is entitled to be a little hedonistic when one reaches seventy, I've decided. There have to be some compensations in the lonely life of a widower.'

'Except that you're not a widower, are you, Mr Robson? Your former wife is alive and well and living in the house you used to occupy with her in Bristol, before she divorced you.'

For the first time, Robson looked shaken. His voice no longer carried its suave ring as he said, 'A harmless deception, I felt. I have found that one receives a little more sympathy in a new environment if people think one's wife is dead.'

'And someone with your habits needs sympathy.'

'I resent that. You have proved nothing against me and to imply that you have is not acceptable.'

'You have been divorced for four years. Why did it happen?'

He gave an elaborate shrug, as if the physical movement could restore his equanimity. 'Why does any relationship fail? It was a mutual decision. Things weren't working and we decided to go our separate ways.'

'That isn't your wife's view. That isn't what she stated in court. According to the court records, she said that you had agreed to her ultimatum that you must abandon your unsavoury interest in children if you were to remain a couple under the same roof. But you broke that agreement repeatedly, both in materials you brought into the house and in your activities outside it. She'd had enough and she wanted you out.'

'How very well informed you are, Mr Lambert! I suppose that is part of your expertise as a policeman. Edith was a bitter and unbalanced woman. Having agreed to a divorce, I thought it better to let her have her way. I did not trouble to contest even her grosser accusations.'

'So you left her in full possession of the family house and made also a generous financial settlement. Very generous – unless, of course, it was part of an agreement to prevent her making further revelations about your activities.'

He was plainly anxious to get them off this ground. 'Edith was vindictive. I was glad to be rid of her. I didn't count the cost.'

'And you retain an unhealthy interest in children.'

Lambert had expected him to deny this, but he made what they now saw as a characteristic attempt at philosophic diversion. 'I find young people fascinating. They retain an innocence that is not possible for adults, who are inevitably affected by the views and actions of the people around them. In some other societies, my love of children would be seen as laudable. Perhaps it will be here, in another couple of generations. We used to send people to prison for sodomy; now it seems to be positively applauded.'

Bert Hook rose abruptly to his feet. It looked for a moment as if he was outraged by Dennis Robson's sentiments, but he spoke calmly enough. He didn't ask for the man's permission to move out of the room and into the rest of his single-storey home. He merely said, 'Excuse me for a moment,' and slipped through the door and into the hall.

Robson looked as if he would like to rise and follow him. Then, with an effort to remain seated that was palpable, he said sarcastically, 'With an agility surprising in one of his bulk, Bulldog Drummond left the room. Bulldog Drummond was very popular, when I was a lad, Chief Superintendent. I'm afraid it wasn't long before I found all that blood and thunder rather boring.' He glanced at the door. Hook's absence was plainly worrying him, but he would lose face if he tried to find what he was up to.

Lambert, noting his quarry's unease, repeated his earlier query. 'Where were you at eight o'clock this evening, Mr Robson?'

'I was here. Probably washing up my dinner dishes at that point. I don't rate a dishwasher; I have too few items to warrant that. But I prefer to complete the menial tasks before I relax with my glass of port; I find I enjoy my hedonism better that way.' He was back into his stride now, enjoying taunting his visitors, showing them how little he was worried by their presence here.

'Is there anyone who can confirm that for us?'

Robson lifted his hands a little from his thighs to show how ridiculous that question was. 'I live alone. It would be quite odd if anyone could attest to my presence here at that time, don't you think?'

'I shall ask you formally: were you in Church Lane at that time?'

'Ah! I now divine that you are investigating an incident that took place in Church Lane, Oldford, at around eight o'clock tonight. That is the limit of my knowledge, as I have been in here listening to our New Zealand diva for most of my evening. Thoroughly enjoyable, but I fear of no use to you and your worthy sergeant.'

It was as if Bert Hook was responding to a cue. There was but the slightest of noises before he stood in the doorway, almost filling it, staring accusingly at the man who was settled so comfortably into his favourite armchair. Like many burly men, Bert moved almost silently. He had entered every room in the bungalow and its garage during his brief absence, searching for any sign of a boy who had been captured and imprisoned. He had found none.

He had discovered something else, however. Something that demanded an explanation. He said simply, 'You've been out this evening, Mr Robson,' but he invested the simple words with an enormous weight. 'You've been lying to us about that.'

Dennis Robson was plainly shaken. He began to rise from his chair, then settled himself determinedly back into it. He would face this out, if that was even faintly possible. 'And so the worthy detective sergeant returns from his spying mission in my home. What makes you think I've been out, DS Hook?'

Hook looked at him with steady distaste for a few seconds. Then he produced a pair of suede shoes and held them in front of him. 'These are damp. They have traces of moss and mud in the soles. I'd say they've been worn outside earlier this evening.'

'And that makes me guilty of some yet undisclosed crime, does it?'

'It makes you a liar. And I don't believe you lie just for the pleasure of it. You've got a reason.'

'A perfectly innocent reason, which I don't have to reveal to you.'

He was still looking up at Hook, trying hard to remain insouciant. It was Lambert who now cut hard across their exchange. 'A reason that you would be well advised to reveal to us, if it's innocent. The alternative would be arrest on suspicion and more formal questioning at the station. You'd be entitled to a brief, of course.'

Robson looked at him evenly, trying desperately to disguise the fear in his heart. 'Let me make it plain that I disapprove of this type of tactic in our police service. Against my inclination, I shall reveal to you that I went out to walk a dog. I miss having my own dog, but my solitary lifestyle makes it impracticable. I am away too often to keep a dog of my own.'

'And a dog enables you to stalk and approach children. I seem to remember that you were accused of using your own dog for that purpose when you were questioned at length by police officers eleven years ago.'

'I denied that I used my dog for that purpose and it was never proved. I presume that always wanting to think the worst of people is part of the equipment considered necessary for CID officers.'

Hook said, 'You'll need to give us the address of tonight's dog.' Bert contrived, thought Lambert, to brandish his notebook aggressively, a feat he would have thought impossible.

'Fourteen, Gleeson Terrace. The dog's name is Hector and he's an Airedale. But it's no use your trying to check that. Neither he nor his owners were at home. That was no great surprise to me. There was no prior arrangement on this occasion. It was just an impulse of mine to get a little exercise because I'd been stuck in here all day and I thought Hector might like a run.'

Hook noted the address nonetheless, then said, 'So you now admit being out of the house this evening, but with no one to confirm exactly where you were. I note that the coat hanging in your utility room is also wet. I believe it began to rain at around eight o'clock this evening.'

'I'm sure you're right about that – if you want to confirm the time, ask a policeman.' Dennis Robson smiled at his own witticism. Skilled in subterfuge, he was fighting to recover his self-control. 'A light drizzle. Nothing at first, even quite refreshing, but very wetting if you stayed out in it for a lengthy period. I didn't do that, but I obviously got wet enough for a diligent and highly intrusive DS to note the condition of my footwear and topcoat.'

Lambert believed in letting suspects talk. They often revealed far more of themselves than they realized. The most difficult ones to crack were usually those who said least. But he'd had enough of the elaborate verbosity of Dennis Robson, who combined fluency with insolence so effectively. He snapped, 'Where were you at eight o'clock this evening?'

'On the common. Breathing in my allowance of fresh air and getting my exercise without a dog. Feeling rather foolish as it began to rain.'

'Were you in Church Lane, Oldford, at any time this evening?'

'No.' For once, he was reduced to a monosyllable, as if recognizing the gravity of the issue. Robson and Lambert stared hard at each other for a moment. Then he said, 'And now I'd like you both to leave my house, please.'

He'd included Hook in his injunction without even glancing at him. Hook had still scarcely moved from the doorway into the big, rectangular room. It was from there that he said, 'You took your car with you when you went out. The bonnet is still warm. You didn't tell us that.'

'You didn't ask me.' But he'd been caught out again and he knew it. 'I went round to my friend's house in the car in the hope of collecting his dog. When that wasn't possible, I drove to the edge of the common and parked there. I'm glad I took the car. I'd have got much wetter if I'd had to walk back here without it.'

'Did anyone speak with you whilst you were parking or walking?'

'No. I like my own company.'

Hook didn't voice the thought that not many other people would wish to share it. He told the man brusquely not to leave the area without informing them of his destination. Then they left him in a sour silence.

Bert Hook sat beside Lambert in the big car, reflecting that they had tried unsuccessfully to speak with their least articulate suspect, Big Julie Foster, before moving to the other extreme with this great balloon of words. There was no doubt which of the two Hook preferred as his prime suspect.

THIRTEEN

Raymond Barrington was better fitted for survival than many eight-year-olds. He had spent many nights on his own before he had been taken into care two years ago. It shouldn't have been so, but that is what had happened. He was used to dark and to loneliness. He had also grown used to fear in those days, and to coping with fear.

But this was a different and greater fear than anything Raymond had known before. He was frightened, very frightened. He had no idea where he was and that made things much worse. But he was still alive. He had thought when he was first seized that he would be dead by now. That girl Lucy Gibson, who was in the class below him at school, had been killed. She'd been strangled. It said so in the paper.

Mrs Allen had tried to stop him reading the print beside the photograph on the front page of the paper. She'd said it wasn't good for him. Well, what was happening now wasn't good for him, was it? This wasn't good for him at all. This is what Mrs Allen should have protected him from, not some silly old newspaper.

He wished he hadn't thought of Mrs Allen. The thought of her kindly bosom and her arms around him would surely make him cry. Yet, miraculously, it didn't. For a minute or two, Raymond couldn't move at all. Then he shook his head hard, as though he was jolting tears angrily away.

But there were no tears. Raymond was surprised by that. He clenched his fists and told himself he'd been through much worse things than this with some of the men his mother had brought home. They'd hit him when he spoke out of turn – or if he spoke at all, some of them. This man hadn't hit him yet. If it was a man. It might be a big woman. Raymond still wasn't sure, with that scarf wrapped round so much of the face. He wondered if he'd ever heard that voice before. But that only helped to make the thing more scary.

He decided that he would think of his captor just as the monster. That would be best. Or at any rate it might be better than wondering if this was someone who knew him. A monster was definite, not vague. The vaguer things were, the more he feared for his future.

He wondered where on earth he might be now. A long way from Oldford and the care home and Mrs Allen, he thought. He'd been flung into the passenger seat of some sort of vehicle and told to stay still whilst the belt was buckled tight across him. Then he had cowered in the dark with his eyes tight shut as they had bounced and skidded over narrow roads, made slippery by the falling rain. He had thought he was going to be killed when they stopped, and because of that he had wanted that bucking ride to go on for ever. He tried to think now how long it might have taken, but he had really no idea. You were too terrified to think of time when you were wondering how you were going to die.

But now they were stopping. They jolted to a halt outside a house which rose all on its own against the night sky. The monster undid his belt, then took his arm and pulled him towards the darkness of the door. Then he was dragged into a room and told to be quiet, for the fifth or sixth time. That was all the monster ever seemed to say to him through the scarf: be quiet. This room must be on the ground floor; they hadn't gone up or down any stairs. The monster switched on a light in the hall, but not in the room where they were. Raymond crouched fearfully on the floor and looked up at the monster, who was breathing heavily from what seemed many feet above him. But there was only the dim light from the hall behind his captor. Everything seemed to be just a collection of dark, threatening shadows.

Both of them gasped for breath and Raymond wondered what was going to happen to him. In that moment, when nothing moved, he wondered whether perhaps the monster was wondering about that too.

The monster stood very close to its victim for a moment. Raymond was very conscious of heavy shoes and trousers with splatterings of mud upon them. Then it turned and stood in the doorway, looking down the hall and towards the front

door through which they had come. Raymond wondered
whether he might gather his strength and escape. He would
crouch on the floor like a coiled spring, then catch the monster
off guard and make a run for it.

Boys did that in stories. But stories were different from real
life. Raymond Barrington's real life had taught him that years
ago. And where would he run to if he managed to slip past
the monster and get to the front door? He would have no idea
which way to turn in the darkness outside, so that the monster
would easily catch him and kill him.

Perhaps the thing could read his thoughts. Anything seemed
possible on this strange and horrific night. The monster reached
up to the back of the door, pulled something from there and
tied it round Raymond's leg. Then it tied the other end of it to
something heavy, a few feet away to their left in the darkness. It
was the leg of a big, heavy bed. The monster knew his way
around in this house. That was one more thing that added to
Raymond's fear and helplessness.

Then the monster was suddenly standing above him and
Raymond cringed against the carpet, breathing in the dust
and praying pitifully for the creature not to hurt him. When he
dared to open his eyes, he saw the dark outline of a pillow above
his head. He thought in that moment that the monster was going
to bring it down upon his face and smother him, whilst he pleaded
hopelessly for his life into the softness that would not let him
breathe. But the monster placed the pillow almost tenderly
beneath his head as he flinched, turning him upon his side, trying
ridiculously to make him relax.

It brought cushions from somewhere else, whilst Raymond
kept his eyes resolutely shut, fearing that any sort of movement
on his part might lead to sudden violence from above. But there
was no violence. The monster rolled him over, slid the cushions
beneath him, then rolled him roughly back again. Raymond
stared up at it between eyelids that were almost closed; he was
still afraid that any sort of reaction might provoke this strange
and unpredictable presence.

There was a gruff command that he should not move, an
assurance that the monster would be back. Was he supposed
to find that reassuring? Then the thing was gone. The light

went off in the hall and the front door closed softly in the distance. Raymond was left in a darkness so profound that it seemed to press down upon his small and helpless limbs.

He didn't dare to move for quite a long time. Then, as his body relaxed, he shed his first tears. They came as a relief after the tensions he had endured in the previous half-hour, when he had felt that he might be killed at any time. Tears also brought a heavy, releasing lassitude. The boy who had thought he would never relax again fell into a deep and dreamless sleep.

It was after ten now, but the CID section was crowded and busy. The house-to-house reports were already coming in and being logged by Chris Rushton, but nothing significant had been discovered yet. There had been no random sightings of a boy with an unauthorized adult.

Lambert exchanged views sporadically with DI Rushton, watching the flickering additions to the DI's computer screen. He was there when the young man in uniform came in to say that Big Julie Foster had returned home. The officer had followed instructions. He had watched Julie park her old car behind the house where she had her flat, then enter by the front door. As his orders dictated, he had not made any contact or revealed himself to the woman. He'd shone his torch through the window of the locked car but not attempted to enter it. He had seen nothing there to indicate the presence of an abducted minor.

John Lambert glanced at his watch, nodded at Rushton and took a quick decision. 'I'm going out there right now to see her. I know it's late, but a kid's life's in danger here.'

As if by some private understanding, Bert Hook appeared soundlessly at his side. Lambert had told him ten minutes ago to go home; neither of them was surprised to find him still here. Lambert parked his old Vauxhall at the end of the road rather than right outside Julie Foster's house. The woman would receive enough unwelcome attention on the morrow when news of the second child abduction was made public. There was no need to create difficulties for her now. It was still possible that she had no connection with this latest outrage.

Lambert had thought that Julie might be on her way to bed, but she was still in corduroy trousers and heavy, flat-heeled shoes when she opened the door to them. He expected her to be shocked, even resentful, when he said they must speak to her at this hour of the night, but she evinced no surprise. She merely turned and led them down the dimly lit passage and into the bedsitter where they had spoken to her two days earlier.

This time the curtain at the far end of the room had been drawn to one side, exposing the bed that lay behind it. The portable television on top of the chest of drawers was blaring noisily, the sound of the ITV adverts as usual louder than the programmes they divided. Lambert asked her to switch it off and inspected the soles of her shoes as she moved to the set. The place was tidy, but even more depressing than it had been in daylight. He and Hook sat as they had on Monday on the battered sofa, leaving the big armchair with the green buttoned back for the woman who normally occupied it.

'You were out earlier this evening, Miss Foster,' he said.

It sounded like an accusation, so that Julie wondered if they were going to take her in at the end of this. She'd spent nights in the cells before, and in much worse places too. That didn't really worry her. She was more disturbed by the tall man coming back here and calling her 'Miss Foster' again. No one called her that. 'Miss Foster' was a written thing, confined to the odd letter she received from the council, which Karen the social worker usually helped her to read.

She said, 'I was out tonight, yes.' She wondered if she should snap out, 'There's no law against that!' or 'Why the hell shouldn't I be?' as some of the lads at work would have done. But Julie Foster didn't do that. She didn't want any trouble, and these people were much cleverer with words than she would ever be. It would be much better to stick to something straightforward.

Julie said carefully, 'I went to Tewkesbury.'

'Did you take anyone with you?'

They watched her carefully, studying her face even more keenly than they listened to her words. Would she give them any sign that she had carried a small, terrified boy in the old car?

'I was on my own. I don't have friends.'

It was a flat statement of fact, not asking them for sympathy, leaving them to make of it what they would. It was Hook who now said to her gently, 'That's not true, is it, Julie? You've got friends at work, at the supermarket.'

'They're not real friends. We're friends at Tesco's, not anywhere else. They talk to me at work. Some of them are quite good to me. But they don't want me anywhere else.'

She wasn't looking for consolation. She would have resented attempts to tell her it was not so. She was talking about the life she lived, the life she was compelled to live, and no one knew about that except her. Hook said softly, 'But you like children, Julie, and they like you. We were talking about that when we were here on Monday, if you remember.'

'I remember. But all I said was that I chat to some of them at the store, if they come to me. It's only there, when I'm at work, that I talk to the kids. The parents don't like me to do it anywhere else.'

They were getting a troubling insight into her bleak life again. She was content that it should be so. Better to keep life simple, as she was trying to do now. It was safer just to recite simple facts for as long as you could. She folded her hands in her lap, the only movement she had made since she sat down in the big green chair. She was happier here than on the sofa. It was the chair she always sat in, during the long hours she spent in this place alone.

Hook looked at those hands; her movement had drawn attention to them. They were the nearest parts of Big Julie Foster to him, scarcely four feet away. Strong hands, which would have been perfectly capable of taking an eight-year-old by the scruff of his neck and flinging him into that car now parked thirty yards from where they were sitting. She was a big, powerful woman, filling the wide green armchair in which she sat. Bert had not realized that her shoulders were so broad. He wondered why her very strength and potential, her lack of femininity, should compel this odd sympathy to well within him.

He strove to keep emotion out of his voice as he said, 'Do you know a boy called Raymond Barrington? Perhaps you've chatted to him.'

He had expected a straight denial, but she suddenly had that air of sly cunning that the unintelligent sometimes unexpectedly adopt. 'Not at Tesco's, I haven't. He doesn't go there.'

'But you know him.'

'Might do.' She folded her massive, powerful arms, but she was not being truculent. She was merely inviting them to talk on, because she had knowledge they had not thought she would have. Make them work for it, make them ask the questions. She wasn't often in this position, with educated men like this.

Hook didn't react as he would have done to one of the aggressive, anti-fuzz young thugs they encountered more frequently each year. This was a woman of thirty-eight, finding herself in possession of more knowledge than they had expected. Treating her kindly, encouraging her to talk, might be the best way to discover the whereabouts of this boy she had known and perhaps kidnapped. He said quietly, 'You need to tell us all about this, Julie.'

'Is he in the care home? Is he in Bartram House?'

'That's where he lives, yes. Have you talked to him there?'

She nodded vigorously, as if the vehemence of her reaction was important to her as well as to them. 'Karen got me to go there. I was there myself at one time. But that was a long time ago. There's no one there now who was there when I was there.'

This wasn't unusual. Social workers often got former residents of care homes to go in and talk with the present occupants, on the grounds that they might bring a steadying influence and give good long-term advice. He wondered whether that was a good idea in Big Julie's case. Would the younger children in particular get anything useful from her? Wouldn't the older, more streetwise ones find her a figure of fun rather than a role model? He found himself hoping irrelevantly that she had not been bruised by the experience; Julie Foster seemed to collect a lot of bruises from life. He just hoped she hadn't decided that she needed to hit back.

'So you've talked with the children there. Do you remember Raymond Barrington?'

'I think so. Is his house-mother Amy Allen?'

'Yes.'

'And is Raymond a fair-haired boy? Thin and spindly?'

The description they had from Mrs Allen hadn't used either of those words. But someone as heavily built as Big Julie would no doubt think of any healthy growing boy who was less than burly as being spindly. He wondered if the adjectives derived from her handling of Raymond Barrington earlier in the evening. 'That would be him, yes.'

'He asked me about my mother. He wanted to know how I came to be in the home. I think his mother was a junkie. She didn't look after him properly. People shouldn't have children if they're not going to look after them.' She looked sadly past him at the silent television and the wall beyond it. He knew more clearly than if she had stated it how much she wanted the babies she would never have.

'Did you see Raymond earlier tonight, Julie?'

'No.' The monosyllable came dully. Then, as she realized the implications of his question, she said more loudly, 'No, I didn't. Has something happened to him?'

'Did you pick him up in Church Lane? Did you take him for a ride in your car?'

'No I didn't!' She was shouting now. 'I was on my own. I went up the M50 and then down into Tewkesbury. I like the motorway at night, when it's quiet.'

'Is there anyone who can give us confirmation of that?'

He spoke quietly, trying to calm her down, to preserve the embryonic relationship he had built with her. But he had used the familiar police term and Julie did not understand it. 'Confirmation' was something they'd talked to her about long ago in school, something that was supposed to follow on after baptism. She looked at him suspiciously and repeated the syllables carefully. 'Confirmation?'

'Is there anyone who saw you in Tewkesbury? Did you go into any shops there? If you spoke to people, they might remember seeing you.'

The big, open face frowned a little as she gave the matter her full concentration. 'No. I didn't speak to anyone. I'm used to being on my own. People don't like you speaking to them, unless you already know them.' She spoke as if giving him guidance on how he might behave in company, and in doing so offered him another glimpse into her loveless life. 'I walked up and down for a while, looking into the shop windows. I thought I might go to the pictures, but when I got to the Roses Theatre there was a play on, not a film. I don't like plays – they're hard to understand. And it costs more than the pictures.'

'Do you think anyone will remember you from when you were walking up and down?' Bert wanted desperately to throw her a lifeline, but he was pretty sure that no lifeline existed.

'No. There weren't many people about. It started to rain and most of them were hurrying along. I went to look at the abbey. It's nice at night, when they have the floodlights on. It looks like something out of fairyland.'

'And you weren't in Church Lane tonight? And you haven't set eyes on Raymond Barrington?'

'No. I wouldn't recognize him in the dark if I did. I don't know him that well. I just remember him talking to me about my mum and my house and thinking that he must have had a rotten time before he was taken into care.' Then her voice rose again. 'Something's happened to him, hasn't it? Someone's taken him. Have they killed him, like they killed Lucy?'

'We think that someone has taken him, yes. We very much hope that he's still alive. But if you can help us at all, if you know anything about this, you must tell us now, Julie. We need information very quickly if we're to help Raymond.'

'I didn't take him!' Her voice rose towards a scream.

Was this panic because she was innocent but feared they would not believe her? Or was it panic because the enormity of what she had done was pressing upon her? Both Hook and Lambert felt a searing sympathy for her, but an even greater and more fierce desire to find and rescue that lonely boy who might be trapped and terrified as a result of her actions.

Just when she had become used to DS Hook's friendly and understanding manner, it was the older man who now took over. John Lambert's long, lined face seemed a huge threat to Julie as he said, 'You really must tell us everything you know, Miss Foster. If it's you who has taken Raymond, you must tell us now. We'll do everything we can to help you, But you must help us before we can help you. Where is Raymond?'

'I don't know! I've told you I don't know! Why won't you believe me?'

'A lot of people tell us lies. When one child has been murdered and another one goes missing, we can't afford to believe anyone. That's why DS Hook was asking if you'd seen anyone who could support your story about where you've been in your car tonight.'

'I was in Tewkesbury. I walked up and down the main street and I looked at the abbey in the lights.' She spoke as if she no longer expected to be believed.

Lambert stood up slowly, as if it was important not to alarm her by moving quickly. 'We'll need to examine your car for fingerprints and any other evidence, Miss Foster. It's just routine. Two of our officers will be round in the morning. Will you be here then?'

'Yes. I'm working ten to six tomorrow.'

She stood up, moved quickly to the door and held it open for them. There was a small scratch on the back of her hand. A tiny trickle of blood, no more than an inch long, had run away from it and dried on the brown skin there. Three pairs of eyes fastened upon it. 'I don't know how that happened,' said Big Julie Foster.

FOURTEEN

Raymond Barrington woke when the night was at its blackest. For a moment, he had no idea where he was and he did not care. His whole frame was consumed by the need to pee. Raymond had been beaten for wetting the bed when he was small, but he had stopped doing that now. He felt almost superior about it, because some of the kids in the home still peed their beds. He didn't tease them about it, as some of the others did when the adults weren't there, but it gave him a feeling of superiority that he didn't do that anymore.

Now he was going to piss himself and soak the cushions and the floor where he lay. It wouldn't be his fault. He'd been grabbed and brought here and not been allowed to clean his teeth or go for his last pee of the day, those rituals they taught you at Bartram House until they became habits. But he was bent nearly in two, with his knees against his chest, and it was coming any second. As he twisted hopelessly in the darkness, the back of his hand touched something hard and cold. He ran his fingers cautiously along its cold, curved surface, found a handle, pulled it towards him. A chamber pot.

He'd never used a chamber pot. Now he pulled it against him and used it thankfully and copiously. The long, exquisite sound of his relief tinkled very loud in the stillness that surrounded him. He pushed the pot as far away from him as he could, moving it an inch at a time across the carpet. You mustn't spill this stuff.

He couldn't remember the monster leaving him a chamber pot. But then he couldn't remember the blanket that covered him. He remembered a pillow and cushions, but he'd had his eyes shut most of the time and been too terrified to recall much of what was going on around his small, prone frame. He only remembered that he was tied when he felt the pain in his ankle as he stretched to push away the chamber pot. He panicked for a moment when he realized that he was roped to the leg of a bed he could not see, that he could not move away from this spot on the floor where he had been covered and left for the night.

For the night. Would it be for as long as that? Or – he hadn't thought of this before – would it be for much longer? Would he be left tied here until it became light and then for long hours, even long days, after that? Had he been dumped here for ever, to live out in solitude the last days of his young, unimportant life? He tried to think about that, but even the fear he tried to summon could not keep him awake. His whole body was dominated by the overwhelming relief that he had peed, and peed not in this makeshift bed but in that great, cold chamber pot which now lay stinking several feet away from him.

Raymond was young, exhausted, filled with the short-term relief of his urination. He turned on his other side, facing away from the invisible chamber pot. In two minutes, he was asleep again.

It was getting light when he woke for the second time. He must have slept for many hours, he thought. He watched the oblong of the window at the far end of the room appearing, then passing through various shades of grey as dawn moved into day. He knew what time it was now: about half past seven. That was when it came light in Oldford at the end of October. They'd be dressing themselves at Bartram House now, having breakfast and getting ready for school.

He wondered if Mrs Allen was missing him, as he was so fiercely missing her at this moment. She'd have told the police about him last night when he didn't come back from cubs; he was sure of that. He wondered if the police might be looking for him. He supposed they would, but he wasn't sure how much they would care about one small boy who had gone missing. They'd probably have other and much more important concerns.

Raymond lay on his back and looked at the ceiling and tried to forget that his leg was still tied to the bed. He had attempted to undo the rope, but it was knotted hard and he couldn't do that. It was the cord from a dressing gown, he thought; that was another sign that the monster knew his way around this house. He thought for a while that he might bring his ankle to his mouth and try to chew his way through it. But he didn't think he could do that with his small teeth. Even if he succeeded, it might annoy the monster; he couldn't afford to do that.

Raymond wasn't sure how long it was before he heard the engine of a car outside. It was an old car, he thought, because the engine sounded quite noisy. For a moment, Raymond was glad that he wasn't to be left alone and forgotten in this strange place. But when he heard the monster turning a key in the lock, he was abruptly very frightened again.

It seemed to be a long time before the door of the room opened and the monster stood looking down into the wide blue eyes of the boy on the floor. The thing seemed not quite so tall, but broader than ever, in a big blue anorak. It had a balaclava helmet and a scarf round the bottom half of the patch of face that showed, so that Raymond could see only its eyes. The eyes stared at him for a moment, then a hand with fat, strong fingers picked up the chamber pot and took it away. He heard the sound of it being emptied, then the noise of a toilet flushing.

It took the monster a long time to come back. Raymond wondered if it was washing its hands, the way he'd been taught to do in the home. That didn't seem the kind of thing a monster would do. Not a monster that kidnapped and killed small boys. He wondered if he would be killed today. Perhaps right now. He didn't know what it was like to be strangled, but he thought he'd prefer it to having his throat cut. He was surprised that he could even think about such things.

The monster had a big plastic bag with it when it came back. It put the bag down on the bed, above the leg to which Raymond was tied. Then it stood looking down at him for what seemed a long time. It had its feet apart and it scarcely seemed to breathe, let alone speak, as it towered above him. Raymond wanted to say something, just to break this long and threatening silence, but his tongue wouldn't work. He knew that he mustn't risk annoying this strange and powerful thing that had complete control over him. Eventually he managed to gasp out, 'My leg hurts.'

The monster looked at the bed and the tie, then back at Raymond. It said, 'Will you promise not to run for it, if I untie you?'

They were the first words it had spoken since the car arrived. Raymond nodded, not trusting himself to speak again. The monster had a gruff voice, indistinct through the scarf. It could have been male or female; to Raymond, it sounded scarcely human. He tried to think of the thing as the Gruffalo, which he'd read about in a story when he was younger. That should have made the monster less frightening, but it didn't work.

The monster still didn't move towards the dressing-gown cord that held him. Perhaps it hadn't seen him nod, or had forgotten about it. Raymond said tremulously, 'I won't run.'

The monster said nothing, but it moved its big hands suddenly down towards Raymond's face, so that he cowered against the floor, throwing one arm across the cushion he had pushed away. But it didn't touch him. Those fingers must be very strong, because they untied the knots he'd been unable to loosen, however hard he'd tugged. He flinched away as the hands moved towards his leg, but the thing moved almost tenderly – like that big ape in *King Kong*, the video they'd been allowed to watch at Bartram House. He wished he hadn't thought of the care home again. It seemed a very long way away now. He rubbed his ankle gingerly, because he didn't want the monster to handle it.

It didn't try to touch him. It stood over him for another moment, then turned and moved quickly through the door. This time it came back quickly. It had a small square table in one hand and a chair in the other. It put them together, reached into the bag and put a bowl and a spoon on the table. Then it produced a packet of cornflakes and poured a big helping into the bowl, so that it piled up and almost overflowed. The bottle of milk looked small in that huge hand, but the monster poured carefully, until the bowl brimmed and one or two cornflakes fell off.

Raymond cringed away as the monster turned towards him, trying to avoid its touch. But there was no doing that. The hands picked him up as if he weighed nothing and plonked him on the chair by the table. A big dribble of milk overflowed and trickled across the table as Raymond lurched against it, so that he wondered if he would be punished. But the monster only said, 'Eat now!' behind his head, and Raymond bent swiftly to do its bidding.

It was good, the cereal. He was surprised to find he was hungry. He even felt a little guilty. Shouldn't he have lost his appetite, after the awful things that had happened to him? There was half a loaf of sliced white bread in its wrapping, a tub of margarine, a plastic knife, even a pot of jam which the monster opened for him. He was glad it didn't stand over him and watch him eat, because he felt very clumsy as he tried to handle the very full bowl of cereal without spilling any more milk.

The monster seemed anxious to be away. It went out of the room again and Raymond heard the sound of the front door opening. Perhaps the thing was leaving him. But no. It came back quickly, carrying a bucket, which it set down without a word where the chamber pot had been. It stood looking at Raymond for long seconds, as if wondering what to do with him. Then it said in that harsh voice that was all it used, 'You won't run. You promised that.'

'I won't run,' said Raymond quickly. You surely couldn't annoy the thing as long as you agreed with it.

'Make sure you don't, then!' And then it was gone, turning a key in the lock of the room this time. It hadn't said what the bucket was for. It was much later in the morning that Raymond discovered that.

Rory Burns decided on aggression. That was the way he reacted to most challenges.

On this occasion it didn't work. The fairground worker told the two young constables that he had work to do and it wasn't convenient to talk. Chief Superintendent Lambert and that big ox he used as a bagman could wait. He was a free citizen and he'd help the police in his own time, if he saw fit to help them at all. The filth produced handcuffs and said they'd use them if necessary. Then they arrested him on suspicion of abducting a child and took him to Oldford police station.

Now he was waiting in a square box of an interview room with a single light in the ceiling. His strategy had failed. When he was a small boy and the troubles had been rife in Ireland, a fanatical republican soldier had tried to explain the difference between strategy and tactics to him. Burns was still hazy about that, but he decided that he had better concern himself now with the narrower issue of tactics.

He had been in places like this often enough before, but never in connection with anything as serious as this. And he'd never before had a chief super questioning him and watching his every move. He'd need to watch this bugger Lambert, who seemed to have quite a local reputation. They hadn't charged him with anything yet, but he knew very well what this was about. He was in deep. They were leaving him alone in this room with nothing but the four green walls to gaze at. That was supposed to make him nervous. It was an obvious enough ploy – the police were nothing if not obvious. But it was working. Rory Burns was already much more anxious than when the young coppers had dumped him here and shut the door on him.

As was usual with him, nervousness translated itself into aggression as soon as there was someone to shout at. When John Lambert pulled up a chair and sat down opposite him at the other side of the scratched square table, Burns said aggressively, 'This had better be good and it had better be quick.'

'How useful it is to us and how quickly it is concluded will depend very largely upon your attitude. I advise you to remember that. We can hold you here all day and all night if we consider it necessary, Mr Clancey.'

He was stunned by the name. He said roughly, 'What the hell are you playing at now? You know bloody well that I'm Rory Burns. The pair of you spoke to me at the fairground on Monday.' It was the first time he had acknowledged the presence of Hook, who was sitting quietly beside his chief, studying the tattoos on Clancey's forearms and enjoying the discomfort of this powerfully built man.

Lambert didn't hurry. He allowed himself a sour smile before he said, 'You are Michael Clancey. You were charged with offences against children under that name in Cork six years ago. You also committed a severe assault on a man and severely wounded him four years ago.'

'I wasn't guilty with the children.'

'Not what the law said, Mr Clancey. You were lucky to get away with six months, largely because it was a first offence. Or the first one you'd been charged with. Lucky to be out after three of those months, I expect. Good conduct isn't a phrase I'd associate with you.'

'It's a long time ago. It's all behind me now, part of another world. Or it was until you dug it up.'

'It's our job to dig such things up, Mr Clancey. Especially when we're investigating a child murder. It's just under six years since you received a custodial sentence for indecent assault upon a junior. That isn't very long ago, in our book.'

'It is when you're going straight and trying to make an honest living.'

'You were accused of touching an eleven-year-old girl's thighs, looking up her skirt and propositioning her only last Saturday. Doesn't sound very honest to me. Later on that same day, a younger girl, Lucy Gibson, was abducted and subsequently murdered. You're in trouble, Mr Clancey. Deep trouble, with separate convictions for both child abuse and serious assault. Perhaps you should be considering getting yourself some legal representation.'

'I don't need no brief, Lambert. I've committed no bloody offence.'

'You've taken no legal steps to change your name, Mr Clancey. You're a convicted criminal operating under an alias, which implies to us that you have much to hide. We're not pursuing that this morning, because we are concerned with much greater crimes.'

His face set into the sullen, uncooperative mask they had seen a hundred times before in men who settled differences with their fists. 'I didn't kill Lucy Gibson. And I know nothing about this boy that's gone missing.'

It was a mistake and they wanted to be sure that he recognized it as one. Lambert let ten long seconds pass before he said quietly, 'And how do you know that a boy's disappeared, Mr Clancey?'

That old name, the one he thought he'd discarded, was ringing like a knell in his ears. He said dully, 'I heard people talking about it this morning. Someone came into the pub last night and said the pigs were stopping everyone.'

'Which story do you prefer us to record, Mr Clancey? I won't use the word "believe".'

'I don't care whether you sods believe me or not, do I?' When they didn't respond to that, he said more quietly, 'I heard about it in the pub, I think. I'd had a few.'

The thug's usual accompaniment to villainy. *I'd had a few. I was quite drunk. I don't remember things accurately and you shouldn't expect me to do that. And I'm not guilty of anything, because I was drunk and not responsible for my actions.*

It was Bert Hook who now asked quietly, 'You went to the pub for a drink after you'd finished with Raymond Barrington, did you, Michael?'

This was good cop/bad cop, wasn't it? The stupid ox was using his first name, hoping to prise things from him that the bugger with the furrowed face couldn't get to. Well, it wouldn't bloody work. It mustn't bloody work, thought Michael Clancey, as panic surged suddenly through his powerful frame. He stared at the table, concentrating hard. 'I don't know that name. I've never met any boy. I had nothing to do with whatever happened last night.'

'What car do you have, Michael?'

'Peugeot 350. I'm going to change it. The engine's knackered.' He sounded apologetic about the vehicle, as if he was talking to one of his mates and needed to explain away its deficiencies. There was no need to tell the filth about it, he realized. It felt like a sign of weakness that he'd done so.

'We'll need to let our forensic boys have a look at your car. See whether you had a passenger in there last night. See if an eight-year-old boy has left anything of himself behind.'

'You can look all you like. You'll find bugger all.' But even as he spoke, he wondered exactly what they would discover among the old newspapers and the crisp papers and the fag packets. He should have cleaned the thing out and left them nothing to bite on. It was too late now.

'Were you in Church Lane in Oldford last night?'

'Very likely I was. It's within a couple of hundred yards of my digs.'

'Were you or weren't you in Church Lane last night?' Hook never lost his temper, but he was finding it more difficult than usual to keep it this time.

'Yeah. I drove along it. There's no law against that.'

'Time?'

'I don't know. Early evening. I wasn't looking at my watch. The clock in the Peugeot's buggered.'

'Before or after eight o'clock?'

'I don't know, do I? Before, I should think.' He'd been tempted to lie, but for all he knew, they already had a sighting of the Peugeot.

'Where did you take the boy when you picked him up?'

'I didn't take him anywhere. I never saw any boy.' But they wouldn't believe him, would they? They'd nabbed him for changing his name and they'd got his criminal record to hit him with. They wanted someone for this, someone to get the public off their backs, and anyone would do. Preferably someone with previous, like him. He said, 'I went into Gloucester. Went to a pub there.'

'So you'd be able to provide witnesses. Someone who could confirm you were there and tell us how long you spent there.'

'No. It was casual, like. I don't have friends. I'm always on the move, see, with the fair. We don't get the chance to make friends.'

Hook smiled a little, registering Clancey's unease, letting it build. 'And no one in a Gloucester pub would be talking about what the police were doing fourteen miles away in Oldford. Not so quickly. So where were you really last night, Michael? You'll find it's much better to talk to us now. We might even be able to say you cooperated with us, if you can take us to the boy and we find him unharmed.'

'I never touched any boy. You've got the wrong bloke here. It's time you realized that and let me out of here.'

But they didn't do that. And as he fretted in a cell, he was more and more certain that they'd find things when they went over the Peugeot.

FIFTEEN

Dean Gibson was five minutes late for work. You didn't want to be late when the job wasn't permanent. You wanted to convince your employer that you were reliable as well as skilful.

The death of his daughter had brought him sympathy from the people who worked alongside him in the houses, but it hadn't pleased his employer. Frank Lewis wasn't interested in being popular. He was a man interested in keeping a business going in a recession, not in looking after a man who had suddenly become both a grieving father and a murder suspect.

The four men were working on an extension to a large house in a village just south of Hereford. Dean had his story about traffic hold-ups ready when he drove into the quiet road, but he was relieved to see that the boss hadn't yet arrived. He parked the battered white van near the gates, moved hurriedly within the house and began assembling the materials he needed for his morning work.

His fellow workers were glad to see Dean because they needed his skills. The extension was nearing completion. The brickwork of the new walls was completed and Dean was scheduled to begin the plasterwork this morning. He was the only one with the skills to provide a smooth and even finish over large surfaces; that was his specialism. The householder was paying well for this, but he expected high standards. They couldn't afford any blemishes in the plastering, or they'd end up stripping the wall down to the bricks and beginning again. Any such disaster would mean a severe blow to Frank Lewis's profit on this job and possible reductions in his workforce. Frank played things close to his chest, so that none of his workers was sure as they moved towards winter how much work he had in the pipeline for them.

Dean was nervous; perhaps he realized how much his work this morning meant to all of them. His hands even shook a little, but that didn't prevent him doing an excellent job. He worked steadily throughout the morning, not even stopping for the normal tea break with the joiner and the bricklayer who were working on other parts of the extension. He said continuity was important with plastering: when the material was at a certain delicate stage, you had to use it immediately. Pausing even for quarter of an hour would leave it less workable than if you carried on without a break. This was a big surface to cover and he didn't want to risk the possibility of a join showing when his work was finished.

The others raised their eyebrows at each other behind him, wondering if he was trying to impress the boss with his industry. You couldn't blame Gibson, really. He needed the work and he was the most recent addition to the team, so he had to show what he could do and how he could be trusted. It was only later that it occurred to them that he might want to work rather than talk, that the loss and subsequent murder of his little girl might be preying on his mind and making him wish to avoid the normal bawdy, brainless banter that carried them along.

Frank Lewis was impressed. The boss inspected Dean's work closely when he had finished and congratulated him on a good job. Dean nodded and gave him the briefest of thanks, as if praise was no more than he had expected – or as if his mind was preoccupied with other things.

It was at the end of the morning that the lady of the house came uncertainly into the room. Her policy was to avoid contact with the men, apart from the ritual of supplying them with mugs of tea at appropriate intervals. She was happy to let her husband handle their payment and any queries about the quality of their work. She inspected the workers' progress with her husband each night, when they had gone home, but she had only minimal contact with them during the day.

This time she had no alternative. She looked around the men, who had bent automatically to their tasks as they registered her presence. 'Is there a Dean Gibson here?' she said. Plainly the name had not registered with her as having any connection with that of the girl who had died at the weekend.

The plasterer put down the trowel he had been cleaning. 'I'm Dean Gibson.'

'There's a phone call for you. It's the police.' She couldn't keep disapproval out of her voice. Her carriage and her air suggested that anyone whom the police needed to contact should not be working in her elegant house. 'You'd better come through and take the call.'

The cool female voice said calmly, 'Oldford police station here. You're very elusive, Mr Gibson. We've been trying to contact you all morning.'

'I left home early because I had a fair way to travel. We're working near Hereford. Sorry, you already know that.'

'I do now, Mr Gibson. It's taken me hours to track you down. Chief Superintendent Lambert wishes to speak to you as soon as possible.'

'Has he found who killed Lucy? Has there been an arrest?'

'I don't know and I'm not at liberty to discuss cases, Mr Gibson. I know you're Lucy's father and I'm sorry I can't tell you any more. Please call in at Oldford police station as quickly as possible. Unless you wish Chief Superintendent Lambert to contact you there.' It sounded almost a threat,

'No. I'm almost finished here for today. I'll call in before I go back to my lodgings in Ledbury.' He was surprised how calm he felt at the prospect.

The man who had stepped into Dean Gibson's home and then into his wife's bed was nervous. Matthew Boyd had opted to go to the police station at Oldford rather than be interviewed in his rather seedy digs. Now he was wondering if that was the right decision.

A youngish man in plain clothes who said he was Detective Inspector Rushton installed him in an interview room and told him he would have to wait for a while because Chief Superintendent Lambert wished to speak to him in person. Rushton managed to imply that this made Matt a very interesting specimen indeed, who might well be banged up in a cell before the day was out. Then he studied his reactions to this as though he was a fish on a slab, awaiting dissection by an expert filleter. DI Rushton said he would arrange for a mug of tea to be sent into him whilst he waited, much in the manner of an American jailer offering a man on death row a final hearty breakfast.

Matt Boyd was glad when he was left alone. Perhaps they intended to increase his tension by leaving him in here. Well, he could counteract that by using this interval to calm himself and plan his own tactics for the ordeal to come. He tried hard to do that, but his mind raced ahead and ranged over all sorts of things – things that weren't going to be helpful to him when he was eventually interviewed.

Lambert brought Hook with him, the stolid detective sergeant whom Matt remembered from their meeting four days earlier about Lucy. Lambert apologized for keeping him waiting. Then both men studied him for a few seconds, as if assessing his state of mind before they moved in on him. It was one of the things about police interrogation: coppers didn't feel any need to observe the normal social conventions. They didn't try to put you at ease and they didn't see any reason why they shouldn't stare directly at you to discover your thoughts and emotions. If you were used to people feeling their way in, it could be very disconcerting. He told himself it wasn't any worse than when he met some truculent nobody who didn't want to buy, but he knew immediately that the stakes here were much higher.

It was Matt who eventually felt an overwhelming need to break the silence. He said, 'What's happened? Your uniformed man said there'd been new developments.'

Lambert was studiously low-key. 'Do you know a boy called Raymond Barrington?'

'No. I don't know any children in Oldford. I only knew Lucy Gibson because she was Anthea's daughter.'

'Raymond attends the same school as Lucy did. He's one year older than her. He's disappeared. He appears to have been abducted last night, in much the same manner as Lucy was on Saturday.'

Matt was intensely conscious of their scrutiny. They were almost accusing him of the crime by the way they were studying him. And being looked at like that made you self-conscious, so that you behaved as if you were guilty anyway. 'It wasn't me. I didn't kill Lucy and I didn't even know of the existence of this boy.'

'I see. We think this might have been an opportunistic action.

The person who seized Raymond last night might never have seen him before.'

'And why would he take the boy?'

Lambert shrugged. 'Because he – or she – is unbalanced? Because this person has been excited by the abduction and subsequent murder of Lucy and is now looking for another minor to attack? Motive is not easy to establish in cases of child murder. Sometimes it is not even a very useful concept for us to pursue.'

'And so you think that I took this boy that I've never even seen.'

'Did you, Mr Boyd?'

He was shaken by the calmness of the question. He had anticipated nothing so direct, had expected something much more apologetic. Shouldn't they be talking about the need to eliminate people like him from their enquiries? Shouldn't they be assuring him that this was merely a routine that had to be observed? He said as vigorously as he could, 'No, I didn't take him! The first I've heard about this wretched boy is your mention of him a moment ago.'

'Wretched boy indeed, Mr Boyd. Poor Raymond is in a wretched situation, if indeed he is still alive. Do you think he is still alive, Mr Boyd?'

'I don't know. I told you, I don't even know the boy.'

They both stared at him without comment, making him wish he'd been able to state what he had just said even more vehemently and convincingly. It was Hook who now said to him, much less aggressively, 'What have you been doing since we spoke with you on Sunday, Mr Boyd?'

Matt couldn't believe it was only four days ago. It seemed to him much longer than that. He tried to be conciliatory, in response to Hook's quieter approach. 'I've been working. Trying to earn an honest penny and keep the car industry going.' His nervous giggle fell oddly into the echoing cube of the interview room. 'I've now taken a couple of days' leave; that is why I am available to speak to you now.'

'Getting on well, are you, in this second choice of career?'

Matt tried to ignore the last phrase, but his mind reeled in the face of what might be coming next. 'I'm doing well enough.

People always need parts and accessories for vehicles, even in a recession. If people are forced to hang on to their cars for longer, they need batteries, exhausts, tyres. Headlights and side-lights get broken. Cars are more reliable and they rust less than they did thirty years ago. But if people use them for longer, that makes good business for people like me.'

It was a spiel he had delivered many times before and it fell a little too readily from his lips. It echoed in his ears like a rehearsed speech. To Hook, it sounded exactly what it was: a rather desperate attempt to divert attention away from the mention of a second career that had been thrown at him. 'We've spoken to your ex-wife. That's how we heard about your earlier career.'

'There was no need for you to contact Hannah. That's the action of someone operating in a police state.'

'It's routine procedure in a case as serious as that of Lucy Gibson. When the last person seen with a girl who is later found dead has no alibi, we investigate his background thoroughly. We do the same thing with other people who might be suspects.'

'And how many of those have you followed up in this kind of detail?'

'You wouldn't expect me to answer that, Matthew. Tell us about your previous experience with children.'

'Why should I? You seem to know all about it.'

'We know a little. Perhaps, indeed, we know quite a lot. But we'd like to have your version of events. That would surely be much fairer.'

'It's a long time ago. Ten years and more. I was training for teaching. I decided it wasn't for me. That's all there is to it.'

'Wouldn't it be fairer to say that others decided that it was not for you? That you were given little choice in the matter and were relieved to extricate yourself without the matter going to court?'

'No! The matter was blown out of all proportion by a hysterical parent. I offered comfort to over-excited seven-year-olds; that was all I did. And the thanks I got for it was to be hounded out of my training by a head teacher and governors who weren't prepared to listen to my arguments!' He had been over this so often, both in his own mind and with that sour-faced ex-wife of his, that he had almost convinced himself of the righteousness of his case.

'Teachers, let alone trainee teachers, are not allowed to touch children nowadays.'

'It's ridiculous!'

'However ridiculous it may be, you were well aware of the rules. Why did you break them, Matthew?'

'I was offering comfort. I behaved perfectly reasonably.'

'That wasn't what others thought at the time, was it? It was only by signing a statement to the effect that you would withdraw from teacher training and undertake no employment that involved contact with children that you avoided charges of indecent assault on two minors.'

'It was all rubbish! It was blown up out of all proportion. I wish I'd gone to court and fought it. I'd have won the case.'

'We'll never know that, will we? Such evidence as there is does not support your view. When you applied with your wife to become adoptive parents five years later, you were turned down because of this history.'

Matt stared hopelessly at the table in front of him. 'We should never have applied. You get turned down for any little thing. They're talking of making it easier to adopt now, but they rejected you for piddling little things then. We should never have applied after the way I was driven out of teaching, but Hannah wanted to try and I went along with it.'

Hook gave him a few seconds to see if he would add anything to this. Then he said quietly, 'If you put yourself in our position, Matthew, you will see that we cannot simply discount this. It doesn't make you guilty, but it strengthens the case against you. Have you seen Anthea Gibson since the weekend?'

He thought he had been prepared for the question, but the sudden switch back to the present from events of a decade ago caught him off guard. His mind wouldn't work as he wanted it to. He decided he had better tell them the truth. For all he knew, they'd had him followed; perhaps they had even spoken again to Anthea herself. He said sullenly, 'I called in there on Tuesday. I wanted to tell her how sorry I was about

Lucy. I didn't know what sort of reception I'd get. I still feel guilty because I was with Lucy when she was snatched.'

'But Mrs Gibson didn't send you packing.'

It sounded as if they knew, as if they were inviting him to plunge deeper into trouble. 'No. It was awkward at first, but I'd expected that. She'd only just come back home. She'd been staying with her sister in Gloucester. I think she was finding it difficult, being in the house on her own, without Lucy. Well, you would, wouldn't you?'

'Did you stay the night?'

'Yes. I was going to stay downstairs on the sofa, but I ended up in Anthea's bed. At her invitation, I should add, since you seem determined to think the worst of me.'

He wondered if they would ask if there had been intercourse; being a suspect in something like this seemed to rob you of any shred of privacy. But all Hook said was, 'Have you been staying there since then?'

'No. I'm staying in the digs in Oldford where I used to stay before I ever knew Anthea. I wanted to be nearby if she wanted me, but not in her house. Apart from Tuesday night, I've stayed in my digs. I think I shall do so until after Lucy's funeral. I'll let Anthea decide on that – she knows that I'm around, if she needs me.'

Simple words were concealing the intense and tangled emotions of two people who had been through unspeakable things in the last five days. Hook wondered what Lucy Gibson's mother really thought of Matthew Boyd, whether sexual attraction could survive his connection to the death of her daughter, even if she did not believe that he had any direct connection. He said quietly, 'Where were you last night, Matt?'

'That's when this boy went missing, isn't it?' He wondered if Hook would tell him that he was here to answer questions, not ask them, but both detectives merely maintained a watchful, expectant silence. He said heavily, hopelessly, 'This has nothing to do with me.'

'We need to know where you were last night, Matt.' Hook was quiet, almost apologetic, but nonetheless insistent.

Matt gave a deep sigh. 'I was in my digs. I can give you the address.' He did that, then looked hard at them, wondering if they already knew it, wondering if he had been followed ever since he had left them on Sunday.

'Is there anyone who can confirm that you were there throughout the evening?'

'No. My landlady was out from around seven until ten thirty.'

Hook wondered a little at the precision of this. It sounded like a prepared answer, but he couldn't see why Boyd would have had it ready, when it was so unhelpful for him. 'Did you receive any phone calls?'

'No. I rang Anthea on my mobile at about six thirty to check on how she was feeling. She didn't invite me round and I didn't suggest it. To tell you the truth, I wasn't sure whether I wanted to go.'

Hook nodded. 'It's a funny expression that, don't you think? "To tell you the truth." It almost makes it sound as if you haven't been telling the truth up to that point. Did you take your car out last night?'

'No. I've already told you that I didn't leave my digs.'

'Which, unfortunately, no one can confirm. Were you in Church Lane in Oldford at any time between seven and eight last night? You should realize that it would be much better to admit to it now, if you were.'

'But I wasn't. That is what I wish you to record.'

'I now ask you formally: do you know an eight-year-old boy named Raymond Barrington?'

'No. I've never even heard the name.'

'Have you any idea of his present whereabouts?'

'No. Of course I haven't. You must have better candidates to pursue than me.'

'Matt, you are a man we have not been able to clear from involvement in the murder of a child last Saturday night. You were forced to leave your teacher training course because of child abuse. You are unable to establish where you were last night at the time a boy disappeared within a quarter of a mile of your lodgings. Do you really expect us to ignore you?'

Boyd tried not to panic. It sounded very damning when Hook itemized it like that. And DS Hook seemed to be the sympathetic cop. Matt said, 'That must seem impressive, from your point of view. From where I stand, knowing that I am completely innocent of both these crimes, it seems unfair and bizarre.'

'We shall need to examine your car.'

'You're welcome to do that.' He kept his face as neutral as he could. 'It's being valeted as we speak.'

Hook felt Lambert tensing beside him. 'A process that is no doubt removing anything that might be of interest to our forensic team. Why is the car being valeted?'

Matt didn't shrug his shoulders; they were far too tense for that. 'I took advantage of the fact that I wasn't working to have the car made spick and span. It's important that I present myself decently when I'm selling vehicle spares. That extends to the condition of my car, inside and out.'

They stared at him for a moment, challenging him to say more, inviting him to condemn himself by elaborating his case. Then Lambert asked quietly, 'When was your car last valeted?'

'I put it through the carwash every week, but it was last valeted about a month ago, I think. I could check it for you, if you think it necessary.'

'It is necessary. Give me the name and telephone number of the firm who did it, please. We'll check the date with them.'

Matt felt his pulse racing, but he gave them the name of the company as calmly as he could. 'I don't have their number here, but you'll find it easily enough.'

'We will indeed. We'll need to check this date out with them, and also the normal intervals between the valeting of your car. We'll do that before you leave the station.'

The implication was clear. They didn't trust him. If the car hadn't been due for a valeting today, they'd be all over him again about why he was having it so thoroughly cleaned this morning. He said woodenly, 'I understand that. I don't know this boy who was taken last night. And I'd rather you didn't tell Anthea Gibson about that nonsense that ended my teacher training.'

SIXTEEN

R aymond Barrington wasn't dead. He told himself that, told himself that so far it had not been as bad as he had expected. Then he tried not to think about what might be in store for him.

After the monster had gone, Raymond lay for a little while on the cushions where he had spent the night. It seemed the appropriate place, simply because it was where he had been tethered for so long. Settling down again there felt like returning to a prison cell after being let out for breakfast. He knew that he was free to move around the room now. In a while he would feel bold enough to do that, but for the moment it felt to him that it would be breaking the monster's rules to move away from where he had been tethered.

That was a silly thing to feel, because his leg had been freed from its cord. Even though he had been tied to the bed for no more than ten or twelve hours, he could hardly believe that he could now move his leg freely, could climb slowly and gingerly to his feet. He did that, then glanced fearfully around him. The monster's presence seemed to hang over the room, so that Raymond feared being seized again by the scruff of his neck and flung to the floor. But he forced himself stiffly upright, then put his shoulders back, as Mrs Allen said he should do. He was going to be a big boy, and tall boys shouldn't slouch, Mrs Allen said. As he wondered how far away she was, he found himself biting his lip to keep back the tears. Raymond had done that quite a lot over the years.

He moved around the big room, very slowly. He felt as if every step might activate some screaming alarm and bring the monster racing back to kill him. He checked the door and the window. Both were locked, as he had known they would be. He found that rather a relief, as he wouldn't have known where to go if he'd got out of this place, and he feared what the monster would do to him if it caught him and found that he'd even tried to escape.

He pressed on the switch beside the door, but the light didn't come on, as he had somehow known it wouldn't. He tried not to think about what the monster might be planning for him. Was it like the giant in *Jack and the Beanstalk*? Would it shout 'Fee, fi, foh, fum!' in that huge voice? Would it eat boys for lunch? He didn't think so. It didn't seem quite as huge or as awful as Jack's giant. Raymond thought it had been a little more friendly this morning. It had brought him some breakfast, hadn't it? And it had left food for him in the big plastic bag.

He still wasn't sure whether the monster was male or female. It was so muffled up and it spoke so little. And all of its words came in that strange, gruff voice that he could scarcely interpret. Raymond wondered for a while whether he wanted it to be male or female. Females hadn't been very kind to him, apart from Mrs Allen. He wouldn't mind it being male if it was anything like Mr Kennedy, the only male teacher in his school. Mr Kennedy brought him books and talked to him at lunch-times. Mr Kennedy had told him that he was an intelligent boy who must make the most of his schooling, because that was how he would make his way in life.

Raymond wasn't quite sure what it meant to make your way in life, but it sounded impressive. He couldn't see any similarity between Mr Kennedy and the monster.

The day passed slowly, but Raymond didn't mind that, because he didn't want the monster to come back. There was a small bookcase against one wall, with all kinds of rather battered books on its three shelves. There was one with a picture of a woman with her tits threatening to burst out of her dress on the cover. The big boys in school and at Bartram House talked a lot about tits, when the girls weren't there. One of them had said Mrs Allen had luscious tits, and the others had all laughed and made funny groaning noises. Raymond hadn't liked that, even though he didn't know what 'luscious' meant. But he'd kept quiet and been careful not to annoy the big boys. He had a go at reading the book with the tits on the cover, but it had lots of big words and didn't seem very interesting, despite its cover.

It was at this point that Raymond found he needed to do number twos. He looked in panic at the locked door, then round the room. He saw the bucket and realized why the monster had left it there. Raymond didn't want to use it. He held out for perhaps twenty minutes, then knew that he would have to go. The bucket felt very uncomfortable, but he did ones and twos in it quite quickly. He looked in the big plastic Tesco's bag the monster had left and found a toilet roll there. He'd made a horrible stink, but that wasn't his fault, was it? Please God the monster would realize that.

Raymond had never been quite sure about God – he'd heard very little of him until he'd been taken into care. Now he asked God fervently to look after him. Raymond listened carefully, but he couldn't hear the answering voice he would have liked to hear. In those stories of saintly boys he had heard at school, they usually seemed to hear Jesus calling to them. Perhaps he wasn't a good enough boy to be that close to Jesus.

Raymond found a magazine on the bookshelves and placed it carefully on top of the bucket to keep in the smell. Then he found some Enid Blyton books, but he thought the Famous Five were a bit below him now. His teacher had said that he was ready for more advanced books than Blyton, and that had made him feel quite grown up. He found a book that he hadn't read by someone called C.S. Lewis. It was called *The Lion, the Witch and the Wardrobe* and he'd seen one of the older girls at school reading it.

Raymond set it upon the square table where he'd eaten his cereal and began to read. He was soon caught up in it, despite the danger he felt here. He went through the back of the wardrobe in the book and moved out of the prison of this room. He understood nearly all of the words and the book gripped him, making him forget for minutes on end where he was and the awful peril he was in.

Presently, he became very daring. He took his shoes off and lay on top of the big bed to which he had been tied during the night. He turned so that the light from the window fell directly upon the book and read on. He lost all sense of time. When he felt hungry, he went to the window and put his face right against it, gazing up to see as much as he could of the sky.

The sun had risen as high as it was going to go and was definitely dropping now, he judged. That meant it must be well past midday. He went back to the table, took some slices of bread from the packet and spread them with the margarine from the tub. On some of them, he spread chunks of the jam the monster had left for him.

He hadn't realized quite how hungry he was until he began to eat. Even the plain white slices without the jam tasted wonderful. He couldn't believe it wasn't butter he'd spread thickly over them; he looked twice at the tub to check. Some of the women who worked at Bartram House joked about that. Raymond didn't understand properly, but apparently there'd been some television advert once about not being able to tell margarine from butter. The thought of the care home and its safe and cheerful rooms brought him near to tears, but he seized the bread with jam on it, and that tasted even better. He closed his eyes and deliberately ate it very slowly, wondering again why this simple stuff tasted better in his mouth than any food he had ever eaten before.

Perhaps it was danger that made you extra hungry and able to enjoy your eats so much. Raymond poured some milk from its container into the plastic cup and sipped it slowly. It tasted as good as the bread and marg.

Raymond looked out of the window. The sun was behind clouds now, but he could see that it was getting quite low. He climbed on to the bed again, stretched himself luxuriously and plunged back into *The Lion, the Witch and the Wardrobe*. He read on and on, conscious of the fact that the light would go soon, wanting to cover as many pages as he could before dark. Presently, with the book clutched still in his hand and the room growing dimmer, Raymond Barrington fell softly asleep.

Dean Gibson was in his working clothes when he came into the station at Oldford. He looked years older than when they had talked to him at his digs in Ledbury three days earlier. He was quite tall, but what little hair he had around his prematurely balding head was dishevelled and held traces of the white plaster he had been working during the morning. His face was grey with fatigue, his eyes were watery and he looked much older than his thirty-three years.

'You look as if you haven't been sleeping well,' said John Lambert, who was himself feeling the strain of a child snatch and murder which had been followed by a second child abduction only four days later.

'I haven't. Would you sleep well if your daughter had been murdered at the weekend?'

Lambert nodded. 'Fair point. I have daughters, but I won't even pretend that I know what it feels like to lose one like that.' He sighed. 'But it's our job to find out who took Lucy and killed her, Mr Gibson. I'm sure you want us to do that.'

Dean nodded, tight-lipped, waiting for the real business to begin. He didn't want to talk about Lucy, unless they were near to a solution. But Lambert delayed matters further by saying, 'You aren't under caution, Mr Gibson. But I'd like us to have this conversation on record, to avoid any misunderstandings. We have a query about what you told us on Monday, which we'll take up later.'

Dean was conscious of the two men studying him, as if looking for a reaction. Perhaps they were waiting for a break in his concentration, but he was beyond worrying about that now. He wasn't even going to be alarmed by the mention of what he'd said to them on Monday. He just wanted this latest ordeal to be over, so that he could be out of here and alone with his thoughts. Eventually, because it seemed to be expected of him, he said dully, 'Have you found who killed my girl yet?'

'No. We have our thoughts, but we haven't established anything definite yet. We need evidence. Or a confession from someone.' Gibson's grey, hunted eyes looked up at him on that challenge, then blinked two or three times in quick succession, as they had done in their first interview on Monday, when they'd been forced to give him the news of Lucy's death. It was the first time his eyelids had fluttered so violently in this meeting. Perhaps his weariness and the fact that he was so near to breaking point had atrophied his normal physical reactions. Lambert was watching him as intently as ever as he said gently, almost apologetically, 'And now we have this new horror to contend with.'

'What horror is this?' Dean spoke flatly, as if convention demanded that he ask the question, when he had no real interest in the answer.

'You haven't heard?'

'If it's something round here, I wouldn't have. I went straight to my work from Ledbury this morning. We're working on an extension to a house in Breinton, up near Hereford. I spent the morning plastering.' He lifted his hands a little, then dropped them back to his sides, as if explaining his appearance. Bert Hook wondered if he was aware of the white plaster powder in his sparse hair.

Sitting beside Hook, Lambert seemed not to be blinking at all, as if he sought to balance the reactions of the man across the table, who was now blinking furiously and unpredictably. He stared grimly at Gibson as he said, 'A boy a year older than Lucy was taken last night. He was snatched from Church Lane in Oldford when he was on his way back to Bartram House. No doubt you know the place.'

'I know it, yes. Church Lane is not far from where I used to live, when I was still with Anthea.' It was a relief to confess something so undamaging. He said suddenly, 'How is Anthea?'

'Our family liaison officer tells me that she is doing as well as can be expected. I understand she stayed with her sister for a few days.'

The faintest of smiles twisted the bloodless lips for no more than a second. 'In Gloucester, yes. That would be Lisa. She never liked me, Lisa. She thought Anthea could have done better. I suppose she was right.'

'Forgive me, Mr Gibson, but we need to—'

'Is that man with Anthea? The one who was with Lucy when she went missing. That Matt Boyd?'

'I don't think so. But we are not here to talk about Mr Boyd, Mr Gibson. Do you know a boy called Raymond Barrington?'

'No. Is that his name – the boy who was taken from Church Lane? It is, isn't it?'

'That is his name, yes. Where were you last night, Mr Gibson?'

'At home. Or at least in the place I have to call home now, in Ledbury.'

'And is there someone who can confirm that for us?'
Furious blinking. 'No. I don't think there is.'
'What about your landlady in Ledbury?'
'She wouldn't do that. She's a right cow who hasn't any
time for me. She'd like to see you arrest me over this boy.'
'Are you saying that she'd tell us lies to get you in trouble?
Are you saying that she'd say that you were out last night,
even if you were in your room all night?'

There was such a long silence that it seemed he wasn't
going to respond at all. Then he said wearily, 'I *was* out last
night.'

'At what time?'

'I can't be sure of that. I was tired after work. I had a good
wash, then lay on the bed for a while. Then I went out for
something to eat. I'm not sure what the time was when I went.'

'Where did you go for your food?'

'Fish and chip shop.'

'In Ledbury?'

'Yes. I doubt if they'd remember me. The place was busy.
Often is on a Wednesday night, apparently.' His eyes blinked
furiously, but they couldn't interpret that as a sign of strain
or dishonesty; it was plainly a nervous reaction to stress which
he could not control.

'So can we presume that you weren't out for long?'

'I don't know how long I was out. I sat and ate the fish and
chips in the van. I had a Mars bar for afters. But then I sat in
a lay-by for a long time. I was thinking about Lucy and Anthea
and everything that's happened.'

He spoke with such conviction that Lambert was sure that
all this had happened at some time. Whether it had happened
last night was what concerned him now. And Gibson's mention
of the van provided the cue for questioning, which they had
already agreed was to be DS Hook's concern.

Hook said quietly, 'You told us on Monday that you rode
a bicycle.'

'Yes. It's old but it's reliable. I've got lights on it. It's all
quite legal.' When Hook didn't respond, he added impetuously,
'It's a Raleigh. The gears work well and the change is easy.'
He'd hoped that piling on the detail would make his story more

convincing, but he knew as he spoke that it merely sounded ridiculous.

'You told us that you'd ridden this bike to the fair in Oldford on Saturday night. That wasn't true, was it, Dean?'

Dean tried to control the welter of eyelid flutterings that now hit him. They were so fierce that they seemed to move his head about. He needed to look and sound convincing, and he couldn't do that with this damned affliction. He gripped the edge of the table and said, 'No, that wasn't correct. I'm sorry. I came in the van.'

'And did you put Lucy in it and take her away?'

'No!' The tortured monosyllable thundered his pain around the walls of the interview room.

'Then why lie about it? Why did you pretend that you had ridden over from Ledbury on your bike?'

He stared at the table. 'The van isn't mine. It belongs to the man who is at present employing me. I'm allowed to use it for work and to collect supplies from the builders' merchants. I thought Frank Lewis might be annoyed if he found I was using it for pleasure.'

'Even for a short trip at the weekend to see the daughter you'd had to leave behind enjoying herself at the fairground?'

Dean clamped his eyes shut. It was surely better to speak with them shut, however odd he might look, than to have them fluttering ridiculously as he tried to convince these two watchful, experienced men. But it was no good. He was blinking again as he said, 'I haven't worked for him long and I need the work. He's a bit – well, a bit unpredictable, Frank Lewis. But he pays well and I can do the work. Frank might take me on as permanent if I can impress him and he thinks I'm reliable. I did a good plastering job for him this morning – there aren't many casuals as can do good plastering.'

'But isn't it understood when you're allowed the use of a van in these circumstances that you're going to use it in your private life as well? Not to drive to Cornwall or up to Scotland, perhaps, but to run around locally, to see your daughter or go to the chip shop?'

'I suppose so. I suppose Frank Lewis expects that: he's not

daft. But I didn't want to go telling the police I was using his van like that. Not with the situation I'm in at present. I need the work.'

He repeated the phrase plaintively. Hook studied him for a moment, then nodded. 'So we need to amend the statement you signed on Monday. On Saturday night, you came to Oldford in Frank Lewis's van, not on your Raleigh bicycle. Did you in fact arrive at the fair in time to watch Lucy on the rides, rather than too late to see her, as you told us on Monday?'

'No. I never saw Lucy on Saturday night.'

Hook went on as if he hadn't spoken. 'And did you in fact seize Lucy, on the blind side of the roundabout where Matt Boyd could not see you, and whisk her away into the woods?'

'No! I didn't see Lucy on Saturday. The last time I saw her was a fortnight ago!' Dean strove to make it sound convincing, but the words seemed too simple and too bland for his purpose.

Hook's voice was quiet, understanding, but relentless. 'Didn't you in fact bundle Lucy into the van and take her away from Matt Boyd, the man you resented being in your bed and in your position as Lucy's parent?'

Dean felt very weary. He'd hardly slept since the weekend and he had given the plastering all his energy and all his concentration this morning. It felt now that it would be so much easier to agree with this sympathetic, persuasive voice and let these older men have their way. It took an effort for him to say jadedly, 'No. I didn't see Lucy at the fair on Saturday. I keep telling you that.'

'You do indeed, Dean. But you kept telling us that you'd come to Oldford on your bike that night, until we forced you to admit otherwise. We're deeply sorry about Lucy, but if you know anything about her death, you had much better tell us about it here and now.'

Here and now sounded very persuasive to the man on the other side of the table and the recorder. But he said doggedly, 'I don't know anything about my poor Lucy. I just want you to get to whoever killed her. Can I go now?'

'Not just yet, Dean. You were out in your van last night. At least we've agreed on that, this time. Were you in Church Lane in Oldford?'

'No. I didn't go more than a couple of miles from Ledbury.'

'Do you know Bartram House?'

'Yes. It's at the end of Church Lane. It's a home for children who are taken into care. I wish my Lucy had been in care. She'd have been safe then.'

'Perhaps she would, Dean. But Raymond Barrington was in care, and he wasn't safe, was he? Do you know where Raymond is, Dean?'

'No. I didn't take him and I don't know where he is.'

'Did you put him in that little van and take him somewhere secret, Dean? Somewhere you'd taken Lucy, perhaps?'

'No! I didn't take him and I didn't take Lucy. Why can't you believe me?'

'It's our job to ask these questions, Dean. Sometimes we believe what people say, sometimes we don't. But we have to go on asking the questions until we are sure about the truth.'

It sounded very convincing in his exhausted ears. He nodded, his eyes shut, his hands clasped together on the table in front of him.

Hook said, 'Did you come here this afternoon in Mr Lewis's van?'

Dean nodded again, feeling that if his eyes opened they would see only fear in them, that if his mouth opened they would hear only uncertainty in his words.

'Our forensic team is already on site. I'd like them to have a quick look at that van before you go.'

Dean Gibson nodded hopelessly, giving the consent he was in no position to withhold.

Hook glanced at Lambert, received his nod of consent and said, 'If you come with me, Dean, I'll get you a large mug of tea and a sandwich from our canteen. You look as if you need them.'

SEVENTEEN

It was almost dark when the monster came back. Raymond Barrington woke with a start of fear as he heard the vehicle reversing outside the window.

There was very little light left in the sky. That meant it must be about seven o'clock, he thought. He scrambled hastily off the bed as he heard the key turn in the lock. Seconds later, the room blazed with light and the monster stood in the doorway, looking at him fiercely. Perhaps it was trying to assess what he had been doing during the long hours in which he had been left. Raymond blinked his eyes, dazzled by the sudden light. He could see only nose and eyes between the scarf the monster had wrapped around its face and the cap above it.

That nose was now wrinkled in distaste. Raymond glanced at the bucket with the magazine on top, then fearfully back at the monster. 'I had to use it. I thought that was what it was for. There's a stink, isn't there? I'm sorry about that, but I couldn't help it.'

He poured the words out rapidly, fearful that he might be punished before he could make his explanation. The monster didn't speak, didn't even look at him again. It marched across to the bucket and threw the magazine on the floor. Then it picked up the bucket without even looking at its contents; Raymond was glad about that. Then it marched to the door with the bucket and disappeared.

Raymond thought for a moment that he might make a dash for it whilst the monster was attending to the contents of the bucket, but even as the thought entered his head he heard the key turn in the lock. There was the sound of a toilet flushing somewhere above his head, then other, more muffled sounds. He tried to follow the directions of the monster's footsteps, but he couldn't do that. Then the key turned again in the door and it was back in the room, setting the bucket down at one side of it, taking something out of a new Tesco's bag and putting it on the square table.

The monster hadn't spoken at all yet. That made Raymond more afraid of what it might do to him if he annoyed it. He said, 'I ate some of the bread you brought. And the margarine and the jam. It tasted very good. Thank you.'

There was a grunt. The thing didn't look at him. It stood between him and the table, keeping its back to him. Raymond realized now that it didn't want to be seen, that it didn't want him to recognize it. He tried to think of people he had seen before, and whether it might be someone he would know if he saw the complete face. He couldn't. But the fact that it feared him, just a little and just in this one small thing, made him bolder. He nodded towards the now empty and shining bucket. 'I had to use it. And I couldn't wash my hands, when I'd been. I haven't been able to wash any of me, not since you brought me here. I want to wash myself.'

He could never remember wishing that in his life before. It wasn't what you did, when you were a boy. You approached soap and water reluctantly. Adults drove you to it and then checked that you'd washed the bits you might choose to miss, like behind your ears. It wasn't until he'd been put in the care home that he'd known people washed their hands when they'd been to the lavvies. But he'd got into the habit now, and he remembered all those dire warnings about germs that Mrs Allen had given him. Once he had voiced the thought, he felt an overwhelming need to wash his palms and his fingers, which must surely be teeming with germs.

He thought at first that the monster was going to ignore him. Then it turned suddenly and nodded. It came swiftly across to him and reached out a hand, so that Raymond cringed instinctively towards the floor and prepared himself for a blow. But the thing didn't hit him. It took him by the scruff of the neck and pulled him towards the door. But it handled him quite gently. There wasn't the violence it had used to seize him and fling him into the passenger seat of the van on their first contact. It led him to the door and then out of the room. When he stood uncertainly in the hall, it pushed him up steep, narrow stairs. Raymond saw a small red light, bright in the darkness beside a cupboard.

Then they were at the door of a room and the monster spoke for the first time on this visit. 'Wash here. Have a bath or a shower, but don't take too long. Shout for me when you finish. You don't try to escape. Deal?'

'Deal!' Raymond agreed hastily. The monster had asked him for something, rather than giving him orders. Raymond was certain for the first time that he was going to survive this.

Then he was thrust into the room. It was suddenly ablaze with a clear white light as the door shut behind him. It was a bathroom. There was a bath along one wall and a separate shower beside it. They were new and gleaming, much shinier than the ones at Bartram House. They were so clean and shiny that Raymond didn't want to soil them. He looked at the door behind him, then turned to it and drew the small bolt there with elaborate care, trying to make sure that it did not even squeak. He was sure the monster wouldn't like it if it found that he'd drawn the bolt and locked it out.

Raymond breathed a little more easily when the bolt was drawn without any reaction from the landing outside. He tiptoed across to the lavatory in the corner and peed, making sure that it went against the porcelain, not into the water at the bottom of the bowl; he wanted to be as quiet as possible. The cistern seemed to make a great noise in the silent house as he flushed it. But that seemed to help Raymond to think, as if the noise of flushing water was disguising his thoughts and keeping them from the monster.

He wasn't going to have either a bath or a shower, despite what the monster had said. He wasn't going to take all his clothes off with that thing anywhere near him. He went to the washbasin, turned the hot tap, then stripped off the top half of his clothing. He thought it might be filthy, but the collar of the grey shirt he had put on for cubs was still quite clean. It seemed impossible that it was only a day since he had been at cubs. Was it really only twenty-four hours since the monster had snatched him on his way back to Bartram House? It was, but Raymond went over what had happened several times before he could accept it.

The water was hot. He realized that the red light they'd passed must be for an immersion heater. They had one with a similar light at Bartram House, but they weren't allowed to switch it on, except for emergencies. The monster must have switched this one on earlier to warm the water. It seemed to know its way around this cottage pretty well. Perhaps this is where it lived some of the time. He wondered where it went to when it went away, and how far they were from Oldford and Bartram House. Raymond washed himself quickly, dried himself on the softest towel he'd ever used, then put his shirt and his green cub sweatshirt back on.

He was glad he'd promised the monster that he wouldn't try to escape. He wouldn't have fancied making a bolt for it across country he'd never seen in the dark, not with that thing after him. He slid back the bolt, opened the door and called tremulously, 'I've finished my wash. Thank you.'

The monster was at his side in seconds. It took his hand this time, not the collar of his shirt, and led him back downstairs. It was so gentle with him that he wondered if it might be female. It would need to be a big woman, though, because it was a strong hand that was clutching his. He realized with that thought that he knew the monster was human, not some creature from a book. He wasn't sure how good that was. There were some nasty humans about. He'd met some of them, when he'd lived with his mother. And it was something human that had done those things to Lucy Gibson, the girl from his school.

He was back in the familiar room now, seated obediently at the small square table. The monster brought him cottage pie in a plastic container. It was very hot. Perhaps it had been heated in a microwave. Raymond scarcely remembered his mother now, but he remembered the microwave, which was all they'd had to cook with.

The monster went back to the room next door, which must be a kitchen, because it brought Raymond a dish of sliced peaches from a tin, a chocolate digestive biscuit and a beaker of hot, sweet tea. Raymond didn't take sugar, but he sipped the tea obediently and munched the biscuit with it. The tea was much too sweet, but he didn't dare to leave it. The monster took his dishes away whilst he drank the tea. He heard the sound of them being washed in that other room which he had never seen. It didn't lock the door on him this time, perhaps because he would have had to pass the door of the next room to get out of the house.

The monster came back and stood looking at him for what seemed to Raymond a long time. Then it said, 'I won't tie you up tonight. And you can sleep in the bed, if you want to.'

'Thank you.' He'd never in his life slept in a bed as big as that. He was surprised to find that he was almost looking forward to it.

'I'll have to lock you in here, though. You'll have the chamber pot.'

'All right.' Raymond wasn't going to argue. The monster had been good to him this time, but he wasn't going to risk upsetting it.

'And you can't have the light.'

'I'd like to have the light. I won't switch it on unless I need it. I get frightened when I know I can't put the light on.' Raymond felt very bold saying that, but he'd felt suddenly that he didn't want to face another long, black night locked in this room.

The monster shook its head. It didn't move, but those eyes, deep-set above the nose which was the only other feature he could see, studied Raymond as if he were a dog that had been called to heel. 'Will you promise me not to use the switch unless you're really frightened?'

'Yes. I probably won't need it. It'll just be good that I know it's there if I do.' Raymond tried not to sound too eager. He felt that if he showed excitement of any kind, it might annoy the monster and make it hostile again.

The monster looked at him again for a moment, then went and drew the curtains very tightly around the window, pushing the edges of them into the corners of the frame so that not a chink of light would slip past the edges. 'I'll be back in the morning.' It had spoken more now than at any time before, but still in that strange, gruff voice that was not its own.

As the monster passed Raymond on its way from window to door, it stooped and gave the fair hair on top of the boy's head the briefest of fondles. Raymond wanted to ask what was going to happen to him tomorrow, but he sensed that he should not do that.

The search for the missing boy was proving no more successful than the one for Lucy Gibson.

Because it was Thursday and not Sunday, there were fewer volunteers from the ranks of the public than there had been when the police organized the search for Lucy. It was also a little less of a novelty than the one conducted at the weekend. The disappearance of a second child was sensational, certainly, but the combing of the area around Oldford was not the breathtaking innovation that the weekend search had been for the civilians involved in it.

The failure of that exploration hung like a ball and chain upon this one. The police officers and the few members of the public who searched outwards from the centre of Oldford for any trace of Raymond Barrington were weighed down by the knowledge that the first victim was dead. It was inconceivable that the person who had seized this eight-year-old boy was not the same individual who had taken and murdered the seven-year-old girl four nights earlier. The searchers worked diligently and urgently, but they could not thrust away the thought that the boy, like the girl, might have been killed within an hour or two of his abduction.

Inspector Cameron, the same uniformed man who had handled the unsuccessful hunt for Lucy Gibson, deployed his depleted army of searchers systematically around the area. He would not have thought there were so many garden sheds in such a small town, but land had been cheap when the older properties in Oldford had been erected and most of them had substantial plots. The scrutineers liberated two cats which had mysteriously got themselves locked in sheds; they also heard numerous rodents scrambling away from them as they opened the doors of the less-frequented sheds. The more experienced of the searchers tied string around the ankles of their trousers as a precaution against rodent intrusion. Mice fled to some very strange places when they were alarmed.

The searchers found no trace of a small boy.

They worked outwards from the spot where Raymond Barrington had been snatched. They found no trace of him in the outbuildings of Oldford. At four p.m., Cameron dispatched six of his more experienced officers to examine the banks of the Wye at the nearest points to the town, with instructions to search for any sign of recent access to the river. They knew exactly what they were looking for as they conducted their melancholy mission: any traces at the edge of the quietly flowing river that would indicate that a second child's body had been recently consigned to its waters.

They found none. That could not be considered conclusive. Unless they found some distinctive article dropped by the side of the river – a possession or an article of clothing, perhaps – they could not be certain that either Raymond or the person who had seized him had been here. Negative results were good in this case: they meant the boy might still be alive. But finding nothing, as they moved along the bank of the river with the light dying in the west, felt nonetheless like sad and unrewarding work.

There were still working barns with hay in them at a couple of the farms. There were also disused barns in various stages of decay. These seemed the likeliest sources of a find, and Cameron instructed his team in muted tones. 'You need to search every nook and cranny of these places. Bear in mind that we don't know definitely what we're looking for. We all want a live and healthy boy, but we have to bear in mind that what we eventually discover might be a body. If that's the case, it's important that we find it, even if we can no longer help the boy. It's our job to get the mad sod who did this, whether male or female, before any other kids are put at risk. The body might be hidden, so make sure you search properly. I don't want anything turning up later in a building we're supposed to have searched.'

The majority of his team on this joyless day were professional police personnel. But it was a new experience for many of them. Young men and women, many of them with children of their own, found themselves beset by a variety of emotions as they moved apprehensively into the unknown. They all knew the rules; part of professionalism was to be as detached and unemotional as possible. But they were also human. When a child who had offended no one was in danger or dead, they couldn't proceed with the brisk efficiency of automatons.

They wanted to find things. There was even a small part of each of them that wanted them to be the one who discovered whatever there was to be found. There must be kudos in it, even if there must also be a huge amount of luck. But it couldn't do you any harm to discover key evidence in the most high-profile case that had come to Oldford in many years. But each man and each woman wanted it to be a positive finding, to find the boy Raymond Barrington alive and well and return him to the tearful Mrs Allen at Bartram House.

The British police service is not noticeably religious. The things officers see, the victims they find and the people they have to deal with militate against a belief in any beneficent higher agency. But as the light died on that Thursday in late October, many silent prayers were uttered by those not normally given to such supplications.

A search of this kind is a strange business. For much of the time, you are content to find nothing, consoled by the thought that at least you have discovered nothing dire and that the worst may still be avoided. Yet confirming that a series of huts and more substantial buildings are empty is a bleak experience. You want something more positive. Best of all, you want an excited, laughing boy falling into your arms and being carried back triumphantly to salvation.

Inspector Cameron called off the search for the day at seven thirty. The light was gone and the team was exhausted. They could have carried on with torches, but that wouldn't be either effective or sensible. He ticked off all the buildings they had investigated on his large-scale map of the area. They would recommence their search on the morrow – assuming always that there was not bad news from some source to make further investigation unnecessary.

Cameron paused at the bridge below Ross-on-Wye on his way home. He knew he would see nothing there, but some superstition made him stop and look at this long stretch of what many considered England's most beautiful river. The Wye flowed black and silent beneath him as he leant on the parapet of the bridge, its waters concealing who knew what. A crescent moon was already low in the sky, conspiring with the last glimmering of daylight to show him the silent eddies of the dark waters as they moved beneath him. It was a couple of miles south of here that the body of Lucy Gibson had been discovered. Cameron wondered what those dark, slow-moving waters concealed. Beauty became sinister when it was overlaid with human behaviour like this.

It was a little over twenty-four hours since Raymond Barrington had been snatched on his way home from cubs. No trace of him had been found. Every police officer knew what that suggested.

EIGHTEEN

D I Rushton thought he had never seen Detective Superintendent Lambert looking so old. Chris had just recorded on his computer the information that the search for Raymond Barrington had been abandoned for the day at seven thirty-three p.m. It was what they had expected, but a blow nevertheless to the three senior men at Oldford CID who were reviewing progress, or the lack of it.

Rushton looked at the faces of the two older men and voiced the thought that none of them wished to contemplate. 'Do we think the lad's still alive?'

There was a long pause – this was the moment when Chris thought how grey, gaunt and tortured the long face of John Lambert looked. But it was the chief who said, 'I think the boy's still alive, somewhere. I'm assuming for the moment that it's one of our five suspects who took him. We've seen them all; to my mind, none of them is behaving like someone who has just murdered a second child. I might be wrong, because I'm on ground I've never trodden before; we all are.'

It was DS Hook who voiced the second appalling thought that lay darkly behind everything they were doing. 'What are the possibilities that these crimes are the work of someone else entirely? Perhaps someone who might be among the fifty-odd people seen by the team, but not thought worth further follow-up? Is there perhaps someone who presented an alibi for the Lucy Gibson snatch, which was accepted at face value when it shouldn't have been?'

'Thanks, Bert!' Lambert's weary face produced a mirthless grin. 'You're quite right to raise the question. We can't afford to neglect any possibility in this situation. What do you think, Chris?'

Rushton frowned. Hook had raised the query he'd been putting to himself all day. Every CID man is wracked by the knowledge that in some previous high-profile investigations, such as the one conducted into the multiple murders of the Yorkshire Ripper, Peter Sutcliffe, crass mistakes had been made. Obvious lines of enquiry had been ignored. Sutcliffe himself had been missed when he should have been picked up, with the result that his later victims had been needlessly killed. Chris said, 'I've been over things today. I couldn't find other possibilities. In some cases, we're dependent upon the perceptiveness of the men and women doing the questioning, but there have been at least two officers involved with every person we have cleared from further questioning.'

Lambert nodded. He and Hook sometimes made fun of Chris Rushton's earnestness and ambition, but the DI was at his best with issues like this. He was confident that Rushton wouldn't have overlooked anything that should have been investigated further, that the officers answering to him wouldn't believe for a moment that they could get away with anything slipshod. He said, 'We're all on unknown ground with a case like this. For what it's worth, it's still my belief that one of our five killed Lucy Gibson and has taken Raymond Barrington. What I find most difficult is establishing which one might have killed Lucy. Even if we allow that snatching her is the action of someone unbalanced, for a variety of different reasons none of the five seems to me a likely killer. Yet if we're right, one of them surely must be.'

Hook nodded. 'We've seen them, Chris, and we're baffled. Sometimes experience actually gets in the way of objectivity. When you meet people face to face and probe their personalities, your own prejudices play a part, however much you try to guard against it. In that sense, you're standing outside this. You're logging everything that comes in from all sorts of sources, but you haven't confronted, face to face, the five people we regard as our leading candidates for this. From everything you've recorded, which one would you say is likeliest to be a killer?'

Rushton smiled grimly. 'If I saw any of these as obvious, it would be my duty to say so and I would have done that by now. If you want my thoughts, I tend to follow the old copper's instincts. I believe in recidivism; those who have offended before are the ones most likely to do it again. I know you don't always like that, Bert, but the statistics support me.'

Hook bridled a little. 'We're not daft, Chris. We don't ignore previous records. We very often throw them at people when we're questioning them. It's just that we don't wish to close our minds to other possibilities.'

Chris Rushton grinned. It always amused him to find the staid and homely-looking Bert Hook such a dangerous liberal – in police terms, anyway. 'In my view, your outstanding candidate has to be Gerry Clancey – Rory Burns. Operating under this alias because of a previous conviction for child molestation six years ago in Cork and with a later conviction for violent assault. He's handy with his fists and certainly not averse to violence as a means of resolving his problems. We know he'd already been touching up an eleven-year-old girl on the fair rides on the same day that Lucy Gibson disappeared. He lives by his wits and by his fists, and the fists are sharper than the wits.'

Lambert sighed. 'It's a fair summary and you make out a persuasive case. We haven't a lot of evidence beyond what you say, but Clancey is probably the one among our five who would cover his tracks most effectively. Let me put the other side of the case. Clancey is a nasty piece of work with a previous record, but perhaps the most sane and clear-sighted about the implications of murder for himself. He knows that killing a child would land him inside for a very long time, and that he'd almost certainly suffer whilst there from other criminals, who dislike child murderers as much as do more law-abiding citizens. Do you see Gerry Clancey volunteering himself for a life sentence?'

Chris pursed his lips. 'Not volunteering, no. But perhaps he didn't mean to kill Lucy. Perhaps he had a moment of panic and did what he never intended.'

'That's perfectly possible. It's also possible, perhaps even likely, for the rest of our candidates. It would be much easier for us if one of them was the homicidal maniac who features in lurid fiction and in the more sensational efforts of our popular press. But there's no sign of that. These are emotional crimes for all of us, and we'd probably all prefer Clancey to be our man: he's an aggresive lout and a dangerous individual. But I scarcely need to remind you two that that is a dangerous line of thought unless we have facts to support it.'

It was Chris Rushton's turn to sigh. 'Point taken. My second favourite for this would be Big Julie Foster.' He glanced at Hook, anticipating some sort of reaction, but there was none. 'Again, she's got previous. She took a baby seven years ago.'

Now Hook did speak. 'A little girl, which she looked after perfectly. A baby who, by all accounts, was returned to the negligent parents in better condition than when she left them.'

'Nevertheless, Julie is of limited intellect and attracted to children. She's a powerfully built woman who might well have taken Lucy and panicked when the girl struck her or tried to get away. Moreover, she's been into Bartram House and talked to the children there. Because she'd been brought up in care herself, the authorities thought that was a good idea. Maybe it wasn't, because when Big Julie decided to take another kid, the home was a natural place for her to turn to.'

Hook shook his head. 'Big Julie's got limited intelligence, but she likes kids. I can just about see her taking Lucy Gibson, but not harming her.'

Lambert grimaced. 'We can't presume that, Bert. If we could, Big Julie wouldn't still be in the frame for this. I can't see Julie taking either child with the intention of harming them, but I can see her panicking under pressure. If she did that, who can say what might happen? She's a powerful woman, as Chris says – possibly more powerful than she realizes.'

Hook nodded dolefully. 'All right. I can't deny that possibility. But any of them might have panicked, faced with a terrified, screaming kid and the prospect of being discovered. I'd prefer to bet on Dennis Robson if we think that's what happened.'

Rushton said, 'You said you wanted my view from the outside, so to speak. Well, I've never even seen Robson, let alone spoken to him, but from what I've filed on him he seems to me the least likely killer of the lot. He's a man of seventy without any history of previous violence. OK, he's another nasty piece of work: a known paedophile, whose wife divorced him because he continued to offend. I can see him doing all sorts of unspeakable things with children and I wouldn't want him within a hundred yards of my kid. But although I can see him taking Lucy, I can't see him killing her.'

Lambert nodded slowly. 'That sounds convincing as you say it. But we should bear in mind that Robson had studied these kids on their school playing field. He may actually have targeted Lucy weeks beforehand, for all we know. And then followed up four days later with another kid he already knew, from the same school.'

Hook said, 'Robson doesn't know children. He never had any of his own, which we might now consider a blessing. But that inexperience might be crucial here. Lucy would scream when he took her and even more if he attempted to abuse her. He would have had no idea how to shut her up. He's more likely to have panicked than any of them.'

Lambert said quietly, revolving the thought that Hook had just prompted, 'The forensic psychologist thought that the person involved almost certainly had some sort of personality disorder. Robson, like many paedophiles, has that. As far as most of his neighbours are concerned, he's a cultivated and highly respectable elderly man who lives alone and causes trouble for no one. His perversions are part of a completely different life, which no doubt fills him with excitement. Apart from the pressures Bert accurately describes, Dennis Robson might exhibit a different personality when he becomes an active paedophile.'

'Which leaves the two men who were closest to Lucy Gibson,' said Rushton. 'The discarded husband and the man who replaced him. I saw Dean Gibson when he came in to see you yesterday. He looked at the end of his tether.'

'I agree. But Gibson was pretty broken-up when he had to leave the marital home a few months ago. According to what everyone tells us, he's been barely coping since then. And he lost a daughter he loved at the weekend. Even if he had nothing to do with her death, you'd expect him to look shattered. Which he does, as you say. He's prematurely bald and he has this habit of blinking violently and repeatedly when he's under any sort of emotional pressure. His appearance doesn't do him any favours, but he hasn't any previous history of violence, towards his child or his wife or anyone else. He's in the frame because we know that he was around on Saturday and we haven't been able to clear him. And, like the others, he has no one to alibi him for last night, when Raymond Barrington was snatched. One of our problems is that all five of our suspects are loners, in very different ways. Gerry Clancey has opted for the single man's freedom, Matt Boyd and Dennis Robson are divorced, Dean Gibson and Big Julie Foster have had the solitary life forced upon them. That helps to account for the fact that none of them has a witness to prove he or she was elsewhere when Raymond was snatched last night.'

It was a long speech for Lambert. It was also evidence of his uncertainty and of the agony this case was causing him. He was trying to rationalize his own thoughts by voicing them aloud and testing the logic of them. There was a pause before Hook said, 'Could you see Dean Gibson killing his own daughter?'

'No. But I also can't rule him out. He lied to us about Saturday when we first saw him, pretending that he'd come to Oldford on his bike and missed seeing her altogether, when we now know that he'd come in a van and might well have been there at the moment she was snatched. I can't see either Dean or Big Julie strangling a seven-year-old girl, but we've already agreed that a fit of panic might have overtaken any one of these five. I feel Dennis Robson is creepy enough to do anything under pressure, that Gerry Clancey is certainly violent enough and that we still don't know enough about Matthew Boyd to rule him out. But I think we've still got to have all five in the frame at this moment.'

Rushton said, 'I'm glad you mentioned Matthew Boyd. I feel I should know most about him, in that I've talked to the woman who was sleeping with him; I went with Ruth David to give Anthea Gibson the news of her daughter's death. Anthea spent the whole of that Saturday when Lucy died with Boyd. But I still feel he is the one of the five whom I know least well.'

Hook glanced at the long, tortured face of his chief. 'I think we might agree with that, even though we've twice spoken at length with Matthew Boyd. We know now that his teacher training course was ended abruptly ten years ago because of incidents with children. He denies there was anything improper, and there was no court case, so he hasn't got form like Clancey and Robson. And Foster, I suppose, in a different way, though the psychological reports saved her from any real punishment when she took the baby.'

Lambert was troubled. 'You're right; Boyd's elusive. He spent Tuesday night with Anthea Gibson, three nights after her daughter was snatched and killed while in his care. That argues that she at least doesn't believe Boyd killed Lucy.'

Hook allowed himself a tiny, doubtful shake of his head. 'But Anthea must be so shattered that she hardly knows her own mind at present. And Boyd's kept his digs in Oldford. He's living within four hundred yards of the spot where Raymond Barrington was snatched last night.'

Rushton smiled. 'Be fair, Chris. So are the others, apart from Dean Gibson.'

'Yes. But Boyd has taken two days off work. Had he planned to snatch a child? He also had his car very thoroughly valeted this morning, conveniently removing any traces of a boy carried in it against his will last night.'

Rushton nodded, glad as always to have a chance to display his efficiency. 'We checked that. Matthew Boyd does have his car valeted regularly, at about monthly intervals. The last one was only three weeks ago, but it's conceivable, as he claims, that he was taking advantage of the fact that he isn't working for a couple of days to have the car cleaned. This is, however, an extremely convenient valeting for anyone who had an unwilling passenger in the car last night.'

Lambert nodded. 'We've had Boyd's ex-wife interviewed. She says that she never really felt she knew him and that she always felt that he lived some other sort of secret life away from her.'

'Which sounds exactly the right background for someone perpetrating crimes like these,' Rushton pointed out. He'd been waiting to say that ever since he had filed DS Ruth David's report on her interviewing of Hannah Boyd, the woman who had divorced their suspect.

'Agreed,' said Lambert promptly. 'But we have to remember that ex-spouses have their own agendas. It's not often that they want to see the best in their former partners. Nevertheless, it reinforces our own thoughts about Boyd, that he's a difficult man to fathom. He was pretty vague about his present relationship with Anthea Gibson and how she's reacted to someone stealing and murdering her daughter when she was in his care.'

Hook smiled ruefully at the memory of Matt Boyd's troubled face. 'That may be because neither of them is sure yet of exactly how they feel about the other. What happened to Lucy must be traumatic for both of them. I imagine Anthea in particular isn't sure what she wants or needs at the moment. I expect her feelings change hour by hour. I know mine would.'

The three were silent for a moment, pondering once again the uniqueness of these happenings for them. Even with their vast combined experience of crime, they were feeling their way into unfamiliar areas.

It was Lambert who wrenched them back to the practicalities of the investigation. 'We've given it twenty-four hours. I think we need to set up surveillance of all five of these people. If we put a tail on each of them, we'll soon know if that boy is still alive. I'd have done it today, but as you know I was afraid of scaring an unbalanced kidnapper into violent action. But we can't leave it any longer. I'll discuss who we're going to use with you in the morning, Chris.'

'It'll be expensive,' said Chris Rushton. He was a natural bureaucrat and this was the standard bureaucratic reaction.

'Expensive but warranted,' said Lambert grimly. 'Refer any queries from the chief constable about the overtime budget to me. I want good people on this – perhaps as many as fifteen, if we want twenty-four hour surveillance. Each of them needs to be aware that a child's life might depend on his or her actions. We'll assign them first thing tomorrow, Chris, unless we have any further news by then.'

It was nine o'clock and each of them was exhausted. They left the station at Oldford sadly, mindful of the fact that the further news Lambert mentioned in his last phrase was likely to be of the death of a second child.

NINETEEN

The five people the detective trio had discussed were pushing ahead with their own lives, unconscious of the intense examination of their characters that was being conducted in the CID section at Oldford.

Dean Gibson was both exhausted and confused, as they had surmised. He had spent a long morning without any break plastering the wall of the new extension they were building near Hereford, which had taken all his skill and concentration. His afternoon had seen the very different pressures of a grilling by Lambert and Hook in the interview room at the police station. It would have taxed most men, he supposed, and he had been in a fragile condition even at the beginning of his day.

He couldn't remember when he had last slept for any decent length of time. He was so tired that he was not thinking straight. It seemed scarcely possible that it was only five days since Lucy had been seized and killed. His mind had not been clear since then; his brain, his stomach and his whole body were beset by a mass of conflicting emotions. He scarcely felt the same from one minute to the next, let alone from day to day. He sat in the dismal room in his Ledbury digs and wondered what he was to do and what was to become of him.

He wasn't even sure whether he was hungry or not. He ought to eat something, he supposed. There would be more plastering for him tomorrow, more long hours without a break whilst he covered another raw wall of the newly completed extension at Breinton. He didn't want to collapse whilst he was working. That would draw the kind of attention he didn't want. It might lose him the steady work he had toiled so hard to secure. But that didn't seem anything like as important as it had a week ago. He kept telling himself that he needed the work, that he might even get back with Anthea some time in the next few months. But Dean didn't really believe that was going to happen any more. He wondered if he had the energy to work, or even the energy to think, beyond the next few minutes.

He heard Mrs Jackson moving about in her kitchen downstairs, and the thought of another confrontation with that mean-spirited woman gave him his first strong feeling in several hours. He didn't want to speak to her, wanted with a passion he could scarcely understand to be away from her. He crept down the stairs as quietly as he could, treading at the sides of the two he knew creaked particularly loudly. Ma Jackson came out of the kitchen as he pulled the front door softly shut behind him. He heard her heavy, proprietorial steps in the hall. But she did not open her front door to call after him, and Dean, whose head was reeling a little, told himself that was an omen of better things to come for him.

He sat for a moment in the van he had cleaned out hastily before the police examined it. They had left it, if anything, even tidier than it had been when they had taken his keys. Without its usual jumble of tools and materials and discarded food wrappers, it felt at this moment like a different van altogether. And for another very long moment, Dean wished that it was and that he was starting anew.

He set out to put distance between himself and Barbara Jackson and the small, miserable room where he spent too much of his life. He drove slowly through the small town and towards Ross-on-Wye. A roadside pub said that you could have two courses for £8.95 on weekday evenings. He eased the van into the car park, sat for a couple of minutes to compose himself, then went inside and collected the set menu from which he was to select his two courses.

It was quiet in the pub. Even at these prices, people who were hit by the recession weren't eating out as often as they had a couple of years earlier. Dean sat at the smallest and most obscure table he could see. There was a party of eight men at the other side of the room on a lads' night out, and two couples who had arranged a convivial meal together. Otherwise, a room that held fifty when packed was empty. The noise rose from the other two tables, particularly the all-male one, but no one took any notice of the white-faced, balding man in the shabby sweater who munched steadily through his meal at the side of the dining area.

That was the way he wanted it, Dean told himself. He didn't want company and wanted least of all to make conversation. And yet he felt very alone. He wanted someone, not to speak to him, but to wrap warm arms around him and tell him that all would be well. He didn't think that would ever happen again. It couldn't now, could it? Not without Lucy.

He refused to order a drink, because he knew how tired he was and he was trying to keep his thinking straight. He had gammon ham and pineapple, with chips and broccoli, and he found that once he started to eat he was surprisingly hungry. He ate it all; he managed to answer the waitress's cheerful query with a routine assurance that he had enjoyed his meal, then a request for a sticky toffee pudding for his second course. No coffee; he would use the old kettle in his room to make that when he had crept past La Jackson and up the stairs.

He was glad now that he had come out. But his head was teeming still with conflicting thoughts as he drove slowly back to the room and his bed. He would need to sort things out tomorrow, but he couldn't think about that now.

Dennis Robson had made his plans for the evening far more methodically than Dean Gibson.

He needed to leave the bungalow at twenty to eight, he had decided. He waited impatiently whilst the clock hands crept slowly towards that time. He had put a suit on for this meeting, but it scarcely mattered what you wore, as long as you paid your dues. A low profile was the order of the day, but Dennis wasn't quite sure how you dressed to secure that. He'd always worn a suit when he'd gone to the Masons, but it was a long time now since he'd ceased to do that.

He'd put the car in the garage, but the bonnet as he brushed past it was still quite warm from when he'd used it earlier. He wasn't going to think about his earlier journey in the Audi now; he wanted to give his full concentration to the evening ahead. There seemed to be more police about than usual as he drove through Oldford. Perhaps he was extra-sensitive since he'd been the subject of their enquiries. He checked his mirror repeatedly as he drove out of the town and turned south, but there was no sign of any vehicle pursuing him.

The car was warm and the roads quiet. He opened up the Audi's two-litre engine and tried hard to enjoy the drive. He felt the old stirrings of conscience, the conflicts within him, which he had felt a thousand times before. But he thrust them away and concentrated on the road, with a quiet, unconscious smile lifting the edges of his mouth. Tonight was about excitement, and for the moment eager anticipation thrust down all other feelings.

He turned off the A38 when he saw the sign for Thornbury, his elation rising with each passing mile. There was a car behind him now; he watched the headlights on his tail for four miles, whilst the seed of alarm germinated and grew in his head. Then, when he was within a couple of miles of his destination, it turned quietly left and disappeared into the darkness down a narrow lane. Dennis breathed more easily again, smiling mockingly at himself for creating fear out of a harmless coincidence. The clock on his dashboard told him that he would arrive at the very minute he had planned, and such exactitude restored his feeling of well-being.

There were no instructions about caution in parking and approach. He liked that. At the gatherings he had formerly attended in a Bristol suburb, they had been instructed to park at least two hundred yards away and walk to the venue, keeping a wary eye behind them for any evidence of unwelcome attention. He much preferred this venue and these companions, where you drove right to the house and parked openly. That was what a gathering of friends meeting for an evening of intelligent conversation might well do.

He had his story ready, as instructed. They were opera buffs, meeting to enjoy a recording of Renée Fleming's incomparable *La Traviata* at the Metropolitan Opera in New York. Dennis Robson had no difficulty with that explanation; it was an evening he might well have genuinely enjoyed, in a different place and with a different set of friends.

He had no difficulty finding the place; this was his third visit. It was a big, modern house, slightly elevated from its nearest neighbours, which were over a hundred yards away.

It had a view of the Severn estuary and the motorway bridge in daylight, but none of that was visible now. *Valley View*, it said on the sign by the gate: each time he came, Dennis was amused by the uninventiveness of the name. A residence like this deserved a little more originality, he thought, though tonight they would all be glad of its dullness. It was better to be conventional, if you didn't want to excite attention.

There were three other cars parked here already, and the lights of a couple of others visible on the lane behind him. There was a convivial atmosphere inside the house. There was a judge here, and the leader of a town council, and at least two captains of industry, but anonymity was the order of the day. He passed through a well-lit hall and was offered white or red wine at the door to the big lounge. His £40 fee was pocketed without even being checked; it was rather as if you were attending one of the charitable functions he had often patronized in the past. There was a buzz of conversation, about politics, about sport, about music, about books, about the latest unwitting cabaret perpetrated by the London mayor. By tacit agreement, none of them talked about why they were here, even though there were most of the trimmings of a civilized gathering.

Dennis had been in the house for twenty minutes when the host tapped the table gently and introduced their 'speaker for the evening', without troubling to name him. Dennis hadn't even known there was to be anything so formal. A man who reminded him of Mephistopheles in *Faust* stepped forward and began to talk about the bond that united them and had brought them together tonight. He had a well-trimmed moustache which curled up sharply at the ends, plentiful slicked-back hair, and dark eyes which flashed with humour; he was entirely confident and gave every evidence of being beguiled by his own intelligence.

The man's theme was that although they had necessarily to recognize that their tastes and activities were at present against the law, and had thus to be indulged in secret, they should privately feel no shame. They were merely a little in advance of their time. Enlightenment among the leaden public must surely follow eventually. Homosexuality had been against the

law fifty years earlier; those with a taste for it had needed to
be as secret as they were being tonight. But now homosexuals
were not persecuted; indeed, it sometimes seemed to him that
they were positively encouraged. He paused for laughter
and the nodding of heads.

And so it would be with people who loved children, in due
course. For they should remember that the word paedophilia
meant, in fact, the love of children, just as Anglophilia was the
love of England and Francophilia indicated a love of France.
(Dennis smiled a little patronizingly as he recognized the argument he had put to those police plodders three days ago.) A recent
court case had proved that sadomasochism was nowadays
recognized as a private matter, a sexual preference, which should
be tolerated, not persecuted. In fifty years, perhaps sooner, their
own sexual preferences would be recognized as just one more
aspect of the infinite variety of human instincts.

Mephistopheles received the applause he expected and
demanded, which he acknowledged with a practised smile. It
was a little like a politician addressing a party conference,
Dennis Robson thought ungenerously. When you were speaking
to those of a like mind, you had no need to convert. He put
his hands together politely with the others, though a small,
persistent voice within him said that children were not capable
as adults were of deciding what they thought about sex with
grown men and women, or any of the other things that he and
the men around him found desirable in them.

Despite his theme, Dennis decided he didn't like
Mephistopheles, and he took care to keep his distance when
others were fraternizing with him after his address. Perhaps,
he thought, it was the very fact that his perversion was illegal,
as well as outrageous to the majority of people around him
from day to day, that gave it an edge. Dennis had never really
rejected that word 'perversion'; he prided himself on seeing
other people's point of view, even when it ran so counter to
his own.

Soon they were setting down their glasses and moving
downstairs, into the cinema room that occupied the whole of
this basement floor. Dennis sat alongside but a little way from
his nearest companions, leaving a vacant seat between them,

as if intimacy was dangerous, even with these men who had the same sexual preferences as he had.

They were all men. Mephistopheles had stressed in his talk how many women were now involved in paedophilia, how some females were more excited and extreme than their male counterparts, as if that brought a sort of legitimacy to what they practised. Dennis hoped this would not become a mixed group; he thought he would have to withdraw from it if it did.

He could feel the excitement rising around him as the images flashed up on the big screen, as the children removed their clothes and the shots became more brazen and the angles more daring. He was sure that the breathing of the others in the room became more uneven, as his did. Why were they abnormal? Why didn't everyone react like this to pictures of naked children? It was easy to think in a gathering like this that your tastes were conventional, that it was the wider world around you that was out of step.

There was a hush when the show finished and the lights were put on. The host stood briefly before them and gave them the details of the websites they were to access on their computers for the illegal materials they wanted. Each man in the room made careful notes, as if they were gardeners recording where they could locate favourite plants and specialist growers. And now everyone was suddenly anxious to be away. The show was over, the information recorded, and there was no need to preserve the rituals and illusions of a normal social gathering.

Dennis Robson threaded his way carefully along the minor roads in the darkness. It wouldn't do to end up in a ditch and have the police asking what had been the purpose of his journey tonight. Especially not in view of the things that were presently going on in and around Oldford. Mephistopheles was immediately behind him in his Jaguar; Dennis imagined him cursing the excessive caution of the man in the Audi in front of him and drove even more carefully. He was glad to see the Jaguar swinging south towards Bristol as he turned north up the A38.

He didn't need to drive right into Gloucester. He turned west as he approached the ancient city and was within ten miles of home when he twisted suddenly into a lay-by, switched off his engine and put his head in his hands. Dennis hadn't known he was going to do this. He had been beset by one of the sudden, overpowering bursts of remorse that overtook him from time to time. He supposed it was guilt, but he wasn't really sure what it was, except that it made him despise himself more completely than he would have thought possible.

It was at moments like this that he ached to be normal, to have those conventional reactions to events and to people that he affected to deride. For a few minutes of searing clarity, he saw himself as the creature that others reviled and he loathed what he saw. The frame within the elegant suit was wracked by a series of violent sobs. Then he lifted his head and stared ahead into the darkness, ignoring the headlights from the other direction as they approached and passed him. Grief was an indulgence. He wasn't going to change at seventy, was he? He drove home and parked expertly within two inches of the back wall of his garage, as if such precision could make him a part of the normal world.

Then Dennis Robson went indoors to the welcoming warmth of his bungalow, where he busied himself with a series of small domestic tasks. He didn't wish to settle into his favourite armchair; that would allow him time for reflection. He took his hot drink to bed with him, tried unsuccessfully to read, downed the pill that he nowadays needed to get to sleep.

As he slipped into unconsciousness, he thought of the small, perfect limbs of Lucy Gibson and of what the morrow might hold in store for himself and for Raymond Barrington.

Big Julie Foster would have been outraged by Dennis Robson's activities on this Thursday evening. Her own evening could scarcely have been more different.

She had come back to work to do two hours' overtime, from eight until ten. Her male supervisor said, 'You look tired, Julie. It's only two hours since you left here. Are you sure you're fit to do this?'

Julie wasn't used to such consideration. She immediately suspected that she was going to be denied the overtime if she gave the man an excuse to do that. And she wanted this little slot. It would buy her twenty litres of petrol for the Fiesta, which she needed. She liked overtime. The work was no harder – sometimes easier, with fewer people around to bother you. She didn't really understand why you got more money for it, but she was very glad you did. She didn't really know what unsocial hours meant, either, but that was fine by her if they meant more money.

There was often overtime on a Thursday. The manager at her branch of Tesco's liked to have everything ready for the weekend. Friday and Saturday were the two busiest days of the week; that was when the store took most at the tills. The supervisor quite liked having Julie in for a stint like this. She never complained, even when she was tired, and she would turn her hand to anything he asked her to do. And she was as strong as any man when it came to carrying cartons and stacking shelves.

Julie worked steadily, anxious to disprove the supervisor's view that she looked tired. Tonight's work was mostly replenishing shelves, so that they were fully stocked for the Friday and Saturday rush. Julie was amazed by how many tins of baked beans had disappeared since she had left the store at six. There was a special offer on – four tins for a pound – so they were flying off the shelves. She liked that expression – 'flying off the shelves'. It took her back to her childhood and her love of cartoons, where anything could happen and tins might indeed fly off shelves.

Big Julie stacked her trolley repeatedly with boxes of tins and filled the shelves quite expertly. She knew now exactly how many tins of different sizes each shelf division was meant to hold. She worked steadily, dropping into the rhythm of the task she had done so often before, happy to show Mr Burton that she wasn't as tired as he'd thought she was. Swiftly and efficiently, she cleared the place in an aisle where a child had dropped and smashed a jar of jam. She made sure that not the tiniest shard of glass remained, then brought her mop and bucket to perform the final thorough cleansing.

Jason Burton watched her surreptitiously through the half-open door of his office and was smitten with a sudden shaft of sympathy for the willing, ungainly woman who so wanted to please. He waited until she finished her cleaning, then brought the sign with large letters 'PLEASE TAKE CARE – FLOOR DAMP', which he set at the end of the aisle. As Julie passed him with her mop and bucket, he said, 'It's quiet now. I'm brewing a cup of tea in my office. Why don't you come in and have one with me?'

Julie didn't know how to say no. She didn't want the tea, but she didn't know how to handle the situation. So she was polite. That was what they had taught her in the home twenty years and more ago, and in most situations it served her well. She said, 'Thank you, sir,' as meekly as a Victorian maidservant, installed twenty tins of mushroom soup on the appropriate shelf, then went into Mr Burton's office to sit on the chair he had set out beside his desk.

He left the door wide open, so that they could see the few members of the public who were shopping at this hour. That was so that she wouldn't think he was going to assault her, Julie thought. And so that she couldn't accuse him of anything afterwards. Julie knew these things, when everyone seemed to think that she knew nothing. She knew because other girls who worked here had told her them. Sometimes, she thought one or two of them would quite like Mr Burton to do these unspeakable things with them. She planted her broad rear carefully on the edge of the chair he had set out for her and sipped her tea dutifully.

They chatted, mostly about work, because they hadn't anything else in common. Mr Burton had a photograph of his two young children in pride of place upon his small desk. Julie Foster was suddenly jealous of the life he lived, of the part played in it by the wife who was not in the picture, who she was quite sure was very beautiful. She said, 'Your kids are very pretty.' Everyone called them kids nowadays; that must surely be all right for her.

Burton looked at them as if they were a part of the fittings he had forgotten about. 'That was taken two or three years ago. They're growing up now. Nothing like as angelic as they look there!'

'Like Raymond Barrington,' said Julie. She didn't know why she'd thought of the boy at that particular moment. It wasn't the right thing to have said; she felt Mr Burton looking at her curiously. She wished again that she hadn't had to come in here. She was never going to be able to make conversation with people like Mr Burton. She didn't know how and she didn't get any practice. She was glad when the tea cooled enough for her to drink it and get back to work.

Half an hour later, she was suddenly conscious of Mr Burton behind her. He said, 'Your time's up, Julie. You should get off home now.'

She said awkwardly, 'I had my cup of tea with you, Mr Burton. I should put in some extra time.'

Burton checked the big square face to make sure she was not taking the mick. But in the same instant he knew that Big Julie wouldn't do that, wouldn't know how to do it. He said rather sadly, 'That was just my little treat for a good worker. You don't have to work any extra time.'

'Thank you, sir. I'll just bring some more tomato soups and then I'll go. They always move quickly, don't they?'

'They do, yes, but we're closing now. You should get off home.'

'I just want to buy a few things. I've got visitors coming tomorrow. I want some cereals and some soup and some of our meals for one. Lasagne and cottage pie, I thought.'

'Better get whatever you want quickly, then. Don't forget your staff discount!'

Twenty minutes later, Jason Burton went out wearily to his car. It had been a long day. He wondered as he drove home what visitors Big Julie Foster might have. He was pleased but surprised that anyone came to see her.

It was half past eight when Matt Boyd rang the bell beside Anthea Gibson's door. 'I don't know why I'm here,' he said.

It wasn't the best of openings. Anthea stared at him for a moment, her blue eyes looking almost black with the light from the hall behind her. 'I suppose you'd better come in,' she said, unwillingly, it seemed.

'I brought a bottle,' he said apologetically. He realized now that it had been a mistake. You did that when you were invited for a meal, not when you were inviting yourself into a house where you might not be welcome. 'I can take it away again if you don't want it. Or I can just leave it here. I don't have to stay.'

She gave him a brief smile, which disappeared as quickly as it had arrived. The dark roots of her blonde hair were more noticeable than he had ever known them before. She had always looked and acted younger than her twenty-nine years. Anthea had had something girlish about her and she had cultivated it. Now, for the first time since he had known her, she looked older than her years. But what else should he expect, after what had happened in the last five days?

She asked him reluctantly, 'Have you eaten?'

'No. I've been rather busy. But I don't need anything.'

She wondered what he'd been busy with, because he wasn't working. But it wasn't her place to ask him that. Not any more. She'd been quite close to him, until last Saturday night. But now she wasn't. Not any more. She said reluctantly, 'That's silly. Of course you need something. I've got bacon and eggs. Will that do?'

'Bacon and eggs would be good. But there really isn't any need.'

His protest must have been feeble, because she was leaving the room, moving away to the familiar kitchen, where he and she and Lucy had so often eaten in the past. He wondered whether he should follow her, should stand behind her and slip his arms round her waist whilst she cooked, as he had often done previously. Even as the thought came into his mind, he knew that he wouldn't do it. He stayed where he was and looked round the sitting room, registering familiar objects but feeling as if he was seeing them for the first time, in a strange house.

She called him through, nodded towards the two glasses she had set on the table, turned back to the grill. He opened his bottle of Merlot and filled both glasses almost to the top, sensing that they were going to need the wine to loosen tongues and emotions. She clattered the plates noisily upon the melamine-topped table, threw cutlery beside them, turned to get salt and pepper from the cupboard behind her. Almost like a resentful wife, Matt thought, as he set knives and forks beside the plates. He said, 'I shouldn't have descended upon you like this, without any warning. I'd lost track of the time.'

'You and me both, then. I hadn't eaten myself.' It was the first conciliatory thing Anthea had said. She took a large mouthful of her wine, shut her eyes, rolled it round her mouth and swallowed it slowly. 'That tastes good.' She gave him her first genuine smile, and he thought how much better her small, pretty face looked when she was happy. Matt drank half his own glass of wine in quick time and felt the better for it. He downed bacon, egg and tomato and wholesome quantities of the brown bread and butter Anthea had set between them. He hadn't realized until now how hungry he was.

He complimented her on the food, made ridiculous remarks about the weather, wondered where on earth he was to go with the conversation if he was not to stray on to dangerous ground. He wanted to let his hand steal across the table and fall gently upon the back of her smaller one, as it had done in happier times. But he sensed that he should not make physical contact. He said awkwardly, 'How are you getting on, Anthea?'

The first use of her name, the first acknowledgement that they had once been intimates. Both of them noticed it; neither was sure whether it was welcome. He poured more wine and she said, 'You'll have to be content with tinned fruit for afters. Do you want ice cream with it?'

Matt felt very stupid as he said, 'We should drink the wine before that. The red won't go with the dessert.' They sipped their way through it in silence. He wondered if she was as conscious as he was of the vacant place where a lively, talkative girl had so often sat beside them.

She said suddenly, 'They haven't found that boy yet. It must be the same person who took Lucy, surely.'

'Yes. I suppose it must.'

'He'll be dead, then, like Lucy.'

'I've a feeling he's still alive.' Matt didn't know why he'd said that. Much better to get off the topic altogether. But he didn't want to deceive her, so he said, 'They questioned me about it. Because of Lucy, I suppose. It isn't pleasant to feel you're still a suspect, when you haven't done anything.'

He wanted her to sympathize, to say it must be awful for

him, to take his hands in hers and say that she'd never ever suspected him. There was a long pause. Then she said, 'Go back to the sitting room, Matt. I'll bring some coffee through. It will only be instant.'

It always had been instant. But it felt as though she was distancing herself from him when she said that. He sat uncomfortably and waited for her. She brought a tray in with cups and saucers, served him as formally as if it had been his first time here. They made desultory, difficult conversation, resolutely avoiding anything that would take them back to Lucy and to Raymond Barrington. In the old days, they would have put the television on and she would have leant comfortably against him on the sofa whilst he put his arm round her. They would have made trivial comments on the programmes and grown closer to each other. Now they were carefully detached from each other. And careful, always careful.

After one of their longer pauses, she said abruptly, 'I don't want you to stay the night.'

'That's all right.' It was a relief, he realized. He'd almost said he didn't want to stay either, but realized just in time that it would be ungallant. Now he only wanted to get out, and he sensed that she wanted that too. He wished he hadn't come. And yet he was glad that he had kept up some kind of contact with her. It was a consolation that she was as uncertain as he was about whether she wanted to get together again.

Anthea went with him to the door, less than ten minutes later. He walked away into the darkness. He hadn't brought his car, because it wasn't far and he'd wanted to make sure that he wasn't being followed. She stood at the door until he disappeared, then went slowly back into the house and stared at the seat where he had been sitting.

John Lambert had been right about Matt Boyd being the most elusive of their suspects. Even the woman who had been nearest to him found that there was a part of Matt that was closed to her.

Gerry Clancey, alias Rory Burns, knew exactly what he was going to do on that Thursday night.

He came into his digs in Oldford at seven forty, leaving his car outside. The bathroom at the end of the corridor was empty – they didn't run to en suites in the lodgings Clancey used. He had a quick shower, washing away the rest of his day and the places he had been, and then lay on the bed for a while, staring at the ceiling. Not many people would have taken him for a man given to introspection, he thought with a grim smile. Well, he'd put it across those English pigs, even when they thought they had him taped.

He put on his oldest pair of jeans, the ones he was planning to discard after they'd erected the fair for the weekend in Stroud on the morrow. His shirt was clean but worn, almost invisible when he put on the navy anorak and the navy cap he used for these occasions. He snatched a quick look at himself in the mirror of his wardrobe door. It was like the old days of the troubles in Ireland, which he scarcely remembered. He felt as if he'd donned an unofficial uniform and must check the details before going on parade. He nodded at himself, then crammed the wad of banknotes into the front pocket of his jeans, beneath the anorak. He'd need to think about a money-belt if things continued to go well.

The Peugeot started first time: the engine was still warm from when he had parked it three-quarters of an hour earlier. He kept his eye on the road behind him as he drove along the winding B road towards Gloucester. He wasn't being followed; there was no sign of any police tail. Perhaps he wasn't the number-one suspect, as he'd decided he was after they'd talked to him.

He'd been watching out for surveillance all day, but he'd seen no sign of it. Perhaps the overtime budget didn't run to it in rural areas like this. Or perhaps they'd got someone else in the frame. The pigs never told you about other suspects when they questioned you. They always wanted you to think that you were the only one and they had you banged to rights. Well, sod the lot of them!

He was running into Gloucester now. It was time to concentrate on this evening's events. The people he was dealing with tonight were far more dangerous than pigs, if you got on the wrong side of them.

He turned away from the centre of Gloucester and drove

towards the industrial estate in the north-east of the city. Some
of the newer and bigger buildings here were still lit and busy,
even at this time of night. But Gerry Clancey turned away
from these, driving through narrower streets until he was in
an older, run-down industrial area, where there were no houses
and almost every building was in darkness. He stopped close
to the door of the tallest of them, paused for a moment to
gather his resources and then slipped out of the old Peugeot
and locked it.

The front of the building rose like a black cliff above him,
so close and so sheer that he could barely see the top of it
against the night sky. He went not to the huge door at the
front, which was wide enough to allow heavy lorries to pass
through, but to a small door in the side of the building which
he would not have found in the darkness had he not been here
before. He had a torch, but he took pride in proceeding without
its use. When concealment was necessary, you used as little
light as possible.

It was a minute before nine o'clock. He was right on time.
The man he was here to meet must surely appreciate that. The
door opened readily to his touch and he went forward to a
small room within the disused warehouse, with a light that was
invisible from the outside of the building. The naked bulb
seemed quite dazzling after the darkness through which he had
passed. There was an old one-bar electric fire at the side of the
small room, which seemed unpleasantly hot after the coolness
outside.

Gerry Clancey thought that the folded forearms of the man
behind the table were the most powerful he had ever seen.
There was very little neck beneath the broad head. The dark
glasses seemed to Clancey an affectation, but no one was ever
going to tell this man that. And the glasses had a disconcerting
effect: Gerry was certain that the man was studying him closely
now, but he could see nothing of the eyes behind the glasses
and divine nothing of what the man was thinking about him.

This was his supplier, the man who provided him with the
drugs he sold on to others. This was the man on the next rung
up the chain, the first of the links with the drug barons who
made millions and, in some cases, did not even live in Britain.

You made good money in this vile trade, especially if you were not a user, as Clancey wasn't. Most of the pushers were users themselves, selling to feed their own addictions. Most of these men and women were condemned to a short and dangerous life, which would end when they were either arrested by the police or eliminated by the ruthless practitioners of this trade because they were considered no longer safe.

Clancey was making good money at present, but he was aware of the dangers. If he tried to find out too much about the suppliers in the ranks above him, or revealed anything to the police drug squad, he would disappear without trace, his body buried under tons of concrete or weighted at the bottom of the sea. Or simply shot through the head and left where he had fallen in some city backstreet, if his death wasn't considered important enough to be concealed. The rewards of dealing were high, the risks even higher. Gerry Clancey planned to make a decent killing and get out whilst he remained intact.

Many others before him had planned to do this and failed.

The man gave him no kind of greeting, sounded no note of recognition. Eventually, he snarled out a hostile 'Well?'

Gerry had to clear his throat. He was surprised how nervous he felt. He was furious with himself when he found it affecting his voice. 'I want skunk. I can shift plenty of it.'

'So can lots of others. Pot's small-time stuff nowadays.' The man reached down to the suitcase beside his feet and set two blocks of dark-brown resin on the table.

Clancey wondered why the man should be so anxious to humiliate him, then whether this fellow in turn was treated in like vein by those ranked above him. 'I can take some E. Not as much as last time – there isn't the demand there was. Ten tablets, perhaps.'

The man looked at him as if it was a derisory order, but banged the ecstasy tablets on the table beside the cannabis. Gerry said as firmly as he could, 'Charlie. Ten grams.'

His supplier placed the cocaine alongside the rest on the table. 'Fifty quid a gram. It's good stuff. You'll get seventy, easy.' His last phrase was the nearest he would come to a concession. The price of cocaine to Clancey had been increased by five pounds a gram. 'We've got crack, too, if you want it. But it'll cost.'

Clancey knew he hadn't the money for the cocaine in rock form. It was both terrifyingly addictive and terrifyingly expensive. He had clients for it, but he couldn't afford the outlay, not with what the rest of his order was going to cost him. He shook his head. 'Speed. Three grams.'

The amphetamines were added to his order on the table. The man with the suitcase couldn't resist a gibe. 'Pity you can't afford the rocks.'

Gerry ignored him. He wanted to be out of here fast and away. 'Four grams of horse. And rohypnol, unless the price has changed.'

His supplier banged the heroin on the table. He hesitated for a moment. The Irishman was small-time, making his way. Not a priority customer yet, and the date-rape drug was in short supply. 'I can't do you the rohypnol. Randy buggers have cleared me out.'

Claney knew the reality of this. Everyone wanted rohypnol; he could move it on faster than anything else on the table in front of him. But the amount that was there made him small-time, not in a position to call the shots. Perhaps if he pocketed his profits and came back with an increased order, he might be in a position to demand his quota of the date-rape drug. He didn't consider suggesting that he could go elsewhere and get a better deal; you didn't threaten men like this. 'That's the lot.'

Gerry peeled off the best part of a thousand pounds and passed it across the table to the man in the dark glasses, who made a great play of counting it carefully. It seemed to Clancey, more and more impatient to be away now that the transaction was completed, to take a distressingly long time. The bull-necked man finally reached down and threw the money into the suitcase beneath him. 'Pleasure to do business with you, Danny Boy. You're the last tonight.'

Gerry Clancey wondered how much money was in that suitcase now. He stood up and turned towards the door.

As if the movement had triggered some device, there was suddenly noise outside the room, in the main body of the huge, echoing warehouse. A voice boomed, 'Don't move, either of you. This is the police and there is an armed response unit covering all exits. Expert marksmen will shoot to kill if there is any attempt to use a firearm.'

Neither of them was so foolish. Police seemed to be everywhere. The words of arrest were yelled fiercely into their unresponsive ears as they were handcuffed. There were yet more police outside, a row of vans and cars where there had previously been bare tarmac. They saw men from the armed response unit, rigid upon one knee with weapons trained on their hearts.

The man in dark glasses yelled final bullying words at Gerry as he was led to a separate car. 'If you brought this lot here, Clancey, you're a dead man!'

TWENTY

John Lambert was indeed very tired. Too tired to eat properly, Christine noted with wifely disapproval. She cleared away the remains of his meal and told him sternly to get to bed and make sure he had a good night's sleep.

John nodded absently. He gave her an exhausted smile when she announced that she was going to bed, promising that he would join her shortly. He stared into space for a good hour after she was gone, revolving the possibilities of each of his suspects, wondering what he had missed, puzzling about the whereabouts and the state of mind of a terrified eight-year-old boy. He refused to contemplate the fact that Raymond Barrington might be a corpse, that his killer might even now be thinking about a third victim. He had convinced himself that Raymond was still alive. Now, left alone in his own home, he wondered whether he had been hopeful rather than objective.

He was in bed by midnight, envying, almost resenting, the quiet, regular breathing of Christine as she slept beside him. Over the years, he had trained himself to sleep, even when the pressures of work lay heavily upon him. Deep breathing was the secret. If you could concentrate on that and continue to do it, you eventually fell asleep. Tonight the theory didn't work. You had to close your mind to other thoughts, let the rhythm of your breathing take over your body and mind, but tonight those other thoughts stubbornly refused to go away.

At some time between one and two, he fell into an uneasy doze. He woke with a start from a ridiculous dream of Raymond Barrington riding a bike through open country, whistling the music of Elgar. The illuminated clock on the bedside radio told him that it was four twenty. He turned on to his back and lay very still, knowing that he was not going to sleep again, trying to ensure that his fevered thoughts would become more rational, organized and useful.

At five forty, he rose, washed and dressed. At five past six, he rang Bert Hook.

The DS didn't sound annoyed. His voice wasn't even sleepy. Lambert suspected that he'd had as disturbed a night as his chief superintendent. Bert was normally very relaxed at home; one of his strengths was that he was able to leave the job behind him, as John Lambert had never been able to do. But child murders were different. They got to the most equable of men, even to those who had developed the carapace of experience which protected them against most crimes.

Lambert spoke quickly and quietly into the phone. As he outlined his thinking, his conviction grew. Bert asked three terse questions as Lambert developed his thesis, but was otherwise silent and attentive. He said at the end of it, 'I'll ring Chris Rushton at home. He needs to know what we're doing.'

'Tell him to hold back on the surveillance, for the moment. And get him to organize a car to follow us at a decent distance, with at least one female officer in it. If the boy's still alive, we'll need separate transport for him.'

'I'll do that. Then I'll pick you up. Say half an hour from now.'

'Thanks, Bert. I'll be ready.'

Bert moved quickly and softly around the sleeping house, imagining Lambert doing the same thing five miles away. He scribbled a quick note for Eleanor, then started and reversed the car as quietly as he could. Lambert was waiting for him at the gate of his bungalow, raising a gaunt smile as he ducked his head to get into the Mondeo. It was still completely dark.

The police car fell in behind them at the station in Oldford, as arranged. Bert had never been a tearaway behind the wheel, but he drove with expert and surprising swiftness now to the point where they would await their quarry. He said nothing to Lambert beyond a clipped, 'Chris says Gerry Clancey was picked up last night in Gloucester. Dealing in drugs. That seems to have been what he was doing on Wednesday night, when Raymond Barrington was snatched.'

Lambert nodded. One of their five eliminated. It increased his conviction that he was right about this. It took him a moment to realize that that was why Hook had been anxious to give him the facts about Clancey. Bert was good on human nature, though he always affected to be merely delivering the obvious. Lambert, crouching a little lower in his seat, was suddenly moved by his old friend's treatment of him. He felt near to tears: this case had really got to him.

It was still quite dark. That was a good thing, since the police vehicle parked a hundred yards behind them would remain invisible. The minutes dragged as they sat tense in the car, gnawed by the thought that Lambert's theory was an elaborate tissue of conjecture, which would not survive examination in the clear light of day.

It was twenty past seven when the dark figure came out of the house and moved swiftly towards the vehicle. Hook had his lights off, but the driver did not look at the crouching duo. Bert waited until the tail lights were fifty yards away, then eased the car quietly in pursuit, relying for the moment on his side lights and the first hint of grey dawn from the east. Once they were on the A438, he switched on his headlights. There was a little more traffic here, even at this early hour. The vehicle they were following wasn't moving very quickly, so that a couple of cars overtook both them and it, making it less obvious that they were in pursuit.

The driver indicated a left turn well in advance, confirming their impression that their presence was still undetected. Bert switched on to side lights again in the lanes, relying on the slowly increasing daylight to help him. The tail lights were intermittently visible as their quarry twisted and turned ahead of them, never more than a hundred yards away. Both detectives were silent and tense, aware that they mustn't lose those tail lights now, when the case was surely moving towards its climax.

Bert prayed silently that Raymond Barrington would still be alive and unharmed.

The van in front of them turned abruptly right into the grounds of a cottage, where there were no lights. John Lambert's hoarse 'Give him room! We can't afford to alarm him!' showed how tight the moment was stretching him. Hook took his foot off the accelerator and let the Mondeo coast almost silently down the slight incline of the last hundred yards to the cottage entrance.

The driver of the van didn't look round. He plainly had no idea that he was being followed; his thoughts were on what he would find within this apparently deserted residence. He collected his bag of groceries, glanced up at the sky and moved to unlock the door. His last action before opening it was to pull his hat down over his forehead and lift his scarf over his mouth, so that his nose and eyes were all that was visible of his face.

The noise of the gravel beneath their wheels seemed agonizingly loud as they turned into the cottage drive. Hook rolled his car tight up behind the battered van, so that there was no chance of it escaping them. The police car closed up behind them and parked between the gateposts of the entrance. Hook glimpsed pale young faces behind its windscreen, one male and one female.

The door wasn't locked. In thirty seconds, Lambert and Hook were standing in the hall, listening to muffled voices and words they could not unscramble from behind the door that was furthest from them. They looked at each other: one of those voices was surely a child's. Then they moved softly past the open door of a kitchen, hearing the voices a little more clearly as they moved towards them. Hook glanced at Lambert, received a nod, took in a huge breath and threw open the door.

Two startled white faces turned towards them, rigid with shock. Hook thought he would retain the scene for ever in his memory: the man and the boy seemed to be frozen, as if they were part of a Dutch interior painting. He heard Lambert's voice say calmly, 'It's over, Dean. Please don't do anything silly.'

Hook tried to be equally calm, even matter-of-fact, as he said to the boy, 'You're quite safe now, Raymond. We're policemen, you see. I think you should come over here.'

The boy hesitated, looked up at the monster, received from him a quick nod and walked a little unsteadily to Hook, who took both his small, uncertain hands into his large and certain ones. Bert looked down at the yellow hair, caught the lad's air of bewilderment and said again. 'You'll soon be home now. Mrs Allen will be waiting. She's been very worried about you.'

He kept the boy's left hand firmly in his as he went to the
door of the room and called softly down the hall to the entrance
door they had left open. The uniformed officers came into
the house and joined them, moving as cautiously as they had
been warned to do when they were detailed to this task. Like
Hook, they tried not to show their enormous relief at finding a
boy safe and well, where they had feared a corpse. The woman
officer was only twenty-four, but she had two children of her
own. She transferred Raymond Barrington's hand from Hook's
to hers and said, 'Let's go now, shall we?'

The boy turned obediently, looking up at her with a nervous
smile. But he stopped unexpectedly at the door, as if it was
necessary to him to record in his mind the room and the
creature that had been his whole world for the last thirty-six
hours. He looked up at the lined, solemn face of Lambert,
which seemed to him impossibly high above him. 'You won't
hurt the monster, will you? I was frightened at first, but he's
been good to me.'

Lambert smiled down at him, his face a mixture of relief
and surprise. 'We're not going to hurt him, Raymond. We're
going to take him away and look after him. We might need
to talk to you a little later, when you've spoken to Mrs Allen
and had a good rest. You should go with PC Miller now. She'll
give you a ride in a police car. You'll enjoy that.'

Dean Gibson took off his hat and pulled his scarf away
from his face. 'Goodbye, Raymond. I'm sorry if I frightened
you.'

Then the boy was gone, and his captor was suddenly
exhausted. He sank down on to the chair he had set for the
boy beside the square table and said, as much to himself as
to the two men who had shattered his plans, 'I could never
have hurt him. I was going to let him go today. I didn't know
what to do with him. I should never have taken him. He's . . .
he's a good kid.'

Suddenly, his face was in his hands and he was weeping.
Lambert gave him time. There was no hurry now. Only when
the sobbing ceased and the man regained a measure of control
did he say, 'Why did you take the boy, Dean?'

Gibson shrugged his shoulders hopelessly. 'I've been

wondering that all night. I thought if I snatched another child who had no connection with me, you'd think it was someone else who'd taken Lucy. I kidded myself I might kill him and convince you that you had a madman on your hands, but that was stupid. He'll be all right, won't he?'

'I expect he will now, yes. The medics will examine him and make sure there's no serious damage. Physical or mental damage. Have you touched him, Dean?'

'What? You mean abused him, that sort of thing? No! No, of course I haven't. I would never do that to any child. I've scarcely touched him, apart from when I grabbed him and put him in the van that first night.' He made it sound as if it was a week ago, rather than a mere thirty-six hours. And indeed it seemed so, to him. The time since he had snatched Raymond felt like a strange, elongated dream rather than reality. 'I'm glad you've got him. Glad you've got me, really. I've been waiting for it.' He could see that he had indeed been waiting for just this, now that it had happened. He felt an immense relief that it was over.

'Why here, Dean?'

'This is a holiday cottage. The guy who owns it is in Florida. I did some work for him in the spring – plastering and decorating. He gave me a key to get in. I found I still had it. It seemed a safe place to bring the lad. It's very quiet here.'

'Very quiet for you. Very quiet for Raymond. Scary quiet. Didn't you think of that when you dumped him here?'

Gibson stared down at his feet, looking for a moment as if he might descend into tears again. 'I was planning to kill him, to make you think it was someone else who'd killed Lucy and gone on to do this. Once I had him, I knew that I could never go through with it.'

It was Hook who now said, 'I believe that, Dean. You've never struck me as a killer. You were going to let him go, weren't you?'

Gibson nodded miserably. 'Today. I was going to let him go today.'

'But you were worried that he'd tell us all about you. That he'd recognize you.'

'I was at first. I kept my face covered with my scarf and

pulled my cap down, so that he could only see my eyes. Pathetic, isn't it? But by today I hardly cared about that.' A long pause, whilst he waited for questions that Hook didn't ask. 'I'm glad you've got me. I wanted to tell you all about it yesterday afternoon, to have it over with. But I didn't.'

'No, you didn't, Dean. But you're telling us now. And the more you tell us, the more you cooperate, the better it will be for you.'

Dean gave Hook a bleak smile, then shook his head. 'Nothing can make it better for me. What was it put you on to me?'

Hook glanced at Lambert, who said, 'You lied about using the van last Saturday. Gave us that silly tale about coming to the fair on your bike, when you'd used the van. We didn't buy that story about only using it for work. And you knew exactly the time when Lucy had disappeared, before we'd released it to anyone. When we spoke to you yesterday about Raymond, you seemed to know more about him and how he'd been snatched than anyone else. And then our forensic boys found your old van suspiciously clean and tidy for a man doing the work you do and living as you do. It began to add up. But it was your manner yesterday as much as anything you said. We had enough to make us follow you this morning.'

'I didn't know you were behind me. My mind was on other things. I was trying to think about how I could let Raymond go without him telling you it was me. But I couldn't concentrate. My mind wasn't in it. I'm glad you've found me.' It was the third time he'd told them that and this time he nodded vigorously, as if confirming to himself that startling fact.

It was Hook who dragged him back six days to the worst confession of all. He said simply, 'What went wrong when you took Lucy, Dean?'

It seemed for long seconds as if Gibson would not speak at all. Then he said in a dull, expressionless voice. 'I only wanted to talk to her. I wanted to hold her in my arms, to see her smile again, to make sure she was happy. I wanted to be sure that she wasn't forgetting me.'

His voice broke on that and he sobbed silently, without any

tears this time. After a while, Hook prompted gently, 'I expect she was scared, being snatched like that?'

'Scared. That's what she was, yes. I should have expected it, I suppose. I thought that as soon as she recognized me she'd be delighted. I thought that she'd smile and hug me, the way she always used to.'

'Did she cry out, Dean?'

He nodded, but didn't speak through more long, agonizing seconds. Then he said bitterly, 'She cried out for him, for that Matt Boyd. Said to let her go to him. I couldn't stand that. I said that it was me who was her dad, that I always would be.'

'That was when things went wrong, wasn't it?'

'Yes. It was suddenly me who was scared, not her. I didn't want her to go to that man who'd brought her to the fair when it should have been me, who was going to come after us as soon as he realized Lucy was gone. I rushed her through the woods towards where my van was parked. She screamed out. Screamed his name again. "I want Uncle Matt!" she shouted. Shouted so loud that I had to shut her up. I put my hands round her neck from behind her as we ran, wanting to stop her shouting. Wanting to scare her, just a little, I suppose, because of that name. Then she wouldn't run, and I had to pick her up and carry her. And she struggled and screamed. And I had to stop her screaming. And when I got her to the van and put her down, she was quiet. I thought she would come round when I hugged her, when I kissed her, when I tried to give her the kiss of life. But she didn't.'

Hook thought the man would put his face in his hands again as he relived the horror of that moment, but he didn't. He wasn't blinking now, as he always had before under pressure from them. He stared steadily at the window and the broadening day behind it, as if light was no longer welcome to him. 'I couldn't believe that Lucy wasn't going to sit up and say it had all been a tease. I drove through the lanes and away from the fair. I couldn't think properly. I followed roads I'd known since I was a child myself. Then I stopped and looked down at Lucy and she hadn't moved. I don't know how long I was there. I didn't want to touch her any more, but I made myself do it. She was very still and getting cold. That was the moment when I knew for certain that she was dead.'

'So you put her in the river.'

Dean Gibson was now as still and unmoving as a statue. He didn't even nod his confirmation. 'I knew I was quite near the Wye. I used to walk that stretch with my dad, when I was a boy. It was very still and quiet. I put Lucy in the water and watched her float away from me. I tried to say a prayer, but the words wouldn't come.'

Hook pronounced the words of arrest more softly than he had done to any other murderer. Then he said quietly, 'You'll get a doctor and a lawyer and whatever help you need, Dean.' They took him out to the Mondeo and installed him beside the chief superintendent on the back seat. Hook drove swiftly back to the station at Oldford. They felt as if they had done a day's work, but it was still not fully light. People stared at them curiously as they moved into busier streets.

As they drove, John Lambert mused anew on the frighteningly small differences between normal and criminal behaviour. And on the tiny, fateful decisions that could transform a man from an ordinary human being into one who could kill a child.